KILLER SHOT

STELLA KNOX SERIES: BOOK THREE

MARY STONE

STACY O'HARE

DESCRIPTION

All bets are off when a madman calls the shots.

After Special Agent Stella Knox's friend and FBI tech ace Mac drops a bombshell regarding the death of Stella's father, she can't wait to follow up on the lead. But that's put on the backburner when six people are abducted from a dinner party—the door open, the table laid, and the meal started. Even more disturbing is that a two-year-old is among the missing.

With no sign of a struggle and the only fingerprints belonging to the guests, there's little to go on. Soon, a body is found in a drainage ditch on the edge of town, shot in the back at close range.

Followed by another.

While Stella and her team scramble to piece together a limited set of clues, a madman is calling the shots in a sadistic game where even the winners lose it all.

Now, it's a race to find the remaining hostages...while they're still alive.

Twisted and spine-chilling, Killer Shot is the third book in the new Stella Knox Series by bestselling author Mary Stone and Stacy O'Hare that will make you wonder how far you'd go to save your life.

1

―――――――

"**W**hat the hell did I do?"

Troy Harvey's first thought upon waking was that he must have been arrested and thrown in the drunk tank from hell. Concrete, damp and stained with liquids he didn't want to think about, surrounded him. The one exception was the single wall featuring thin bars set into a steel frame.

Jail. There could be no other explanation.

As he tried to sit up, tried to better understand his situation, pain as sharp as bolts of lightning shot through his head. His neck was so stiff he wondered if his spine had been replaced with metal. Movement equaled suffering, and no matter how much he longed to cradle his roiling stomach, he could only place a trembling hand over his gut.

None of this made sense. The party hadn't been *that* wild. Had it?

No. Not for him, anyway.

Half a glass of wine was all he remembered drinking. Though he'd only been old enough to legally drink for a couple of years, he wasn't that much of a lightweight. Was he?

The pounding in his head said otherwise.

Shit.

He rubbed his eyes and blinked until the room came into focus. No, this couldn't be a drunk tank. Not unless he'd been transported to some third-world concentration camp, at least.

With no toilet or bed, he sprawled on concrete as cold as ice, with only a bucket for company. Judging from the stiffness in his body, he'd been on the ground a while.

Why? Where?

Fighting another wave of nausea, Troy pushed up to his hands and knees. Unable to walk, he crawled to the bars, attempting to get his bearings. A row of cells—more dog kennel than prison—lined the opposite wall. He blinked, unsure if he was seeing correctly.

"Brenda?"

Curled in a fetal position, Brenda Renelle lay in the cell directly in front of him. Her bright-red hair had lost all its normal vibrancy. Unnaturally still, her pale expression gave no hint of life. Was she dead? Troy couldn't tell.

And she wasn't the only one.

Darrel Dowers was sprawled in the cell to Brenda's right, looking as if he'd fallen through the ceiling. Deathly pale, his chest moved, but barely.

Troy's horror increased when he studied the cell on Brenda's left. Dee Dee Bisgard's face was pressed against the bars, her arm around the little boy curled next to her. Troy couldn't tell if either she or Ashton were alive or...

What was a two-year-old doing in a cell? What were any of them doing here?

Standing on legs that felt like water instead of bone, Troy used the bars to pull himself up. The steel was cold against his skin, even where rust had turned the silver a coarse brown. He shook the gate, but the bars held firm. The *kachink* of metal on metal was the only sound in the quiet room.

"That you, Troy?" The booming growl coming from his right nearly caused Troy to piss his pants. "Forget it. I've tried. These bars don't look like much, but they're set like rock."

Ron too?

Troy couldn't see Ron Bisgard, but the familiar voice was both reassuring and disheartening.

"Where are we?"

The beats of silence that followed were interrupted by Ron's long exhale. "I don't know."

Heart hammering like a drum, Troy dropped back onto the concrete floor and leaned against the wall. Everyone from the dinner party was there.

"What happened to us?"

Another long exhale. "I have no idea."

His mentor's confusion scared Troy more than anything had in a good long while.

Troy's father died before his fifth birthday, and since Ron and Dee Dee had no children of their own—not until they adopted Ashton eighteen months back—they'd taken him under their wings. In those years, they'd become his extended family.

When the Bisgards had invited Troy over for dinner with a couple of their friends, Troy hadn't been surprised. Ron was like a father to him. He'd coached Troy all the way through Little League, showing him how to wrap his fingers around the baseball and land his pitches right over the plate. He'd even given Troy his first job at the family grocery store, making him assistant manager a year later, a level of trust few people had ever placed in him.

Even though he was now an adult, he still ate at their house at least once a month, which was kind of funny. Neither Ron nor Dee Dee was much in the way of a cook, and usually didn't even try, but they knew how to host. And order out.

The atmosphere was always friendly, relaxed, and full of gentle teasing. The conversation would start in the entrance hall, then build steam and laughter around the dinner table before shifting into friendly advice when dinner was done. Dee Dee would put Ashton to bed, and the adults would sit on the veranda, beers in hand, chairs rocking on the stained wood.

That was how those evenings always went, and Troy had expected no different this time.

So, what happened?

Thinking hard, Troy vaguely remembered feeling wobbly not long after tucking into his plate of fried chicken. It had been as though someone had spun him around too fast on a merry-go-round, then stopped it abruptly, magically.

He remembered Brenda losing her dimpled smile. She'd put her arm to her forehead as though the room had started spinning for her too. Darrel, a nice man Dee Dee had been trying to set Brenda up with, was quick to notice his date's discomfort.

He'd draped an arm around the back of her chair. "You okay?" Darrel's voice had seemed strange, the words waving up and down.

Dee Dee had been too busy with Ashton, who had fallen asleep in his highchair, to pay attention. Troy tried to pour Brenda a glass of water, but his hands wouldn't work. From the corner of his eye, he saw Ron drop face-first into the mashed potatoes. The room spun and tilted, and, finally, the world turned black.

Now…here they were. Wherever *here* was.

Troy whacked the bars with the side of his fist. They rattled but didn't move. "Do you remember anything?"

"There must have been something in the food." Ron's voice echoed off the concrete. "We ordered in last night and used some new delivery person who was recommended to Dee Dee. They must have drugged us."

Fear rose in Troy's chest and settled as a ball at the back of his throat. "Why, though? What could they possibly want with us?"

Silence ate at Troy's sanity before Ron finally answered, "I dunno. But, listen, we're going to be fine. I promise."

Are we? You can't know that. You can't.

Whoever had brought them there had gone to a lot of trouble, and Troy couldn't think of a single reason why. None of them were rich. Both Troy and Brenda, a cashier, made little more than minimum wage at Ron and Dee Dee's grocery store, Bisgard's Best.

Darrel, the newest member of their party, was an accountant. He didn't work for a big firm or have billionaire clients who lined his pockets. They were all just regular folk. If they were being held for ransom, what could the kidnappers get? The good olives from the barrel at Bisgard's Best?

At least Dee Dee and the little guy were together. Maybe whoever had taken them wasn't a complete monster.

Clang.

It took Troy a moment to recognize the sound. The footsteps that followed reinforced the idea that a door had just been opened. Alarmed, Troy shuffled over to the wall farthest away from the sound, like an animal crawling from its abuser. Pressing his face against the bars, he attempted to peer past the cages.

Who the hell was that?

The man striding toward them was tall and well built, with a shock of yellow hair that started at the top of his scalp and swooped into a lock hanging over his left temple. He was handsome in a blond Clark Kent kind of way. He wore a long, white coat and carried a metal clipboard, as though he were doing rounds on a hospital ward or had just stepped out of a laboratory.

He stopped in front of Ron's cage. "Awake, are we?" The man's voice was a scratchy alto, sounding strangely high and almost feminine in the confined space.

It set Troy's teeth on edge.

"Excellent."

"Who the hell are you?" Compared to the mad scientist, Ron's voice was deep and resonant.

Ignoring Ron's outburst, the mad scientist banged on the cage opposite, where Dee Dee and Ashton still lay unconscious on the floor. "Wakey, wakey. Time to rise and shine."

"Hey!" Ron roared. "Leave them alone."

Dee Dee groaned and pushed into a seated position. Her face, already pale except for a couple of angry bar-sized stripes on her cheek, turned ashen as she peered around her cell. "What the...where are..." Terror and confusion warred on her expression as she caught sight of her husband. "Ron! What's going on?"

She pulled Ashton into her lap. The child, small for his age, yawned and rubbed his eyes.

Ron extended a hand through the bars and reached toward his wife. "It's okay, honey. We've been drugged, but we're going to be okay."

In the cell opposite Troy, Brenda groaned as she pushed up enough to lean on one arm. Her eyes met Troy's, and in that look came understanding.

"No!" The shrill scream that bounced off the walls was mercifully short before Brenda collapsed into sobs so deep they racked her shoulders. She curled into a ball, her forehead buried between her knees, breathing so hard Troy thought she might be having an asthma attack.

The scream woke Darrel, who, in spite of looking dazed and confused, touched the wall between them. "It's okay. Deep breaths."

Troy wondered if he even knew who he was comforting. Did it even matter?

Ashton's face crumpled into the very picture of misery, and Dee Dee pulled the child even closer to her chest, soothing him the best she could. "Shh, shh, shh."

The man in the white coat rattled his metal clipboard against Ron's bars. "Oh, for the love of god, will you all *shut up?*"

The noise reduced Brenda's sobs into quiet hiccups and drove Ashton deeper into his mother's embrace. Or maybe the room only seemed quieter because of how loud Troy's pulse hammered in his ears.

"That's better." Mad Scientist tucked his clipboard under his arm. "I'm sure you're all wondering what you're doing here."

"You bet your ass." Ron's voice reminded Troy of a bear's growl. "But no one's wondering what I'm going to do to you when I get out."

Mad Scientist rolled his eyes. "Oh, do shut your bleating. You're not going anywhere, any of you. I brought you here because I'm a doctor." He rocked on his heels and began pacing in front of the cages. "I'm engaged in groundbreaking research. You, all of you, are here to help me."

What the hell?

Troy didn't understand. "You brought us here to be lab assistants?"

The man peered down his nose at Troy as though he'd found an unusual mushroom during a woodland hike. "Of course not. None of you have the brains to so much as clean a test tube. I brought you here because I need subjects."

The loud rattle from Ron's cage suggested he was attempting to drag the bars out of their casing. Brenda sobbed into her hands while Dee Dee shuffled toward the back of her cell, Ashton still clutched to her chest.

"Do calm down." The doctor had the audacity to sound bored. "There's nothing you can do. The walls are sound-proofed, the cages have been reinforced, and there is no chance of escape. None at all."

"What are you going to do with us?" The question came from Darrel. He was calm and serious. Troy appreciated the man's steadiness.

"I'm glad you asked." The man reached into one of the deep pockets of his white coat and pulled out a revolver, its six-inch barrel pointed at the ground.

As Dee Dee gasped, Troy's vision tunneled until nothing remained but the weapon and the man's finger resting on the trigger.

"Don't worry. I'm not going to shoot you. I don't have to." He turned in a circle, a false, benevolent smile showcasing too-bright teeth. His icy, reptilian, blue eyes didn't smile, however. No emotion showed in his gaze. "Because you will shoot each other."

Troy shivered as a cold spike settled into his chest. *What the hell does that mean?*

"You're crazy. You're a complete lunatic." Ron's voice contained just a hint of a tremble, a sign that his normally in-charge, capable manner was losing its grip.

The man turned his head toward the cage next to Troy's. His legs and shoulders remained unmoving, like an owl that had spotted movement in the undergrowth but was still unsure whether the prey was worth it.

"And we have a psychiatric diagnosis from the owner of

the grocery store. Are you familiar with the fifth edition of the *Diagnostic and Statistical Manual of Mental Disorders*? Have you read it? Studied it?" His blue eyes were indeed dead, but his voice held the tone of an excited college professor.

"It was a figure of speech, jackass." Ron sounded like he'd recovered some of his fight.

Mad Scientist's enthusiasm didn't waver. "Have you spent years with patients listening to them drone on about their childhood and their ridiculous traumas? No? If you had, you would understand that 'lunacy' is an obsolete term for mental incompetence or insanity. Any previous references to 'lunacy' as a theory that insanity is tied to phases of the moon are also incorrect. So, I would ask you to keep your uninformed comments to yourself."

"Fuck you."

The man glanced at his watch. "It's now midnight. At a designated time tomorrow morning, one of you will shoot a fellow subject in the back. You will shoot that person dead with a single bullet. There will be no namby-pamby wounding. You will shoot to kill. The game will continue each day until only two subjects are left."

Mad Scientist is wrong. Lunacy is alive and well.

Troy pressed his face between the bars and spoke before good sense could keep his mouth shut. "Is namby-pamby technically a psychological term?"

Just as those cold eyes turned on him, Brenda's sobs broke into a loud wail that echoed through the cages. Distracted by the noise, Mad Scientist's white coat reflected the dingy light as he stepped over to her cage. Rubbing one ear, he turned to face the room. "For your own sanity, I recommend you shoot that one first."

Darrel shot to his feet, his arm thrusting through the bars. His fingers were only an inch away from the madman's coat before he could reach no farther. "Why would we do such a terrible thing? Why on earth would we agree?"

Mad Scientist chuckled. "A reasonable question. I wouldn't expect you to cooperate if you didn't have an incentive."

He walked back to Dee Dee's cage and cocked the gun. He pointed the muzzle at Ashton's head.

"No!" Dee Dee covered the boy with her body. "No!"

"Stop it!" Ron rattled his bars, his voice trembling. "No! Don't touch them!"

Troy had never heard Ron frightened before, and the older man's fear spread like a contagion through the group.

Mad Scientist ignored Ron. "That will do you no good, Dee Dee. This gun holds .454 Casull bullets. Hunters use them to take down elephants. Squeezing this trigger is enough to blow a hole through both you and anything, or anyone, you attempt to hide."

"Please, don't."

Watching Dee Dee plead broke Troy's heart.

"If you agree to shoot each other, at the end of the experiment, one of you and the child will remain alive. If you don't cooperate, the child will be the first to die, and the rest of you will follow."

Mad Scientist raised his thumb and eased down the hammer with a slowness that could only have been meant to prolong the woman's terror. He slipped the gun back into his pocket.

"Your choice now is simple. As a group, you will decide who will be the killer and who will be killed. I'll let you enjoy the dawn, so your decision must be made before eight tomorrow morning. If you refuse to cooperate, none of you will see another day."

The man removed a small clock from his left pocket and

placed it on the concrete floor in the middle of the corridor. Both hands on the clock pointed straight up.

Midnight.

"Did I say the choice is simple?" Mad Scientist *tsked* as he walked to the door. Once he'd opened it, he faced them again. "That was an error. I think it will be very difficult. And quite fascinating to observe. You have until the morning."

With a parting smile, the door clanged shut behind him.

No one spoke.

Tick tock. Tick tock.

The clock sounded more like a bomb.

2

Special Agent Stella Knox blinked away the dregs of sleep as she put her 4Runner in park. The Criminal Investigation Division of the FBI's Nashville Resident Agency came into focus. She hadn't slept well last night, not after Hagen Yates's impromptu visit...

"Stella, I need to talk to you. About Joel Ramirez."

She was so startled to hear the name of her father's former partner come out of Hagen's mouth that she very nearly slammed her apartment door in his face. She managed to keep her cool, though, and welcomed him in.

For years now, she'd believed her Uncle Joel was as dead as her father. But, recently, she discovered he might be alive and living in Atlanta under an assumed identity—Matthew Johnson—possibly a witness protection cover.

But she'd never mentioned that to Hagen.

"How do you know that name?"

The great Hagen Yates, super special agent of the FBI, actually blushed. "I overheard you talking with Mac."

Mackenzie Drake was not only the team's technical ace, she and Stella had become close friends in the weeks since Stella joined the Nashville CID. Due to their instant friendship and Mac's technical expertise, Stella had enlisted the cyber tech's help in her quest to find her father's killer.

And Hagen had heard every word?

Before Stella could launch into a lecture about listening in on people's private conversations, Hagen held up a hand. "I don't know what it all means, but it sounds like a mess. And if you need help in Atlanta to sort it out, I'm happy to go with you." He placed a hand on her arm and looked directly into her eyes. "Agents don't investigate alone, Stella. They're safer and smarter in pairs."

The conversation was so strange. Why was he offering to help? Was he interested in her father's case? Or did she *interest him? The way he looked at her, she couldn't tell.*

During their last investigation, Stella thought she sensed an attraction. But as quickly as Hagen had grown warm, he'd become cold again, as though they were nothing more than acquaintances. She didn't know what he was thinking.

And what had caused him to listen to her conversation with Mac in the first place?

The alarm on Stella's phone went off, reminding her that she had a briefing in just a few minutes. Stella groaned in frustration but knew she couldn't mull over the rest of what Hagen had told her last night. She had to focus.

Slamming her 4Runner's door harder than the vehicle deserved, she forced her mind to the present. She had a job to do, even if it was seven in the morning.

Supervisory Special Agent Paul Slade had called last night with a new case. Multiple abductions from a small town called Stonevale outside of Murfreesboro meant they had a busy few days ahead of them.

She wanted to get started. And she wanted to get finished too. Not just because she was eager to find those missing people and bring them home safely, she needed to get to Atlanta…with or without Hagen Yates.

But questions about her father and her Uncle Joel would have to be put on the back burner. She'd chosen this career in part to find her father's killers but mostly to save the innocent and spread justice. Today, that meant Atlanta would have to wait. She was going to Murfreesboro.

Swiping her ID at the door, she headed straight to the briefing room. The rest of the team was already there. Instead of sitting in their seats, though, they were standing along one side of the room.

Chloe Foster grinned as Stella entered. "Dani's idea."

Stella's jaw dropped. "Chloe! What are you doing here? I thought you'd still be on leave."

The last time she'd seen Chloe, her colleague had been unconscious on the floor, blood leaking out of a bullet wound. That was just three days ago. Was Chloe made of steel? Or did she just act like she was?

"Doctor cleared me." Chloe shrugged. When the movement made her wince, she lifted a hand to her shoulder and looked sheepish. She adjusted the sling on her left arm. "It's still a bit sore. But the bullet's out, the hole's sewn up, and I detest painkillers. I'd rather be here than wallow in bed all day."

Stella swallowed hard against the ball of emotion creeping up her throat. "Right. Great. I was so worried, I—"

Chloe lifted a hand. "Tuck in."

She stepped back to reveal a table covered with plates of croissants and pastries. A hot water dispenser and a pile of cups stood at one end.

Three pastries were already piled on Ander Bennett's plate. A fourth was in the agent's mouth. He put down his coffee and gave Stella a small wave.

Danielle Jameson stood next to him, one hand pressed into the small of her back. Now in her third trimester, Dani was limited to desk duty, which meant Stella hadn't had much chance to get to know her. She regretted that.

Dani was always friendly, and she had welcomed her to the team with open arms. If they ever caught more than a one- or two-day break between cases before she gave birth, Stella would try to set aside some time to chat.

Dani raised a cup of chamomile tea. "Thought you guys deserved a bit of a treat this morning. I know you all had a rough week."

Stella couldn't disagree. "Thanks, Dani. You're a gem."

It was going to take more than a good breakfast to knock the memories of two multiple homicides, one after another, out of her system. But sugary goodness wasn't a bad place to start.

"The cocoa's right there." Mackenzie Drake stood on the other side of Dani, her slight frame mostly hidden by Dani's extended belly. She flicked a lock of white-blond hair over her shoulder and pointed to the plastic cup filled with instant hot chocolate packets. "I knew you couldn't begin your day without at least one cup of cocoa. Since the rest of us only drink coffee and tea like grown-ups, Dani had to go to the kiddie store to get chocolate powder."

"Ha." Stella grinned, not insulted in the least as she poured her kiddie powder into a cup. "I'd have gone for a cocktail, but if you're too wimpy to start the day with a dirty martini, I'll just have to make do."

Mac lifted her *Nerd Alert* mug. "Not on a workday. But when we're old and retired and living in neighboring condos in Florida, that's how we should start every day. By the pool with a cocktail and a view of the pool boy."

The door swung open, and their laughter died as Slade's deep voice filled the room. "All right, take your seats."

Stella tossed a pastry onto a plate and took the seat next to Chloe. Hagen sat directly opposite her. He'd skipped the drinks on offer and had a small cup of espresso in front of him alongside a barely touched croissant. He gave her a curt nod of greeting before turning his attention to the SSA.

What's wrong with him?

One minute, he was her best friend, ready to spend a couple of days with her in Atlanta searching for clues about her father's killer and, the next, he was back to being cold and professional. A colleague and agent, not a friend or confidant. She'd never met anyone who could be so different in and out of the workplace.

"Listen up." Slade rested his fingertips on the surface of the table. "We've got six abductees and a police chief who needs our help. Five adults and a two-year-old."

"A toddler?" Ander exhaled out a heavy breath. "Jesus."

"Yup. They were all taken from the home of Ronald and Dee Dee Bisgard in Stonevale, right near Murfreesboro." The faces of a smiling couple appeared on a screen behind Slade. The Bisgards stood before a small mom-and-pop store. "They're the owners of Bisgard's Best, a family grocery that's been in the town for almost thirty years. The two-year-old is the couple's adopted son, Ashton."

The picture changed to show a small boy with jet-black hair, sparkling, blue eyes, and a cheeky grin. He held an ice-cream cone bigger than his head.

Stella wanted to smile, but she knew when they found the family, there would be no smiles or ice cream for a while. Maybe never again.

"The other three are friends who'd attended a dinner party at the Bisgards' house. Troy Harvey, a twenty-three-year-old assistant manager at Bisgard's Best. Brenda Renelle, forty-seven, is a cashier at the store. And Darrel Dowers, forty-nine. He's the only one not connected to the store. He's an accountant and a friend of Dee Dee's."

Slade flicked through images of the three remaining

abductees. Troy looked younger than his twenty-three years. Tall and lanky, he had an awkward smile and narrow chin.

Brenda leaned a forearm on the counter in front of her cash register, her red hair dancing on the edges of her shoulders. She cradled a certificate declaring her to be *Employee of the Month*.

Darrel reminded Stella of a slightly younger version of Jonathan, her mother's husband. With his almost entirely bald head and crumpled, gray suit, Darrel looked every bit like a middle-aged man just waiting to buy an RV and take a slow retirement tour of the national parks.

"Troy's mother reported her son and the Bisgard household missing at five thirty yesterday evening. She went to the Bisgards' after her Bible study because she…" Slade glanced down at his notes, "was 'concerned for my son's moral well-being.' When she arrived, the door was open. All the vehicles were there, but the place was empty. The table had been set, and the meal looked like it had started."

The picture changed to show a dining room table covered in dishes and half-eaten food on the plates. One fork rested in a pile of mashed potatoes. A knife had cut halfway through the leg of grilled chicken. Peas were scattered across a baby's highchair tray.

"There was no sign of a struggle, and the only fingerprints forensics have found belong to the Bisgards and their guests. Food samples have been sent off, but it will be a while before we get those results. Thoughts?"

Slade turned off the slides and faced the agents.

Stella was the first to speak. "At least we don't have to worry about victim profiles for this one. Three are related, and the other three are friends. Maybe we're talking about another relative or a friend? Someone with a personal vendetta or a dispute with the family."

"It would have taken more than one kidnapper." Hagen

tore off the end of his croissant and rolled the pastry between his fingers. "Moving six bodies?"

Ander glanced at Hagen. "Five and a kid. A two-year-old won't put up much of a fight."

"My point is that moving one body is hard enough. Whoever did this didn't work alone."

"People cooperate with a gun in play," Stella reminded him, wrapping her hands around her warm mug. "The unsub could've just pointed them toward the door."

"Without one person in the party putting up some kind of resistance?" Hagen pushed the croissant away as though irritated by the pastry.

Stella knew Hagen was right. "Good point. If it's a kidnapping, we should expect a ransom demand soon."

Mac glanced up from her laptop. "I've got trackers on their cells and will work on tapping their home and work phones."

"Good." Slade stretched his back, and a loud crack sounded through the room. "The police chief in Stonevale is gathering all the surveillance they can find near the Bisgards' home and store. They didn't have a security system of their own, but Chief Houston thinks plenty of their neighbors do. Chloe…?"

The agent dropped her hand from her sling. "Yes, sir?"

"You sure you didn't forge your doctor's name on that medical release?"

A smile played at her lips before she pressed them together. "No, sir. I probably would have but didn't have to."

Slade stared at her so long that Stella started to sympathy sweat for her fellow agent. Chloe, cool as a cucumber, stared right back.

Finally, Slade sighed. "Okay, you're with me. Stella, Hagen, and Ander, I want you three on the road to Murfreesboro right away. If we need them, I'll call in the others. Let's hope it doesn't come to that. Go."

Stella finished her hot chocolate with two long gulps and wrapped her pastry in a napkin, tucking it into her shoulder bag, keeping it away from her laptop and tablet. She knew she'd be hungry later but, mostly, didn't want to waste a good pastry.

Chloe adjusted her sling. "Looks like we've got another strange one, huh?"

"Six people taken from a dinner party? Yeah, that's strange." Stella hauled her heavy bag onto her shoulder. "But when was *anything* normal in this job?"

3

Troy held the bars tight enough to whiten his knuckles and shook them with all his waning strength. After hours of trying, the steel rattled but didn't move.

For the hundredth time, he ran a finger around the edge of the frame, felt for the keyhole, and searched for the pins where the bars met the wall. The cages were old, the concrete stained with dark patches, but the bars were much newer, and their attachments to the concrete were newer still.

At one that morning, he and his fellow captives had all been committed to escaping this place. While his mother worked on their bars, Ashton had turned her shoes into a pair of cars, his soft *vroom-vroom* the only thing keeping Troy sane.

By two, the child had gone silent, as had much of the chatter. Still, Troy worked on his bars. The clock in the middle of the floor continued its relentless ticking as three o'clock became four.

Whether it was due to the lingering effects of the drug from the dinner party or from enduring hours of fear and desperation, Troy was worn out. And as the clock ticked past five, his eyes drifted closed.

Ashton's cries dragged him from a dream of freeing dogs from a pound and running with the animals across the hills. He'd been asleep for only a few minutes.

Brenda slept, curled into a ball on the concrete floor, but Darrel was awake. When their eyes met, the older man nodded, a movement that seemed to contain both a greeting and a confirmation that they were indeed waiting to die. Troy hadn't dreamed it.

Tick tock. Tick tock.

His bladder felt ready to burst. In the corner of the room stood a gray, plastic work bucket, the kind used to mix cement or paint.

No.

But it was either the bucket or his pants. Troy was miserable enough without having to deal with wet clothes. He chose the bucket.

At six, the door creaked open, the noise like a cymbal in their quiet prison. As a different man in a white coat pushed a cart into the middle of the room, Brenda startled awake. He was hunched way over, as if the pot and bowls he delivered took all his strength. A ski mask hid his face.

Why?

Why did he wear a mask when the mad scientist had not?

While Troy pondered the question, Brenda crawled across the concrete floor, tears once again streaming down her cheeks. "Let us out. Please, let us go."

"You better let us go." Ron's voice was much louder, but his threat held little weight. "This is your one chance."

The man ignored them both as he spooned thin stew into bowls. When the scent of vegetable stock floated into Troy's cell, his traitorous stomach growled. Pushing away all thoughts of hunger, his mind whirled with possibilities.

Did the man have a key to the cells? If so, this might be Troy's only chance to take it.

When he brings my food, I'll reach through the bars and grab him.

It wasn't a good plan, but it was all he had.

By the time the sixth bowl was filled, Troy's heart was nearly hammering out of his chest. He wrapped his hands around the bars to keep them from reaching out too soon.

Come on, you bastard.

As if he'd heard him, the masked man picked up a bowl and headed Troy's way.

That's right. Closer. Just a little bit more.

"Back up." The man's voice was nasally and thin, but the dark eyes peering through the slits of the mask held a maliciousness that penetrated Troy's skin.

He backed up a single step. He could still reach the man from there.

"More." When Troy didn't move, the man didn't ask again. He pulled a gun from his pocket and leveled it at his chest. "To the wall."

Hope deflating like a popped balloon, Troy moved back until he was pressed against the cool concrete. He didn't allow his gaze to leave the man, though. Gun or not, he'd attack if he got the chance.

He didn't.

With just enough space between the bottom bar and the floor to fit the shallow bowl, the man shoved it into Troy's cell. By the time Troy lunged the couple of steps from the wall to the bars, he'd moved on. This time, the gun was leveled at Ron.

"Back up."

Defeated, Troy stared at the bowl, his mind warring with his belly. He was hungry, yes, but had the food been drugged? He didn't know.

Tick tock. Tick tock.

In half an hour, would one of them really have to shoot another? Or would the mad scientist smile real big and shout, "You're on *Candid Camera!*"

Troy hugged his knees tighter and rocked back and forth, biting his lip against the cackle that tried to escape at that ludicrous thought. This was real. He'd be a fool to think otherwise.

"Listen to me." Ron's voice was solid, filled with renewed strength. "None of us is going to shoot anyone. Is that understood?"

"Are you willing to bet your child's life on that?" The question came from Darrel, but it was the same question bouncing through Troy's head.

"Excuse me? Am I...?"

"Are you willing to bet Ashton's life against that lunatic's intentions? Because if none of us volunteer in the next half hour, that's what you're going to do." Darrel seemed strangely calm. A five o'clock shadow had sprouted overnight, adding a certain distinguished air to the accountant's face. He sat with his back against a wall, one arm draped over a bent leg.

"I..."

"Ron." Dee Dee stood at the bars, hugging Ashton tight to her chest. Only the black hair at the top of his head was visible in the gaps between her fingers.

"Oh god. My boy..." Ron's voice faded away.

"Maybe he just wants money." Darrel ran a hand over his bald head. In the rising heat, sweat glistened on his pate. "If that's the case, we should just do it now and get it over with."

"I'm not giving that asshole a damn penny." Bars rattled, and Troy imagined Ron ramming home his point by punching the cage. "I'll rot in hell before I do that."

"Please. Just give him whatever he wants." Brenda had

returned to the fetal position she seemed to prefer. "I just want to go home."

"Honey." Dee Dee rocked her child side to side. "If we can buy our way out, I don't care if we have to give him the whole damn store, our house, and then rob a bank to make up the difference. We do it."

Troy paced his cell as he listened to the back and forth. A step-and-a-half forward, a step-and-a-half back. That was all the room he had. Their options seemed even smaller than this enclosure. He couldn't see how they could get out of this mess.

"If he wants money, he picked the wrong people," Troy said. "With all of this preparation, he could have chosen anyone, certainly people much richer than us."

"Do you think the crazy bastard really wants us to go through with it?" Ron sounded dazed. Troy couldn't see him, but he imagined Ron watching his family from across the aisle. "We have to save my son."

Ron was right.

To save Ashton, they might have to kill each other.

"I'll do it," Darrel volunteered, his voice as steady as the certainty on his face. "I'll take the bullet."

"Don't be crazy." Ron's voice sounded weaker, as though the last few minutes had drawn his strength. "I told you. No one's shooting anyone."

The accountant's face finally lost some of its confidence. "I don't see any other way. It should be me."

"Please, Darrel." Dee Dee pressed her son's head to her chest, her free hand covering his ear. "Don't talk like that. I don't want to hear it."

Darrel actually smiled, but the lift of his lips didn't last long. "Believe me, I don't want to say it, but it makes sense. I'm the oldest person here. I've got no kids, no wife. No one depends on me. If anyone's going to die here today, it should be me. Maybe you'll all be rescued before someone has to be next, and I'll be the only one. It balances."

Brenda had uncurled from her ball and now knelt on the concrete floor. She pushed her hand through the bars, reaching for Darrel's cell. "You don't have to do this. Please don't. This isn't some profit-and-loss statement. You matter."

Moving to the front of the cage, Darrel slipped his arm between his bars. His hands were larger than hers, fingers pudgier. Troy had to look away when their fingers touched in the space between the cells.

"I can't sit here and do nothing and let Ashton…" Darrel didn't need to finish the sentence. "How can I live if I let a little boy take a bullet meant for me?" When Darrel laughed, Troy glanced back over at the pair in time to witness the accountant force a bright smile on his face. "If we survive this, maybe you and I can meet up for a drink sometime? Maybe get some undrugged food? Or at least food first, and drugs after."

A small laugh interrupted Brenda's tears. Her fingertips stroked Darrel's. "Sure. I'd…like that. I'd like that a lot."

"Great. I've got something to look forward to." Darrel lifted his head, his gaze meeting Troy's. "Now, I just need someone to volunteer to shoot me."

Troy looked away.

Tick tock. Tick tock.

Who would do it? Who would volunteer?

Not Brenda. No one could expect her to pull the trigger. Not now.

Dee Dee? No, they couldn't let her kill someone in front of her son. How would the boy see her after that? The thought made Troy shudder.

Ron? A sob bubbled up from the deep well of emotions Troy had been holding back, and he covered his mouth with both hands to stop it from escaping.

Ron had been so good to him for so many years. He couldn't let his coach, his boss, his friend carry that guilt on his shoulders.

"I'll do it." The words were out of Troy's mouth before their meaning had settled into his head.

"Troy!"

"I'm sorry." Battling remorse and shame, Troy forced his head up just enough to meet Dee Dee's horrified gaze. "Someone has to…I can't let something happen to Ashton."

"Thank you, Troy." Darrel gripped the bars of his cage. "Let's just hope you don't actually have to do it."

"Yeah. Let's hope."

Tick tock. Tick tock.

Six forty turned to six forty-five and then to seven fifty. Seven fifty-eight.

Troy paced the cell. At the end of each circle, his eyes met Darrel's. The other man's face was as gray as the cell walls. At each glance, he gave Troy a small nod. They were in this together, he seemed to say. But only one of them would come out alive.

Rrring.

The alarm was even louder than Troy had expected, even though he'd watched the hands complete their final cycle. He stopped pacing and fixed his gaze on Darrel's face, which had turned an even paler shade of gray. He wouldn't dishonor the man by looking away.

Click.

The door opened. Three people came in. All wore white coats and ski masks, and each held a gun. The shortest of the three, the one who had brought them stew a few hours ago, stopped in front of Dee Dee's cage.

The taller man spoke, his voice muffled by his mask. "Hello, subjects. I'm One." He jerked a thumb toward the person next to him. "She's Two. And that one over there, he's

Three. That's all y'all need to know about us. That's all y'all will ever know." He lifted the weapon. "Now, I need to know which of you lucky sons of bitches are gonna get the first bullet?"

When silence was his only reply, Three turned to face Dee Dee and Ashton. "Come here, little boy."

Chaos erupted.

"No!" Darrel and Dee Dee screamed the word at the same time. The mother pulled her child into the farthest corner, wrapping herself around the boy.

"Get away from them," Ron shouted over and over, slamming into the bars.

"For crying out loud. Don't make me come in there." Three fumbled in his pocket and retrieved a ring of keys. He jammed one into the lock on Dee Dee's cage before trying another. "Just give me the little shit."

"Get on with it, will you?" Two, the female, said. "Haven't got all freaking day."

"Shut up. Why didn't he key them all the same?"

"No! Stop!" Darrel waved his arms through the bars of his cell. "It's me! I volunteer."

One clapped his hands together once…twice. "Ladies and gentlemen, we have a winner." He nodded at Two. "Go on."

Two pulled a different set of keys from the pocket of her white coat and selected one without difficulty. Seconds later, the cell door was swinging open. "Out you come."

Darrel stepped into the corridor, his head high.

One waved his gun to the opposite side of the room from the door. "Face that wall. On your knees."

Though Brenda had started sobbing again, Darrel didn't look at her as he obeyed the instructions. He dropped to his knees, one hand supporting him as he fell.

"Very good. Now, who is going to do the honors?"

Troy's brain went numb, and he wondered if his racing

heart had stolen all its blood. Would he really have to do this? Could he?

"I am." His voice cracked when he spoke.

The stagnant air was hot, but he was cold. Despite the sweat that glued his t-shirt to his chest, he shivered.

Two unlocked his cage and stood to the side, motioning for Troy to step into the corridor. For the first time, he could see the entire room, but he knew this bit of freedom wasn't free. He'd pay the price for not only the rest of his life but for all eternity.

One dipped a hand in his pocket and took out the revolver the mad scientist had shown them just eight hours ago. "There's just one bullet in it, so don't get any funny ideas. You attempt to shoot one of us, the kid gets it first, you get it second, and your pal down there gets it third. *Capisce*?"

As if on cue, Three turned his gun on mother and child, while Two pointed hers at Darrel's back. One held out the revolver with his left hand while his right lifted the smaller automatic until Troy stared straight down the black barrel.

Ears buzzing, Troy took the weapon. It was heavier than he'd expected. The weight seemed to drag his entire arm down.

Maybe there's a blank inside, like in the movies.

One nodded toward the kneeling man. "Whenever you're ready. I don't think you can miss from here."

A wave of nausea passed over Troy, and he struggled to breathe. He'd never shot a gun before, never even held one. The revolver hung at his side.

It's not loaded. The gun's not loaded.

One sighed. "'Whenever you're ready,' means now. Come on, you might have all day, but we don't. You've got three seconds, then you're out, and I'll pick someone else."

Troy gritted his teeth. Though his arm felt like it

belonged to someone else, he raised the gun. He aimed at Darrel's back and willed his hand to stop shaking.

"One…"

It's a blank. It's nothing more than a blank.

"Troy, don't do it." Brenda's voice was quiet, pleading.

"Two…"

"It's okay." Darrel lifted a hand, two fingers popping into the air in the universal sign of peace. "Now, Troy."

"Three…"

Troy closed his eyes as he pulled the trigger.

Bang.

4

"Who's riding with me? Stella?"

Hagen hoped his question sounded casual, so no one thought he was singling out the pretty agent for any particular reason. But he wanted to talk to her about Joel Ramirez.

Their conversation the previous evening had been brief and inconclusive. When he'd offered to drive with her to Atlanta and help find Joel, aka Matthew Johnson, she looked surprised, even suspicious...

"Why would you want to do that?"

"Because two heads are better than one, especially when they've both been trained by the FBI. Because, if your inquiries lead you into danger, it's better to have backup. But, mostly, because I want to help. I can't leave a colleague to do something like this by themselves. I know what it's like to lose someone."

She didn't say no, but she didn't say yes either. Instead, she simply opened her apartment door. "I think it's best if you leave."

That was how the conversation had ended.

Hagen wondered if Stella thought he was too curious about Joel Ramirez. He'd done everything he could to keep his questions within the realm of inquisitiveness. However, she might already know his father's shooting was drug related. She could connect the dots. They were all FBI agents, after all.

But connecting the dots didn't matter. The records would show his father had been murdered. He'd already told her that.

He hadn't told her about his plan to rain vengeance down on his father's murderers.

All he had to do was find them. The mysterious Joel Ramirez and the death of Sergeant Keith Knox might be just the lead he needed.

"Sure, Hagen. I'll ride with you." Stella sounded annoyingly neutral. "I'll just grab my stuff."

Hagen tossed his empty espresso cup in the trash, followed by the remains of the croissant. As it clunked into the can, he punched the air in victory. His celebration was twofold—two points for the cup and two points for getting Stella alone. The drive to Stonevale was about forty minutes. That was plenty of time.

"You offering Stella a ride in your Corvette?" Ander stuffed his notebook into his bag and threw it over his shoulder. "That's a sly move, man. But you're wasting your time. Stella already knows you."

Hagen gritted his teeth, annoyed. That was exactly the kind of reaction he was hoping not to provoke. "The 'Vette's in the shop. Something with the transmission. I signed out one of the agency's 'til she's all better."

Their small residency agency didn't have the fleet of black SUVs like the FBI television shows depicted. Here, agents drove their personal vehicles or could take one of the few SUVs on hand if needed.

"Slumming it, huh? Cool. Then you've got room for more. I'll ride with you guys."

Hagen studied his fellow agent, not bothering to hide the suspicion in his gaze. Ander, in turn, offered a bright grin that lit up his tan complexion.

Hagen flashed a fake cheery smile of his own. "Yup, sure. Let's go."

He led them out to his appointed SUV, a black Explorer that looked more like the kind of vehicle his father would have once driven. It was exactly the type of nondescript ride Hagen tried to avoid, a symbol of comfort and stability. What good had that stability done for his dad?

"Shotgun!" Ander shouted at Stella, already tossing his bag on the front seat.

Stella's mouth popped open. "Who says chivalry is dead?"

"I'm a feminist and fully support your right to yell shotgun, but you didn't." Ander slammed the door, staking his claim. "Get in, loser. We're going to catch some bad guys."

Stella rolled her eyes and climbed into the back seat. As soon as her seat belt was on, she placed her feet on the back of Ander's seat and pushed hard, causing the agent's blond curls to bounce.

Hagen smiled. That was exactly what one of his sisters would have done. "Okay, children, settle down."

Though missing his Corvette more with each mile, he settled into the surprisingly comfortable leather seat for the forty-minute drive.

Ander turned up the air-conditioning. "Anyone ever been to Stonevale?"

"I have." Hagen turned the air-conditioning back down again. "My sister and her husband just bought a ranch near there. If I get a chance during the case, I'll try to swing by."

"Is that Amanda?"

Hagen glanced in the rearview mirror, his eyes meeting Stella's. She remembered. They'd shared a car ride during the last case when his other sister, Brianna, had called with a long list of complaints about her new brother-in-law.

He smiled. "Yeah."

"I thought she lived in Memphis?"

Good memory.

"She officially does, but they bought this ranch to *escape* to." He held up his fingers, air-quoting the word.

"Neat. I'd love to meet both your sisters, but…" a mischievous glint twinkled in her expression, "I especially want to meet Amanda, so I can congratulate her on her dog-naming skills."

Ander laughed, and Hagen's smile vanished. "Not funny. And Bubs doesn't like it when you laugh at him."

"That's Bubbles," Ander corrected. "Show your beast some respect, man. He earned that name."

"All right, you bullies. Leave my dog alone." Time for a subject change. "What do you guys make of the case? We talking personal vendetta here?"

Ander pulled his iPad from his bag and pulled up the case file. "That's where I'd put my money. All the victims are connected. Three family members. Three family friends. What I don't get is why take all of them? If whoever did this had a problem with one of the Bisgards, why not just kidnap Dee Dee or Ronald? Or even both. Six seems like overkill, and why take a child?" He turned in his seat. "What do you think?"

Stella reached for Ander's iPad instead of pulling out her own. "It doesn't make sense, does it? Kidnapping one person is hard work. Kidnapping six people isn't just six times harder, but it packs in some serious complications. You can't do it alone, which raises the risk of leaks. If your victims resist, you've got a real fight on your hands, which would leave evidence. You've got to have a good reason to take six people. And a good plan for holding them."

Hagen glanced in the mirror again. Stella's forehead was creased, and she was twisting the gold stud in her ear. She always did that when she was thinking. It was like she was winding up her brain.

"Could be the work of one psycho with *Charles Manson style* devotees committed to fulfilling his every desire."

Hagen smiled. He liked how she thought. "True. Think we can rule out a serial killer this time?"

Stella glanced up from the iPad to meet his gaze in the mirror again. "I don't know if we can rule one out, but I've never heard of a serial killer taking on six people at once. They usually take their victims one at a time and savor their killings. But, hey," Stella handed the iPad back to Ander, "we've had some pretty weird perpetrators the last week or so. Who knows what we're going to get this time?"

Hagen moved into the fast lane and gunned the engine, missing his Corvette more than ever. "And one of the victims is a kid, remember, a two-year-old."

"It takes a special kind of evil to take a child." Ander's chipper demeanor disappeared.

They fell silent. Hagen imagined a small boy, terrified, tears streaming down his face. He pushed the gas harder. The Explorer picked up, but not by much.

"Man, if someone tried to take Murphy, god help them." Ander stared at the road ahead. "I think that's one time when training goes out the window, and I just tear someone limb from limb."

Hagen side-eyed him. Ander's face was set, clearly angry just imagining what he would do to someone who tried to harm his kid. Hagen understood that feeling. But, for today, he needed Ander calm. He needed to make sure Ander was thinking clearly.

"If someone tried to take your boy, I think *Murphy* would tear him limb from limb. Remember that time we played catch? I wouldn't want to get on the wrong side of that right arm. Damn near took my hand off with that pitch."

Ander laughed, his expression softening again. "Like father, like son."

"No, man. I'm saying your *boy's* strong. The only thing his dad's biceps are good for is lifting beer glasses, and I've seen you use both hands for that."

Ander swiveled in his seat and flexed his left arm for Stella's benefit. He poked a finger into the top of it. "He's just jealous of this. He likes to drink his European beer from those itty-bitty glasses with the stems. But because I bench, I get to drink from those big German steins. And, yeah, you need both hands to lift one of those bad boys."

As much as Ander annoyed Hagen at times, he had to admit the agent was funny. He chuckled. "Bench, my ass. You got those little bulges lifting Murphy onto your shoulders. I've seen you. Barely put the boy down."

Ander relaxed his arm and faced the front again. "Yeah, what can I do? He asks, and I can't say no. I mean, I don't get to see him that often, and I…kinda like it. Carrying your kid on top of your shoulders? He feels like a king, and I feel like the proudest dad in the world."

Ander's ex-wife had moved to Maine with the ten-year-old, and Hagen knew Ander hadn't seen the boy since Easter.

An unexpected rush of emotion hit Hagen like a brick. He could remember riding on his father's shoulders, feeling like that king. Until someone took it all away.

"Ha, you sound like my dad." Though Stella had lost her father, too, she was grinning, though her eyes didn't quite hold the same sentiment. "He was like that with my brother. Jackson was always asking to ride on my dad's shoulders, and my dad could never say no either. As soon as Jackson was up there, he'd start riding Dad like a horse, making him go faster and jump up and down."

Ander laughed over his shoulder. "Oh, yeah. Murphy does that too. The more I jiggle around, the more he loves it."

"Yeah…well. My dad tried running and jumping onto the veranda one day with Jackson on his shoulders, but he forgot how tall that made him. Jackson smacked his head on the beam above the front door. He had a number from our house's address imprinted on his forehead for days."

Ander roared with laughter. Stella joined him.

Hagen glanced in the mirror. He couldn't remember when he had last heard Ander laugh like that, and Hagen had never made Stella laugh so freely.

He wasn't jealous. That wasn't the strange feeling in his gut. They could laugh. Colleagues could enjoy one another's company. That was fine. Hagen was just irritated he didn't get to talk to Stella on her own.

And he didn't want to hear "happy father" stories.

Rrring.

Saved by the bell.

Glad he'd taken the time to pair his phone to the vehicle, Hagen fumbled for the steering wheel button to take the call. The Corvette was much easier.

"Hagen?" Slade's deep voice rang through the speakers.

Hagen sat straighter. "Yeah. You're on speaker. I'm here with Ander and Stella. We're just coming into Stonevale now."

"Good. Put your foot down. Chloe and I are already here, and Hagen?"

"Sir?"

"We've got a body."

_____

5

"How did it feel waiting for the bullet?"

Darrel Dowers would never be able to answer my question, but I couldn't help but wonder.

He'd been given the privilege of being the first name written in my notes. He had been quick to volunteer as my first subject, and now, he would live in perpetuity.

He'd cited his lack of family and being the oldest as a rational explanation for being the first to go, and I was pleased that Darrel had proven my first hypothesis true. That one of the friends would take the first bullet…and another of the friends would perpetrate the end of life.

The two actions had been executed in quite the unexpected manner, though.

First, I was surprised by how entirely calm Darrel had been from the moment of decision to the point of execution.

Had he no feelings?

Was that why his life meant so little to him?

I sat at my desk in the office of the old dog pound, allowing these questions to spin and turn in my mind as I searched for the answers. When they continued to elude me,

I focused on the workspace in front of me, at how the small lamp and phone were perfectly aligned.

Everything was in its place, just as it should be.

Calmed by the order, I allowed myself to think of the next steps.

My further postulations rested on the premise that the family would stick together as a unit, avoiding the threat as long as possible. And, so far, they had.

The second action I hadn't accounted for was the lack of resistance from the others. There had been some crying, a few shouts of protest, and a lot of pleading. But I witnessed little anger watching them on the monitor. Perhaps, they felt their situation was hopeless.

Had they given up already?

That would be fascinating, if true. So much for resilience in the face of adversity. Most people didn't possess half the strength, mentally or physically, they thought they did.

Perhaps the subjects were collectively relieved someone had volunteered, both to die and to kill.

That would be even more fascinating. I always suspected the human capacity for ruthless selfishness was not as deeply buried as some argued. Instead of fighting tooth and nail in the name of justice, the majority of humans retreated and thanked their lucky stars that misfortune missed them and landed on someone else.

Just apply a little pressure.

But if that were true, what could I say about Darrel Dowers? He'd stepped up without a second thought. He'd volunteered to die to save his friends. I supposed that made him a "good" man. A man of moral integrity, someone prepared to do the right thing even at great personal cost.

Of course, agreeing to sacrifice himself also made him a dead man, so what was the point of all that goodness? It certainly did him no good.

I wanted to laugh at that irony, but the laughter didn't come. Nothing came. Not surprise or disappointment or even relief that my experiment was proceeding so well.

My own disinterest remained unchanged. Therefore, another purpose of this experiment was presently a failure. Even when young Troy had raised the gun and pulled the trigger, I'd remained unmoved. When the boom from the gun had rattled the cages, when the blood sprayed out of Darrel's body, when he fell with a wet thud onto the floor, I continued on, untouched by any basic human emotion.

The Bisgards had cried, all three of them. Brenda had screamed, of course. Tedious, that one. And Troy had just stood there, the gun smoking in his hand, until One took the weapon and shoved him back into his cage.

I might have been watching a movie while flicking through my phone for all the emotional impact the shooting had engendered in me. It wasn't boring, but nothing registered. No rush of excitement. If I had had any emotional response, it was…disappointment.

Perhaps my emotional state would change as the experiment marched onward. After all, I was mildly interested in seeing who would volunteer next and whether Troy would continue to play the gunman. Maybe he'd be the last one standing, the one I'd have to shoot myself.

Would that provide the emotion I sought?

Studying the board I'd fitted to the wall across from the desk, I read my original hypotheses.

One: *A friend would take the first bullet.*

Two: *Another friend would pull the trigger.*

Three: *As the experiment grows more intense, as husband shoots wife or vice versa, my emotional responses will increase.*

That was something to look forward to.

Four: *The family will lose hope of survival after the second shooting.*

Did I still believe that to be true?

It would be remarkable if they still believed anyone, including the child, would survive. People really did cling to the smallest sliver of hope. Of course, not one of them would live. I couldn't risk any of them sharing their experience.

The buzzing of my cell phone broke my thoughts.

Mother. What did she want?

I would take her call, not because I wanted to speak to her but because, occasionally, I had no other choice. No one knew me better than she did. No one else knew all my secrets.

A dilemma I would need to address very soon.

Recently, she'd been spilling them. My secrets. It wasn't her fault. I didn't think she intended to let my childhood stories pass her lips. But that was one symptom of Alzheimer's. Patients forgot who they were talking to. Her blabbing wasn't personal. She wouldn't have stayed silent for so long if she had wanted to hurt me.

Still, if she continued to lose control, if she couldn't stop herself, I'd have to stop her.

"Is that you, dear?"

I winced. Her voice had become shrill as she aged. It was like listening to someone scraping their nails down a blackboard. It reminded me of Brenda screeching in her cage.

"Yes, it's me, Mother. Of course, it's me. You called."

"Frances has taken my glasses again. I told you about that woman. You can't trust her. I have to watch her like a hawk."

"Which must be hard to do without glasses." Sometimes, I couldn't help myself.

"It's not funny."

Dropping my chin onto my fist, I sighed. She'd lost her glasses three times this week. Twice she was wearing them, and once she'd left them in her toothbrush cup.

"Have you looked on your nose?"

"On my…what would they be doing on my nose? Silly boy." A second later, she cackled. "Oh, look. Here they are. I was wearing them all along. Frances must have put them there when I wasn't looking. She's terrible. And I think she's stepping out with that Eric, you know. You'd think he'd know better. At his age. Men! He must be almost ninety if he's a day, but they don't stop, not ever. And that Frances just encourages him. She's like that Ingrid Machin. You remember her?"

I remembered Ingrid Machin all right.

"Mother, it's time you took a nap."

"It is?"

"Yes. Find your bed."

"My bed?"

I waited.

"Oh, there it is. A nap sounds lovely…what's your name again?"

Closing my eyes, I ended the call and returned my phone to its perfect position.

Why had Mother brought up that woman's name?

Ingrid Machin had lived in the house opposite ours. One Saturday afternoon, I heard someone yelling in our front yard. I must have been about nine years old and was playing in my room. From my window, I saw her. Her long, lank, black hair framed her splotchy face, which was red from hysterics.

"Your boy killed my cat!" I'd lifted my window just enough to hear her words. "He cut her open and pulled out her guts."

Mother had been good in those days. She stayed calm. "Why on earth would he do such a thing?"

Ingrid balled up her fists. "Because he's a little freak and everyone knows it. Just like we all know he set the church on fire. He's a nut, and he's going to get someone killed."

Mother just shook her head. "Ingrid, do you have any proof at all to back up these horrible accusations?"

"Proof? I don't need no damn proof. That boy of yours is a—"

"Then I'll ask you to remove yourself from my property before I call the police and have you removed."

Not waiting for an answer or to even see if Ingrid would do as she was told, Mother turned on her heel. The door slammed shut beneath my window. Ingrid stood there for a moment longer, calling my mother to come back out.

I returned to my toy soldiers, expecting my mother to come up the stairs immediately, but she didn't. It wasn't until my red soldiers had defeated the blue that she appeared. She sat on my bed, her eyes red. Had she been crying? I wasn't concerned. Tears came often when I was a kid.

She patted the blanket next to her. "Come and sit next to me."

I dropped my soldiers and did as she instructed.

"Why do you do these things, huh?"

I knew exactly what she meant, but I wasn't sure how to answer her, so I shrugged. With the cat, I'd been curious. I wanted to see what it looked like from the inside. With the church, I wanted to see how high the flames reached when the spire burned.

But, deep down, what I really wanted to know was how it *felt* to watch those things die and burn. I didn't understand Mother's crying, her emotions. Turning the cat inside out, burning the church, all of it meant nothing. I felt the same as always. No joy, no sorrow, not even fear that I might be caught. I felt nothing except a vague curiosity.

I'd spotted an irregularity in nature—me. And I wanted to experiment.

She wouldn't have understood. Mother felt too much.

"You know, I can't protect you like this forever. If you

don't stop, they'll take you away from me. Do you want them to take you away from me?"

I shook my head. But I didn't not want them to take me away either.

"Then why do you do these things?"

Knowing from experience that she wouldn't leave until I spoke, I attempted to answer her question—this time with the truth. "I don't know. Maybe I should talk to the doctor about it. Maybe I have a disease or something. Maybe he can give me something to fix it."

My mother grabbed my arms, gripping them hard.

"Ow, you're hurting me." The physical sensation of pain was interesting.

She stared into my face. "You never tell anyone what you've done, y'hear me? You don't tell the doctor. You don't tell no one. Anyone hears, they'll lock you up and throw away the key. Just like that." She mimed throwing a key over her shoulder.

I hung my head because that was what she expected me to do. "All right. I won't tell."

Mother released my arms and stood. "And neither will I. Not ever. It will be our secret, so help me God."

God might just have to help you, Mother. Because you're not very good at holding onto secrets anymore.

The door to the office swung open. Three stood in the doorway. His ski mask was pulled up to his forehead as though I wanted to see his weaselly, acne-ravaged face.

"Knock next time."

Three stared at me. "Say what now?"

"Knock. On the door. Before you come in."

Three turned to the door, and turned back. "But it wasn't closed proper. You were just sittin' here, man."

"I was working. I am working. And I am not your man. What do you want?"

Three shifted his weight from one foot to the other. He looked like he was dancing, badly, to a song with no tune.

"It's these experiments of yours. When am I gonna do something real, man…er, sir? All I do is point the gun at the kid's head. One has all the fun. You should make me One, man, not Three. I'll make a much better One."

I sighed. Three and One had been arguing since I'd picked them both out of the gutter. But that was their problem. I didn't need them to get along. I just needed them to do what they were told. As long as they received food and enough drugs to stave off withdrawal, they behaved. Still, I had to keep them in separate places, so they wouldn't kill each other. Their constant fighting gave me migraines.

I massaged my temples. What could I do? One, Two, and Three were necessary evils.

Six people…five now…were too much work for me alone.

Glancing back at my phone, I had an idea.

"Don't worry, Three. I might have a job for you soon. A job that's very dear to me."

6

The Stonevale Police Station contained little more than a reception area. A desk in the corner staffed by a single uniformed officer, pen in hand, was it. A room to one side had a narrow board with the word *Chief* nailed to the door, and a short corridor led to what looked like a holding cell and one more room that could have been a broom cupboard or an interview room. Stella wasn't sure which.

Fewer than ten minutes had passed between Slade's phone call and Hagen pulling up in front of the single-story, brick building. Through each of those minutes, Stella tried to avoid imagining which of the six abductees had died.

Please don't let it be the toddler.

Of all the crimes she could tackle, of all the criminals she could hunt down, a child killer was the worst. The thought turned her stomach.

Slade and Chloe met them in the reception area.

The station in Nashville, where she'd served for two years, had four floors and was staffed by two hundred officers who cycled through the building between patrols, paperwork, and downtime. Each shift, she'd see a new face and meet new officers. She couldn't imagine serving on a force consisting of only a few colleagues, never tackling crimes bigger than DUIs and teenage graffiti.

Maybe she could settle into that life one day when the hunger in her belly to find her father's killer was sated. Maybe then she'd find a small-town police force and ready herself for retirement. But that life felt a long way away from where she was now.

Slade made the introductions. "Agents, this is Chief Buck Houston." He nodded to the man standing next to him.

Chief Houston was slim, almost a foot shorter than Slade, and more than a decade older. His thick, white mustache hung over his upper lip like a little umbrella. His wire-framed spectacles gave him an owlish look. The thumbs nonchalantly tucked into his waistband suggested he was more at home in a rocking chair, reading a book to his grandchildren, than hunting down murderers.

Hagen and Ander greeted him with a nod.

Stella greeted him with a question, "Who was it?"

Slade nodded for the chief to share the news. "Darrel Dowers. He was found half an hour ago in a drainage ditch on the edge of town."

A small surge of relief swept through Stella—not the toddler—with a thin wave of nausea followed by a stronger wave of anger and determination right on its heels. They'd get whoever had done this. They had to.

Chief Houston inclined his head. "Let's go into my office."

He led them into a room with barely enough space for his paper-strewn desk. One wall was covered with a whiteboard that showed traces of red and blue ink. Stella could make out a shopping list consisting of coffee, tea bags, and low-fat milk. An office chair under the window had a thick, yellow cushion strapped to the back of it. The gray metal filing cabinet was old and worn with patches of rust. Had someone left it out in the rain?

Stella found herself squashed shoulder to shoulder between Chloe and Hagen. She pressed closer to Hagen to avoid hurting Chloe's injury. He still smelled of coffee.

Chief Houston squeezed past them, adjusted the cushion on the only chair, and took his seat. "I'd get y'all chairs," his vowels, like many folks in Tennessee, were about a mile long, "but, frankly, I don't know where I'd put 'em."

Slade had found a spot between the wall and the filing cabinet. He pushed aside a half-dead spider plant on top of it and used the space as an elbow rest.

"That's fine. Why don't you just fill us in, and we'll get to work?"

"Sounds good to me." Houston stretched his back, winced, and adjusted his cushion again. "Local coroner identified the body of Darrel Dowers and thinks he was shot in the back at close range. Hadn't been dead long, maybe an hour or two at most."

"No sign of the others?" Chloe's voice was flat.

Only a few days had passed since she'd lost a friend to the serial killer the press was now calling East Nasty's Curator Killer. He'd been shot during their efforts to capture the man who created art out of human flesh. Whatever emotional damage she'd suffered seemed to be buried deep inside. Except for the sling holding her shoulder in place, Chloe didn't appear to have changed at all. Someone must have coated her in stainless steel.

Chief Houston shook his head. "Not a peep. We've got one homicide and five missing persons."

"One of them a two-year-old." Ander had found a spot in front of the whiteboard. His lips, usually tilted upward in a half-smile, were set in a grim line.

"That's right, son, so we'd better find them right quick."

Chief Houston grabbed a file from the top of his desk and stood. "'Scuse me."

Ander took half a step sideways, which was enough to bring him to the window.

The chief opened his folder and pinned three pictures to the whiteboard with magnets. Each image showed the abandoned Bisgard dinner table. Plates were still piled with food. One chair had been turned on its side. A glass had been knocked over, sending a dark stain over the tablecloth. Whatever had happened in that room had happened suddenly and unexpectedly.

The chief scratched his temple. "Funny thing is, there's no sign of anyone having cooked the meal. No pots or pans in the sink or dishwasher, and no takeout containers in the trash."

"The meal didn't appear by magic." Stella made a note and underlined it twice. "How did the food get there?"

Houston nodded. "It's a question that needs to be answered. Already sent the food off for analysis. Maybe we'll get something back that's useful, but it'll take time, and that's one thing we ain't got."

"That's right." Slade tapped the top of the filing cabinet. "We need to get out there now and start asking questions. Stella, you're with Ander." Slade tossed his car keys to her. She caught them, bumping Chloe, who didn't flinch. "I want you to talk to Kay Harvey, Troy Harvey's mother. She's the one who discovered they were missing. Then head to the Bisgards' store. See what you can find there."

Houston returned to his chair, patting Ander on the shoulder as he passed. "You going to see Kay Harvey? I wish y'all the best of luck."

Stella didn't like the sound of that. "What do you mean?"

"Well, she's a...she's a handful, is all. Been widowed best part of twenty years now. Raised Troy by herself. Tried to homeschool him for a while, 'til it got too much." He eased himself into his seat and stroked his mustache. "She's got her own ideas, that one."

Slade pointed at Hagen. "You and Chloe talk to Ronald Bisgard's brother, Wayne. When you're done there, head to Brenda Renelle's daughter and her ex-husband. These people are all local, right, Chief?"

"That's right. This is a small place. You'll get around real easy."

7

H agen watched Stella climb behind the wheel of Slade's black Expedition while Ander folded himself into the passenger seat.

Looked like there would be no shot of speaking to Stella alone today.

Was that envy twisting his gut as the two of them pulled out? Hagen pushed the thought away. What he was feeling, he was certain, was frustration. A day investigating together was exactly what he needed to charm his way into the trip to Atlanta. And it wasn't happening.

"This one yours?" Chloe jabbed him with her elbow. She pointed to the Explorer.

"Hm? Yeah. That's the one."

Chloe pursed her lips. "I think you got old, Hagen. Are we going to investigate a murder or play a round of golf and have an afternoon nap?"

Hagen opened the door. "I think we're going to play *around* at investigating a murder. Now hop in, caddy. You can nap on the way."

Wayne Bisgard's house stood at the end of a cul-de-sac on

the edge of town. They parked in front of a planter, the bushes inside long dead. Two plastic, broken-down lawn chairs leaned against the wall beneath a window.

Before Hagen reached the porch, a man appeared in the doorway. His gray hair was swept to one side, and his belly kept his striped t-shirt from meeting the top of his cargo shorts.

"Wayne Bisgard?" At the man's nod, Hagen pulled out his FBI badge and introduced himself and Chloe. "We're from the FBI. Okay if we ask you a few questions?"

"Lookin' for my brother?" Wayne released a small grunt. "Sure. C'mon in."

An old, coffee-stained sectional with newspapers piled high took up most of the living room. Two empty beer bottles stood on the coffee table. A third was on the floor beside the leg of the couch.

"Sorry about the mess. S'what happens when you live by yourself?" Wayne waved an arm over the living room. "My wife would have yelled at me if I'd left the place in a state like this. Big C got her seven years back. Kids have moved out since then, and now I ain't got no one to yell at me no more."

Hagen nodded as though he understood. He really didn't. He lived by himself unless Bubs counted as a roommate, but he kept his place spotless. This mess had nothing to do with loneliness and everything to do with a lack of discipline. Either you had it or you built it. Or you lived in a pigsty and blamed everyone else for your self-created chaos.

Wayne marched past the couch without stopping to pick up the bottles. "Let's go into the kitchen. Can I get you some coffee?"

"I'm good, thanks." Hagen followed Wayne into a kitchen that was no cleaner than the living room. Orange fur was growing in the bottom of a glass on the table. The flower-patterned tablecloth seemed to be covered with more crumbs than flowers.

Hagen pulled out a seat and sat. "Chloe, you want coffee?"

Chloe took the seat next to Hagen. She brushed away the crumbs and rested her elbows on the table. "No thanks. I'm more of a tea girl."

Wayne scratched his head. "Tea, huh? Let me see. Might have some somewhere."

He opened a cupboard above the kitchen counter. A moth flew out, having escaped the assorted jumble of tin cans, jars, and boxes.

Hagen winced. "Tell me about your brother. Does he have any enemies? Is there anyone who might hold a grudge against him?"

"Ron? Enemies?" Wayne peered over his shoulder, a can of barbeque beans in his hand. "Naw. He's a good man, Ron. Never done nothin' bad to nobody. I always worried that someone'll take advantage of him one day 'cause he's so kind 'n' all."

He pushed the can of beans back into the cupboard, shut the door, and opened the next. A shower of pasta shells rained down onto the counter. "Aw, shoot."

Chloe lifted her sling-free hand. "Please don't bother with the tea. I'm fine, really."

Hagen didn't move. He wasn't going to clean that mess up. "So, Ronald never got into an argument? No issues with customers or suppliers that you're aware of?"

Wayne swept the pasta with his arm into the corner of the kitchen counter. "Naw. The only guy I ever saw my little brother have a beef with was Gerry Renelle."

Chloe flipped through her notepad. "Brenda's ex?"

"That's right. We was all in school together. Gerry was a good student. Became a doctor. Works in a hospital now, I think, but he was a jerk back in high school. Always getting other kids into trouble, running to the teacher, and all that. Far as I know, he never stopped bein' a jerk. Best thing Brenda ever did was walk out on that guy. It cost her a lot, though."

Chloe mumbled something under her breath and stood. "How's that?"

Wayne pulled a slim cardboard box from the back of the cupboard. The lid was creased, and the image on the top had long faded. "Huh, will you look at that? Hibiscus. My wife must have bought that. I'll put the water on."

Chloe reached past Wayne and saved a bag of rice that was in danger of falling out of the cupboard and exploding onto the kitchen floor. "How about you just sit with us?"

"That's probably a good idea." Box of tea bags still in his hand, he joined them at the small table. He seemed confused. "What was the question?"

A flash of annoyance crossed Chloe's expression, but she covered it with a smile. "You mentioned it cost a lot for Brenda to leave her husband. How so?"

"Just that she got nothin' from the divorce. Well, not nothin' exactly. He did buy that little house she's living in because that was part of the divorce settlement, but it ain't much. Just sayin' that she left a good life in a big house with a fancy surgeon for a small place and little money comin' in. He got all the big-ass lawyers, and she got some furniture and some child support. That's why Ron gave her a job in the store. Help her out, you know?"

"Anyone else you can think of who might have had a problem with your brother?" Hagen asked.

"Naw, just Gerry. He's the only asshole I know. And Ron's too good a guy to make a lot of enemies."

"How are their finances?" Warrants had already been filed to retrieve the couple's financial records, but Hagen was interested in learning what Ron's brother might know.

Wayne waved his hand in a so-so gesture. "Up and down. They did all right. On the good months, they'd sock their profits away so that they'd have backup in case of a rainy day."

"Did people in town think they were rich?"

The older man looked at Hagen with a mixture of confusion and interest. "Why?"

Hagen didn't want to share the ransom theory yet. "Just trying to get a better understanding of the community."

Wayne shrugged, his fingers toying with a bag of tea. "I guess folks thought they were doin' okay. Weren't livin' in high cotton or nothin' like that. No fancy house and no fancy cars. Most folks know a little grocery can't compete with the likes of Walmart and Costco."

They spent another twenty minutes asking the same types of questions about Dee Dee and the others. When Wayne touched on Ashton's adoption, Hagen headed down that path.

"What do you know about the adoption? Are the birth parents in the picture?"

"Nope. From what I understand, the girl was only fourteen and didn't want nothin' to do with the baby. Signed away all the rights and said she didn't know the daddy either. Fourteen." Wayne shook his head. "Kids don't stay kids long enough these days."

Hagen hadn't been much older than that when he'd started fooling around with his girlfriend at the time, but he kept that bit of knowledge to himself. "Do you know the attorney?"

"Hmm…not sure. Some highfalutin type who cost an arm and a leg up in Nashville."

Hagen bit back a groan. That wouldn't narrow down their search. Well, if a search was even warranted. He had no reason to believe that the boy's adoption was at the root of this kidnapping, but he wanted to cover every base.

After another ten minutes, Chloe pushed her notebook across the table. "Would you please write down the best number to reach you at, in case we have any more questions?" Chloe tapped her sling, showing him it'd be easier for him to write it out.

Wayne obliged. "I sure do hope you find Ron and Dee Dee soon." His face clouded in anger. "If anyone does anything to Ashton, I'll…" He didn't finish the sentence. He didn't need to.

Hagen stood and nearly groaned. Crumbs everywhere. Doing his best not to think about the state of his ass, he held out a hand. "We'll do everything we can to find them."

Hopefully alive.

They said their goodbyes and headed back to the SUV. Once outside, he brushed the back of his pants, sending bits of toast and other morsels of food he didn't want to think about onto the grass.

"The state of that place," Chloe muttered as she slipped into the passenger seat.

"Yeah. Kind of surprised you didn't go for that seven-year-old tea. Pretty sure hibiscus has a *use by whenever* date stamp." He grinned as he pulled away from the house. "What do you make of what he said about Gerry Renelle? Ron helps an asshole's ex-wife get over the divorce, and Gerry decides to take revenge? Or warn him away? Sound plausible?"

Chloe pointed the air vent toward her face. "He's talking about high school. I don't think we can make a judgment based on what someone thought about someone else back then. You know what high school's like."

He frowned. High school had been a blast. "I was lucky. It was pretty good."

Chloe shot him a look. "Not for me, it wasn't."

Hagen fell silent. He could see how Chloe might have had a rough time in high school. Teenagers could be viciously brutal to people who push against the "norm" and choose their own path. He'd had it much easier. Star of the basketball team, dating the head of the cheerleading squad—followed by three of her friends—and invitations to every party in town.

School had been easy. Outside school was when things had been hard. With no father, a couple of sisters, and a burning rage that refused to die down, things could have gone very differently for him. He'd done a pretty good job of hiding that part of who he was.

If Gerry Renelle was hiding who he was, Hagen was sure he'd be able to tell.

8

"Twenty-three years old and living in your mother's basement." Ander nodded at the narrow window between the bottom of the gray siding on Kay Harvey's house and the neatly cut grass of her front yard. "Could you have lived with your mother at that age? Would you have wanted to?"

Stella shuddered. By the time she was twenty-three, her mother had been remarried for three years, and Stella was about to enter her last year of grad school. The five months she'd spent at home after graduation had been among the least comfortable of her life.

Her mother was still her mother, but whenever Jonathan, her new husband, was around, Mom became more serious and less sociable. She talked more about money and investments and less about Stella's plans or concerns. As those months dragged on, and as Stella applied for law enforcement jobs, she'd felt increasingly alone...and increasingly desperate to leave.

"Not for long, that's for sure."

Ander rang the doorbell. "Me? I couldn't wait to get out.

Soon as I hit eighteen, I was off to college. My parents had to beg me to come back, even in the summer. I'd rather have been out camping or backpacking or surfing in Tijuana. Anywhere but home."

Stella scanned the front of the house. The walls were smooth and free of peeling flecks of paint. Crimson shutters stood open and set off the house's white window frames. The shutters shone in the midmorning sun. Everything was well maintained.

The door swung open to reveal a tall, slim woman with long, blond-gray hair tied into a messy bun. She was wearing a small, gold crucifix hanging low over her long summer dress. She scowled at the visitors.

"Yes?"

"Kay Harvey?" Stella reached for her ID.

"Yes. What do you want?"

Stella opened her badge as Ander showed his. "I'm Special Agent Stella Knox, and this is Special Agent Ander Bennett with the FBI. We're part of the team looking for your son. We just need to ask you a few questions. Can we come in?"

Kay sighed deeply and stroked the crucifix between her fingers. "If you must."

Stella glanced at Ander. Chief Houston might have been right. Troy's mother was going to be a handful. She was responding strangely for someone with a missing son.

They followed Kay into the house. She sat in the armchair opposite the fireplace. A basket of wool rested on the floor next to her. Looking annoyed, she waved at a couch decorated with floral prints and protected by a neatly arranged knitted throw. "Do sit down if you're staying, Agents."

Stella took the end of the couch closest to Kay and pulled her notebook from her bag. "Ma'am, you reported your son missing yesterday evening. I understand you went to the

Bisgards' because you were concerned for your son's well-being?"

"His *moral* well-being, Agent." Kay picked up her knitting, her posture ramrod straight. Troy's mother looked to be halfway through crafting a bright-yellow sweater. "Is caring for your son's morality a crime?" The needles clacked as she spoke.

"Of course not. Do you have cause to worry about Troy's for any reason?"

"After my Bible study, I remembered he was going to have dinner with that family." Her nostrils flared at the last two words. "Often, the Bisgards like to 'set people up.' I disapprove of matchmaking. Our Bible study discussion was about building godly relationships, so the topic was fresh in my mind, and I couldn't rest until I knew Troy was not being tempted."

Ander leaned forward. "Your son is twenty-three years old, ma'am. Don't you think he's capable of building his own relationships?"

Kay straightened her back even more. "I suppose you let your children date whomever they want, with no concern for their moral turpitude?"

"My son's ten, so no, not really. But when he's twenty-three, I expect, if we've raised him right, he'll know how to handle his own romantic entanglements."

Stella wanted to kick him. Why was he letting himself get dragged off subject?

"Well, Agent. I'm afraid there we must disagree." She placed her knitting on her lap. One hand rested primly on the wool while the other grasped the crucifix between her bosoms. "If we have no one to remind us where our duties lie, temptation will soon make us forget them. The devil has his ways. We must always be on our guard. For the sake of our children. That's why I went to the Bisgards', to retrieve Troy from the grasp of illicit temptation."

Kay bent her blond-gray head and murmured a small prayer before returning to her knitting. She clicked away as if she'd forgotten two FBI agents were in her living room.

What the hell?

Stella needed this interview to get back on track. "So, you drove to the Bisgards'. Can you describe what you found there?"

Kay tugged on her wool. "Like I told Chief Houston, the door was open, so I went in. I couldn't hear anything, which surprised me. I just figured they'd be laughing and hollering like hyenas in heat, per usual. Or maybe listening to some heathen music."

When she didn't continue, Stella was forced to provide a soft nudge. "And?"

"And the house was silent. As quiet as a grave. In the dining room, the table was laid with a banquet of food, but there was no one there. I walked out into the garden, thinking they'd just stepped outside to look at the sky or smoke something." Another nostril flare could have told the story of Kay Harvey's thoughts on the subject, but the woman apparently enjoyed her little lectures. "Tobacco and its variants are the devil's favorite tool, you see. I've told Troy again and again about the wages of sin and how—"

"Who was in the garden?"

Kay narrowed her eyes at Stella, clearly not appreciating the interruption. "No one, of course. Haven't you been listening? It just looked like everyone had left in a hurry, so that was when I…that was when I got worried and called the police."

Stella turned to a clean page in her notebook. "We're looking for motives, a reason that someone might want to target the Bisgards or their friends. Did anything strike you as unusual in your son's behavior over the last few days?"

Kay waved a hand. "No, not at all. My boy was the same boy he's always been."

"What about any grudges?" Ander rested his elbows on his knees. "Do you know of anyone who had a problem with the Bisgards? Are there any feuds or disagreements we should know about?"

"Well, aside from God's disapproval of the Bisgards, I don't know of anyone fighting with them." Kay wriggled in her seat as though an idea were creeping up her spine and nestling at the back of her head. "But there's that Gerry Renelle, Brenda's ex-husband. He's a wicked, wicked man. I can tell you that. Very angry and full of envy. Although I can't blame him for being jealous. That one, I can forgive him."

Stella glanced at Ander. Jealousy was an excellent motivator, almost as powerful as revenge. Were they onto something here?

"Why's that? What would make Gerry jealous?"

"Oh, everyone knew what that dinner party was really about. Ronald and Dee Dee Bisgard were trying to set Brenda up with some friend of theirs. Disgraceful behavior."

Ander frowned. "How long have Brenda and Gerry been divorced?"

Kay's knitting needles clacked faster. Stella was almost hypnotized by her speed. "It's been more than five years now, but they should never have done it. Divorce is a sin in the Lord's eyes. Ronald and Dee Dee have no business interfering in holy matrimony. Godless heathens. That's what they are. They should have nothing to do with my Troy."

Stella couldn't imagine Troy relying on his mother's romantic advice. It seemed like he'd found a haven with the Bisgards.

"And it's not enough that they led poor Brenda astray.

They had to take my boy with them too. Troy lost his father when he was no older than five. It's just been me and him since then." The needles slowed. "When he started playing Little League, I thought Ronald Bisgard would be a good role model for him. Troy'd finally have a man he could look up to and learn from. Well, if I'd known then what I know now."

She gave a hard yank on her wool, sending the yellow ball leaping out of the basket and rolling over to Stella's foot.

"Oops." Stella returned the wool to the basket, only to watch Kay pluck the ball right back out and plop it onto her lap.

"I've never once seen either of them in church. I'll tell you that. And Troy is so easily led. It's because he's never had a father, you see. That's why he lets himself be swayed by heathens like the Bisgards."

This was getting interesting. "Swayed in what way?"

Kay waved her needles. The sharp points almost reached Stella's nose. "I knew this day would come. It wasn't enough that God cursed Dee Dee with barrenness. I knew something even worse would happen to that family, and if my poor boy wasn't careful, he'd be caught in the devil's crossfire. I was too late." Dropping a needle, Kay threw a hand up to her forehead, à la Scarlett O'Hara. "Too late. They didn't heed the warning, and now, the Lord's holy judgment is falling upon them and striking my family too."

Stella bit her tongue. Was this woman actually saying that Dee Dee Bisgard's struggle to have children was a curse from God?

"Do you think the Bisgards deserve what's happened to them?"

Drama over, Kay lowered her hand and went back to work. The knitting needles rattled like an express train. Fuzzy springs of her hair escaped her bun in her intensity.

"Not for me to say what folks deserve. Just saying a hard

lesson is the only way some folks'll learn. 'Specially heathens. Troy will have to learn the hard way too." Tears actually filled the righteous woman's eyes.

Stella's jaw set. From the corner of her eye, she could see that Ander was staring hard at Troy's mother too. Chief Houston had been wrong. She wasn't a handful. She was a fistful. A clenched, iron fist that liked the thought of heavy blows.

"Now, I must ask both of you to leave. I think that's enough questions for one day."

Ander popped to his feet. "Do you mind if we just take a look in Troy's room? There might be something there that could help us."

Kay almost dropped her needles. "Absolutely not. If you want to conduct any searches in my home, you will need to talk to a judge and ask for a warrant. I know my rights."

Stella wanted to shove the woman's rights straight up her tight asshole. Instead, she rose from her seat. "We'll do just that."

"Now, if you don't mind…" Kay placed her knitting on the armchair and strode to the front door. The unrelenting straightness of her back made her narrow shoulder blades poke through the back of her dress. Holding the door open, she waited for Stella and Ander to pass through.

"You know, Agents, I have a strong feeling that you are both heathens too. You watch your step, now. Remember that the righteous man is delivered from troubles." She fixed Stella with a glare. "But the wicked walk blindly into them."

Ander replied with a thumbs-up. "You have a good day now."

Seething all the way back to the SUV, Stella held her tongue until she was firmly inside. "What a piece of work." She gripped the top of the steering wheel so hard her knuckles turned white.

Ander's exhale ended in a string of curses. "Man, what do you make of that?"

Stella glared at the house. "No wonder Troy lives in the basement. If I were him, I'd never leave it."

"And if I were him, I'd never go back to it. Do you think she might have had something to do with the abductions? She might just be nuts enough."

Stella pulled away from the curb with a squeak of tire on asphalt. "Maybe. She's nuts enough, but capable enough? I struggle to see her organizing something as complex as a multiple abduction and murder."

Ander frowned. "She was far too okay with what's happening for my liking. If someone took my son…"

They drove on in silence.

After they'd traveled a few miles, Ander threw up his hands. "You know what got me about what she said? Calling us heathens. I was very offended by that. I was a choirboy, y'know. Almost made the top of my Sunday school class."

Stella grinned, feeling her shoulders relax a little. "I want to see a picture of you as a choirboy."

"I was an excellent choirboy. I had a voice like an angel 'til it broke. Within a week, I was more like a frog with a bad cold."

"Ha. We should have a karaoke night." Stella tapped a hand on her chest. "She might have been right about me, though. I once took *two* communion wafers."

"Wicked child. If Troy's mom knew about that, she'd have brought the wrath of holy vengeance down on your head." Ander pointed toward a grocery store that stood next to a café at the end of the road. His voice flattened. "There it is."

Stella read the sign with its red letters on a dirty-white background. *Bisgard's Best.*

Wherever the Bisgards were, she didn't think they were at their best anymore.

9

The curses reached Hagen as soon as he climbed out of the SUV. Across the street, a row of fir trees, trimmed to resemble fat candle flames, reached almost to the roof of Brenda Renelle's brick house. A low hedge ran across the front of the property, dividing the street from the small lawn, which was cut in alternating lines of light and bright green.

In the middle of the grass, a middle-aged man in long chinos and a sweat-stained polo shirt kicked one of those ecofriendly electric lawn mowers that had to be plugged into a socket. "Work, you stupid, idiotic machine. You brainless lump of scrap metal."

Chloe leaned into Hagen, her sling brushing his elbow. "Is that an electric lawn mower?"

"Yep."

"Well, that's not something I see every day." She nodded at the cursing man. "That's gotta be Renelle, right?"

"Reckon so." Hagen watched the cursing man, checking his waistband for a gun or other weapon. When he detected no bulge, he allowed himself to relax a bit. "Think we should let him finish beating up his garden equipment before we grill him?"

"Nah. Better chance he'll let something slip if he's already fired up. Let's go." Chloe, moving surprisingly fast for someone who had been shot a few days earlier, was already halfway across the lawn, her badge in her hand. Hagen strode to catch up. "Mr. Renelle? My name is Chloe Foster. I'm a special agent with the FBI."

Gerry Renelle gave the back of his lawn mower one final kick before turning and jamming his hands on his hips. "FBI, huh? Well, first, you should know that I'm paying for this damn house, and technically, I still own everything in it. That means I have a perfect right to be here."

The front door opened to reveal a teenage girl, a loose t-shirt hanging over her cut-off denim. Gerry spun toward the house. "Go back inside, Angela. Now."

Shaking her head in what appeared to be disgust, the girl stomped back into the house. The door slammed behind her.

Hagen watched her go before turning his attention back to Renelle. "Of course, you should be here, sir. Your daughter needs you at a time like this."

"My daughter?" Renelle shook the lawn mower. "She can't stand the sight of me."

Hagen raised an eyebrow. He wasn't entirely surprised. "Can you tell me the last time you saw your ex-wife?"

"Sunday morning, I guess. I came round to make sure the lawn guy hadn't screwed up the yard again. It is *my* yard. I paid for this place, you know? And he *did* screw it up, didn't he?" He waved his arm over the front part of the immaculate lawn. "Look at this."

The grass on the tiny lot was perhaps a quarter of an inch too long, but no more than that. If this were Hagen's house, he would have waited before breaking out the lawn mower and spending sweaty hours in the sun. Renelle clearly wasn't so forgiving. And he was on a roll.

"I mean, we pay the guy. *I* pay the guy. And what does he do? Scrapes a few leaves, then sits on his fat ass all day, I bet. And what does Brenda do about it? She doesn't do shit. We might be divorced, but she's still the same spoiled, lazy housewife she always was."

"Your ex-wife has a job," Chloe stated through tight lips. "She's a cashier at Bisgard's Best."

"Call that a job? She's just playing at working for a living. All she does is pass barcodes over a scanner. You know those owners are trying to set her up with the local *accountant*?" He said the word as if it were dirty. "That's probably where she is now, holed up in some fancy hotel room, on my dime, with some dumbass bean counter."

As loud and obnoxious as Gerry Renelle was, Hagen couldn't decide if this was their guy. Were his efforts at lawn-care part of his control freak nature, or was he trying to show what a good guy he was, hoping to throw them off his trail?

Could he be trying to win Brenda's favor? Surely not. Kidnapping her, her coworkers, and killing her potential love interest wouldn't win her over.

This man was certainly going to the top of Hagen's suspect list.

Chloe seemed close to punching the guy in the nose. "You talking about Darrel Dowers?"

"Yeah, that's the guy. What a loser. Can you imagine dating a guy like that? I mean, what the hell do you talk about? 'I saved a guy three dollars in taxes today, hun. What a great day.' Jesus."

Hagen pushed down a smile. He also couldn't understand how anyone could spend their day adding up columns of numbers and looking for deductions, but everyone had their own interests. Tracking down murderers wasn't for everyone either. "So, I take it you're not too keen on the idea of your ex-wife dating Darrel Dowers?"

Renelle took a step closer to Hagen. "Now, you listen to me. I'm a surgeon at a Murfreesboro hospital. I spend my days installing heart stents and performing bypasses. I don't have time to concern myself with whatever losers my ex-wife does or doesn't date. Okay? Her mistakes are her own damn business."

Chloe frowned. "So, you're not worried that Brenda has disappeared? You're not concerned about her welfare?"

Renelle snapped his head around, pure skepticism marring his expression. "Disappeared? Agent, I don't think she's disappeared. I think she's found some guy to spend money on her. She'll show up tonight or tomorrow. Lazy, money-grubbing bitch."

Hagen stared down at the man. Renelle was still a good six inches too close to him for comfort, but Hagen wouldn't step back.

"Do you think the Bisgards are lounging around with the accountant too? She's not the only one missing. Where were you on the evening of the Bisgards' dinner party?"

Renelle frowned. He fixed his eyes on Hagen's face. "I was at the hospital, elbow deep in…Stephen Smith's chest. And you can go screw yourself."

Besides the blatant HIPAA violation, something about his tone struck Hagen as strange. Maybe it was the hesitation before his patient's name. Or maybe just the way Renelle held eye contact, like a kid trying to prove he wasn't lying.

Hagen stepped forward. The tips of his Oxford shoes almost touched the ends of Renelle's white sneakers. He lowered his voice until it was little more than a growl. "You need to watch your tone. Sir. Your ex-wife is missing. And the man you believe to be her lover has been found dead.

And all I'm getting from you is a sense that you can't control yourself."

"Darrel's dead?" Renelle's face paled, the heat of the day and his lawn-mower exertions finally getting to him.

"Darrel's dead."

Renelle took a backward step and shook the dead lawn mower again, a clear indicator that he was attempting to gather himself. "The Bisgards are missing too? And their kid?"

Hagen nodded.

Renelle shoved a hand through his hair. "Look, even if I wanted to bump off my ex and her bean counter, which I don't, what would I do with all the others? I can't stand toddlers. Couldn't bear the screaming monsters even when my daughter was one."

Chloe pointed with her chin toward the house. "We need to speak to your daughter. Her mother might have mentioned something to her that could help our investigation."

The bluster returned with a vengeance. "Oh, no, you don't. If you want to question my daughter in my house, you'll have to do a lot more than wave your badge." He threw an arm toward the road. "Now, if you're done, you can get lost. Both of you. Get a warrant or get off my property."

Renelle turned away. He shook the lawn mower until it rattled, and stomped on the motor twice. The machine still refused to power up.

Furious to his core, Hagen headed back to the vehicle. Before he had covered half the distance, he stopped and turned around.

"Sir, did you hear a bang earlier? Like a balloon popping?"

Renelle looked up. "What? Yes. Why?"

"Because you can kick that old thing all you want. It won't

help." Hagen pointed behind Gerry to a small patch of mown grass that was charred and brown. "You ran over the cable."

The curses from Brenda's front lawn continued to reach them, even through the closed doors. Hagen smiled as he pulled away.

"You enjoyed that, didn't you?"

There was no need to lie. "I did a little. We need a search warrant."

Chloe pulled her iPad from her bag, cursing as she struggled to power it on with only one hand. "For both Brenda and Gerry Renelle's homes?"

"Yup, both of them. I thought we'd find a bully. I think he's closer to a sociopath."

As Chloe waited for the case files to load, she rotated her shoulder and winced. "Damn this thing."

Thoughts of Renelle fled Hagen's mind. "You okay?"

"I'm supposed to head back to the clinic and get the dressing changed today."

Glad they were at a stop sign, Hagen did a double take. "What? Why didn't you say?"

Chloe rolled her eyes. "Because I didn't want to."

Typical Chloe. When they got back to the station, he'd search for the closest urgent care center and drag her there himself.

"What's the cause for the warrant?"

Back to business.

Hagen grinned. "Because he's an asshole?"

"If judges handed out search warrants whenever the FBI said a suspect was an asshole, we'd be doing nothing but digging through people's underwear drawers."

"Then we'll just have to find a better reason." Hagen tapped the steering wheel, thinking through everything the man had said. "Call Chief Houston. Have his guys check Renelle's alibi. I think he might be lying to us."

10

Noon.

That was all the lunatic in the white coat had given them this time. Troy had expected they'd have at least twenty-four hours before needing to make another decision.

But no. They'd been given much less than that.

Why?

Did their captor want to see how they reacted under pressure? Or was he in a hurry for a different reason? Were the cops sniffing too close? Did he need to get rid of them all before he was caught?

Please let that be the reason.

"Quick, quick. Make a decision. Who's going to sacrifice themselves for the child next?" Mad Scientist's raspy voice echoed in Troy's head.

Only an hour to go.

It wasn't enough. The still air stank with the acrid stench of gunpowder and vomit. The odor settled over the stink of the unemptied buckets in each of the cells.

After Troy had pulled the trigger, the gun kicked in his

hand with such a jerk he'd almost lost his grip on the weapon. Troy's immediate thought had been that Darrel's dive to the ground was part of the joke they were currently living. Didn't all guns recoil like that, even when they fired blanks? Wouldn't Darrel soon jump to his feet, a big grin on his face, and wrap his arms around Troy in a big, friendly hug?

But none of that had happened. Blood had sprayed the wall and spread in a puddle under Darrel's body. One, the ski-masked leader, had taken the gun from Troy's hand and shoved him back into the cell even as bile exploded from Troy's nose and mouth.

The other two masked assistants had dragged Darrel's body out through the door, spreading a red stain along the gray concrete. A few minutes later, Three came back with a mop, but only managed to spread the stain farther. With a shrug, he returned the clock to its place and left the room.

To Troy's growing horror, a narrow stream of Darrel's watered-down blood had run under the bars of his cell, chasing him into a corner of his enclosure. Once it had mercifully stopped, he curled into a ball as two flies fed on the gore.

He hadn't moved in hours. He didn't want to move ever again. All he wanted was for the walls to come crashing down and bury him alive. It was what he deserved.

Tick tock. Tick tock.

When the clock ticked to eleven thirty, Brenda's sobs began anew. The noise was an almost welcome distraction from the buzzing flies.

Who was left?

Brenda and Dee Dee. Troy and Ron. Little Ashton, the child they had to save.

And me.

"I'll be next."

Troy sat straight up. *No...not Ron.*

He could picture Ron's face, even though he couldn't see it. His dark green eyes would be puffy from lack of sleep. The permanent frown in the middle of his forehead would look like a canyon. Troy had seen that crinkle every time something stressed Ron out, whether it was how to win a baseball game or reconcile the grocery store accounts.

"No, Ron. No!" Dee Dee grabbed the bars of her cell, Ashton clinging to her arm. The kid had been a champ through all of this. Troy figured the constant state of fear must have sealed his voice box closed. The child didn't even whimper as his mother pleaded with his dad. "Please, don't leave me."

"If not me, then who? I won't let them take you, Dee Dee. Ashton needs you."

Troy glanced at the cell opposite. Brenda was on the floor, in the fetal position, her back to the corridor. Though her body shook, not a sound came from her. Had her voice box been sealed closed too?

Was it bad that he hoped so?

Yes. Yes, it was bad.

Because I'm bad.

Not for long.

"I'm next, Ron. Ashton needs you too."

"Oh, Troy." Ron's voice trailed away.

Troy wished he could see him, that he could look into his eyes and hug him.

He remembered his senior prom. His mother had told him he couldn't go, no matter how much he begged, that no boy of hers would ever take part in such lewdness and immorality. He had stormed out of the house and turned up on Ron's doorstep, crying with rage and frustration.

Ron and Dee Dee had taken him in and put him up for the next two weeks. Ron had rented him the tux for the dance, and it was Ron who had shown him how to knot the bow tie. Even in that stinking cell, Troy could close his eyes and see them standing toe to toe as Ron folded the cloth one way and the other. When he was done, Troy saw a tear in Ron's eye.

"How old were you when you came to Little League for the first time?"

Troy touched the knot under his chin and pulled on his collar. "Don't know. I must have been...what? Ten?"

"Ten, that's right. You had that pudding-bowl haircut your mother gave you, and you sat in the corner of the dugout. Didn't say a word."

Troy grinned. "I was a shy kid."

"Yeah. You've still got that, haven't you?" Ron pinched Troy's cheek. Troy batted away his hand. "You spoke when you got onto that mound, though, didn't you?"

"Did I? I don't remember being very good."

"No, you weren't too good that day. But you were better than I'd expected. You got the ball to move, and you brought it in fast enough. But I heard what you were saying up there that day, that there was something in you that needed to be set free. And you weren't going to find it at home." Ron pulled the end of the tie so that it came loose. "Now, you try it."

Troy arranged the tie so that one end hung lower than the other. He brought the longer end across and tucked it up. "Yeah, I liked baseball. For a few hours each week, I was...I was just like all the other kids." He pulled the tie closed. "There."

Ron wrapped a hand around the back of Troy's neck and pulled him into his chest. "I've watched you grow up, son. I've seen you find who you are. Me and Dee Dee? We couldn't be prouder of you."

"Troy!"

The sound of his name dragged Troy back to the reality of his cell.

"I can't let you do that. You've got to live, son. You need to make it out of here. You and Dee Dee, Ashton and Brenda. I can't let you die." He paused. "But, Troy?"

"Yes, sir?"

"I need you to be the shooter. I can't...I can't ask it of Dee Dee or Brenda."

The floor seemed to open beneath Troy's feet, dropping him into a deep, black pit. He was vaguely aware that Dee Dee was crying, but her voice sounded far away, as though her cell was at the end of a long, dark tunnel.

"Troy?" Ron's voice cut through the distance.

"Hm?"

"Will you do that for me, son? I trust you. You've always done what's right."

The force that was sucking Troy down sucked harder. He could no longer feel his hands or feet. The concrete walls faded. The world disappeared. Nothing mattered anymore, nothing at all.

"No." Troy had never been more sure of anything.

A low growl sounded from the cell next door. "Listen to me, son. This is how it needs to be. If you don't kill me, then I'll kill myself. When they hand me that gun, I'll turn it on myself. I promise. I'm going one way or another."

He would, too, Troy knew it. He'd never known Ron to back out of a promise.

Tick tock. Tick tock.

Troy closed his eyes as if that would shield him from the words he was about to say. "I'll do it."

"Good. Just...make it quick for me, huh?"

Troy didn't reply. He'd do it. And after he murdered Ron, after he killed the man who'd been the closest thing to a father he'd ever known, he'd die next. At least he wouldn't have long to wait.

Only a few hours had passed since Darrel died. Maybe Troy would have even less time after Ron. That would be a blessing.

Rrring.

Noon.

The door opened, and One, Two, and Three entered, their ski masks crooked, their white coats rumpled and stained with blood.

Without a word, Three opened Dee Dee's cage and yanked Ashton away from his screaming mother. A second later, a gun was pressed to the child's head.

Through Dee Dee's screams, through the roaring of blood in Troy's head, a faraway voice was yelling, "No! I'm going. I volunteered. Give him back to his mother."

The world rocked as the cage next to him opened, hinges squeaking to harmonize with all the other noises. Ron landed on his knees in the middle of the corridor.

One lifted the revolver and asked a question.

Troy wasn't sure his mouth would cooperate, but it did. "Me."

It'll be my turn soon.

As if his arms and legs were attached to strings, a puppet master forcing his every move, Troy stepped from his cage and gripped the revolver when it was pressed into his hand.

Two hours, three tops, and this nightmare will be over.

He raised the gun. Ron turned his head. He was saying something. Troy caught the words "son" and "proud" and "love" before he pulled the trigger.

Bang.

A red mist exploded, sending droplets in every direction. A mile away, someone screamed and screamed and screamed.

You're next. Soon, very soon, you'll find peace.

The gun disappeared from Troy's numb fingers, and a hand landed on his shoulder and pushed. Troy slipped in Ron's blood before falling into his cage.

A voice broke through the distance. "Next one in twenty-four hours."

11

Opening my notebook, I turned to where I'd prepared for the second experiment and stared at the name I'd carefully printed at the top of the page.

Brenda Renelle.

With a single stroke of my pen, I crossed it out. One hypothesis negated. Human nature could sometimes be difficult to predict.

But that one? I was strangely unsettled for being wrong.

I was so sure that I would be writing about her death.

No, I hadn't expected her to volunteer. That would have been silly of me. The woman seemed much too selfish for that.

When Three had taken the child from the cage, I'd assumed all hands would point to Brenda in order to save the boy. I'd told One to take her if they did that. It was what they should have done.

Brenda wasn't family. Her attachments to the others were weak. She was entirely expendable.

But she would live another day while Ron, a husband and father, had stepped up.

How noble. And how stupid.

I wrote Ron's name at the top.

Arguments against Ron volunteering to die.

His family depended on him. People loved him. He had everything to live for. Had I not interfered in his life, Ron would have loved to see his son grow up. He would have supported his wife.

How bizarre that he thought abandoning his family was more honorable than persuading the others to gang up on Brenda.

Darrel's sacrifice? That was entirely logical. No one loved him. Someone else could easily perform his work. His life was worthless, and his death was no loss at all. He must have seen that in the end. I respected that decision.

But Ron? His decision was moral and old fashioned. He saved the women and children first. And, yet, his decision harmed the people he loved most. It could almost be described as an act of selfishness. Almost. He had, after all, chosen to turn his wife into a widow and leave a child fatherless.

Why? To save the others from death? Or to avoid living with the burden of killing someone else? Or maybe Ron had figured out no one would be getting out of this alive, so order didn't matter?

Whatever his reason, he'd placed that burden on Troy's shoulders. And the young man had accepted it again.

Interesting.

I laid down my pen and leaned back in my chair. The two men presented such fascinating conundrums. Was Ron's self-sacrifice brave and altruistic, or cowardly and egotistic?

And did Troy's decision to take the gun stem from the belief that he would be the one to survive in the end? Surely not. He could have sat back and let anyone do the killing. His conscience would have been clean.

His sacrifice appeared to be both generous and painful.

The effects of trauma were becoming clearer as the experiment continued. Troy's first reaction had been largely one of shock, as though he hadn't really believed that someone was about to die.

He had vomited and cried after the first shooting.

And, yet, he had overcome that shock and agreed to kill again.

The harm he was causing to himself was becoming quite clear. The trauma was working its way into his bones. He was withdrawn and quiet, behaving like an abused child.

The thought made me smile.

I picked up my pen. *Like little Hank Ferguson*, I wrote.

Hank had been two years below me in middle school, with bright ginger hair and a stammer that made it hard for him to say much. I made friends with him, and how grateful he was for that friendship. He would have done anything for me.

No matter how I treated him.

It was fascinating to watch.

Troy's behavior echoed Hank's. He was silent and withdrawn now. His eyes had developed a faraway look, as though he had already removed himself mentally from his environment.

And, yet, despite the damage he was enduring, when Ron asked him to be his executioner, Troy barely argued. He stepped right up and killed again.

Subject's behavior demonstrates courage in the face of hardship.

Despite his situation and his past, Troy appeared to have kept a mental strength and an emotional depth that he could use to accomplish almost anything.

I stopped writing. What was that little tickle at the back of my throat?

Was that envy I'd felt as I wrote those words?

Perhaps there was just a flicker of jealousy.

And with that flicker came a touch of disappointment. After all this effort, all the planning, the only results I had to show so far were the weakest of roars from the old, green monster. Jealousy was nothing new. I'd felt that before. And the emptiness that followed each mildly dissatisfying tickle.

The door burst open. One stormed into my observation room, closely followed by Two.

"I'm not working with that little fu—"

"Language," I warned.

One pulled himself straight. "I'm not working with that… with Three anymore. I won't. He's dangerous. He's going to kill me. He ain't firing on all his cylinders no more."

I pressed my fingertips together, wishing I found my assistants half as fascinating as my subjects. But they behaved like children. Once my experiment was complete, I could care less if Three killed both of them and followed up his double homicide by diving headfirst into an acid bath.

"He won't lay a finger on you. Trust me."

Two threw up her hands. "We do trust you, but we don't trust that…that lunatic working with us."

So tiring.

"I will talk to him. Now, get out of my office. I have work to do."

The pair turned and left, leaving the door open behind them. With all the patience I could muster, I pushed to my feet and closed it before settling back down with my notes.

Troy Harvey, you're such an interesting specimen. Whatever will happen to you next?

12

B isgard's Best was as abandoned on the inside as it had appeared on the outside.

With the owners and two of their small staff gone missing, the place was shut down. The bright paint on the outer walls had been cheery but walking into the vast place felt like entering a ghost town. With the store's lights off, the shelves were cast in gloom. Cash registers sat dark and lifeless. Somewhere in the back, a refrigerator's hum was the only undercurrent of sound.

Stella didn't like it. It was like being inserted into a horror movie, waiting for some monster to jump out.

Ander exaggerated a shiver. "Closed stores always give me the creeps. Worked retail for a summer when I was at college. Nothing more depressing than coming into a locked store first thing in the morning." He looked around. "Middle of the day, man. This is even worse."

Stella felt the same. When Chief Houston had told them the store had been closed to both staff and customers since the abduction, she hadn't imagined it would resemble an apocalypse so soon. This place had that post-zombie vibe, despite everything being neatly in place.

She moved down the first aisle. Signs hung from the ceiling, indicating where shoppers could find their canned goods, fresh bread, and dairy products. On the wall, a line of tubes offered a variety of muesli, nuts, and dried beans. In the produce section, someone had arranged the yellow, green, and red peppers into a colorful diamond.

Ander stopped and examined the display. "That looks nice, but it's no good for business. No one wants to ruin all that hard work."

Stella glanced at the vegetables that were already showing signs of age and moved on. She never knew what to do with that stuff. Food was something that came put together, like cars and furniture. "Sounds like you missed your calling. You should have been in store design."

"Oh, yeah. I'd have been good at that. I've got a lot of experience buying food, not much rearranging it, though."

"I've got a lot of experience eating it." She pulled her leftover pastry out of her bag. Biting into it brought a jolt of sugary goodness and chased away the creepiness of the store.

"Got another one of those?"

She moved past barrels of olives and gherkins. "It kinda tastes like purse lint now. You wouldn't want it."

They reached a freezer packed with pizzas and frozen tacos, and Stella remembered that her freezer was empty. Again. She'd be ordering in tonight. Again. She gestured with her crumpled napkin to the back of the store. "Let's see what's back there."

Stella moved past the detergent aisle into a back hallway that ended at a closed wooden door marked *Office*. A light shone from beneath the door.

A shadow moved across the light.

Stella stopped and held up her hand. No one was

supposed to be here. Slowly, she drew her weapon and indicated for Ander to take point while she covered.

Ander crept past her until he reached the door. Stella swallowed hard and leveled her gun.

How long had it been since she'd been forced to draw her weapon? Only a few days, and how had that ended?

She could see it now. Chloe sprawled on the ground, a puddle of blood stretching under the desk. And him, pointing his weapon at her.

"Put your gun on the floor for me, Stella. That's it, nice and slow."

And she had done it. A trained agent taken by complete surprise. She hated how easily she'd fallen into that trap.

Not this time. Not again.

She gripped her weapon harder and gave Ander a small nod.

Ander threw open the door and shouted, "FBI."

Hagen sat at the desk, his face just visible behind the computer monitor. His expression showed no surprise or concern. "Yeah, I know. You want me to put my hands up, or shall we just head straight for the strip search?"

The relief that flowed through Stella was quickly followed by annoyance and disbelief. "What the hell?" She holstered her weapon. "What are you doing here? We could have killed you."

Hagen inserted a flash drive. "We got the warrant for the store's electronics. Slade sent me over to download everything from the computer while Chloe's at urgent care getting her wound poked. Forensics will be here soon to cart everything out to Mac, but Slade wanted backups of all the files so we'll have our own copy." He glanced at his watch. "Thought you guys would already be here."

Ander shrugged. "We've been busy."

Stella stepped into the office. The room had more order

than she'd expected for a grocery store office. A Little League pennant hung on the wall behind the desk. A picture of Ronald and Dee Dee leaned crookedly on a shelf on the opposite wall. They looked happy. His thoughtful face smiling, her bright-blue eyes shining.

A metal filing cabinet stood in the corner. Each drawer was labeled by year. Stella tugged on the top drawer. It slid out easily, revealing folders marked as tax documents, invoices, revenue sheets, and employee records.

Hagen stretched in the chair. "Whatever you find over there, Stella, we're going to find in here. And it'll be easier to search too."

Stella frowned and continued flicking through the folder. "Not everything." She turned over the resumé she was holding. Someone had written *rejected* in the corner in red ink and circled it. "People make notes on paper documents they might not put in a file."

Wasn't that why she and the team used notebooks instead of the iPads they'd been issued? They didn't want every thought in their head to go into official records.

"Smart thinking," Ander and Hagen said in unison. They looked at each other, and Stella half-expected them to shout "jinx."

When they, instead, went back to their work, she grabbed all the folders from the top drawer and placed them on the desk next to the monitor. "We should take everything from the last three years back to the station and go over it all there. We need to learn everything we can about the store's current employees, old employees, investors, suppliers, anyone they might owe money to."

Ander flicked open the top folder. "You think this is financial?"

Stella pulled another armful of records from the filing

cabinet. "I think it could be. We might get lucky and find evidence of a big black-market loan they haven't paid back."

"Guess we've got some reading to do." Ander gathered up the files. "The surveillance footage should be coming up soon as well."

Hagen yanked the flash drive out of the computer. "Got it. And let's hope those other search warrants come through quickly too. Gerry Renelle is a jackass. I don't know if he's involved, but I want to dig around in his stuff anyway."

"Gerry Renelle, Brenda's ex?" Stella pulled a sheet out of the tax folder. She frowned and put it back. "You should meet Troy Harvey's mother. If Gerry Renelle gives you the creeps, she'll make your toes curl."

Hagen raised an eyebrow. "Really? What's the matter with her?"

"She's the right hand of God."

Stella sighed at the pile of folders now covering the desk. Crammed into that room with the two men, the place seemed to have shrunk. "Let's get out of here."

Neither agent needed to be asked twice.

Ander locked the door of Bisgard's Best behind them, sealing the gloom still darkening the empty aisles inside.

There had to be a light somewhere, and they needed to find it.

Fast.

13

"How many more hours of this stuff do we have?"

Stella had been sitting in the cramped interview room at the Stonevale Police Station for the past three hours. She was beginning to doubt there were any large spaces anywhere in this small town.

The room wasn't much bigger than Mac's office in Nashville, but Chief Houston had crammed a table, three chairs, and an oversized monitor into the tight space. Since the hard drive that belonged to the monitor was a dinosaur that took five minutes to pull up a single website, Stella was using her laptop instead.

Over the past half hour, the others had all trickled into the space. Chloe, pale and a little sweaty, took the seat next to Stella, leaving Ander and Hagen to stand in front of the door, their shoulders almost touching. Stella pushed the fast-forward symbol on the video.

Slade stepped into the small office and took the remaining chair. He passed her a thumb drive. "Try this. One of the officers just got it from a different neighbor's security camera. It's got the three hours before the party begins up to around one in the morning. Maybe we'll have more luck with this."

Stella pulled up the footage. Since leaving the supermarket, she had done nothing but trawl through grainy images, searching for anything that might give a clue to who had taken the Bisgards. The couple didn't have a security camera at their house, so she'd had to look at footage from their neighbors. So far, she'd found nothing.

She pressed play, and a country road lined with elm trees appeared on the screen. The footage from the wide lens of the camera bent the trunks and stretched the road. The setting sun cast a dim glow over the hills in the distance.

"What are we looking at here?" Ander asked.

Slade squinted at the screen. "It's from a house about a hundred yards away. We get a view of the road, but not much more."

Stella sped up the video. The glow on the hills grew darker. The shadows of the elm trees stretched and passed along the road. A truck sped past the camera.

"Go back." Hagen gripped Stella's shoulder. His fingers were warm and strong, but the contact made her feel…what? Uncomfortable? Alive? Included? Forcing her mind back to her task, she leaned forward and rewound.

As the truck rolled back, Hagen released his grip.

"That's Troy's." Slade pointed at the image. "Chief Houston said that all the guests' vehicles were found outside the house. Looks like Troy was the first to arrive."

Stella hit play again. Darrel's Toyota followed shortly after Troy's old Nissan. A few minutes later, a red Chevy pickup barreled down the road in the opposite direction.

"Stop there." Slade consulted a form in his lap. "Can you see the license plate?"

Stella zoomed in, zeroing in on the truck's back bumper.

The closer she got, though, the blurrier the plate became. "I can't see a thing."

Slade shook his head. "Doesn't matter. One neighbor has a red Chevy truck. Just put it on the list and keep going. We can send the image to the tech team, but it's so pixilated it'd be a miracle."

Stella moved the video on. They identified two more neighbors before Brenda's car turned in shortly before the party was due to begin.

Chloe rubbed her shoulder. "Everyone's there now. The window is tight. Any car heading toward the house could be our guys."

"You okay, Chloe?" Stella glanced at her. "Shoulder not acting up too much?"

"I'm fine." Chloe snapped the words and dropped her hand. "Just hit play, will you?"

Stella mashed play again. Next time she wanted to make sure that Chloe was okay, she'd just bite her tongue. It would probably be less painful.

The road was dim now. About fifteen minutes passed when a new pair of headlights flashed on the screen.

"Roll that back, Stella." Ander's direction was entirely unnecessary. Stella was already rewinding the video. A brown pickup with a covered bed reappeared.

She glanced at Slade. "Does that belong to any of the neighbors?"

He shook his head. "Can you get the plates on this one?"

Stella rewound until she reached the point where the truck first entered the frame. The registration plate glowed at the bottom of the screen, but the numbers and letters were bleached by the light from the neighbor's house.

"Best I can get, I'm afraid. We wouldn't have been able to make out the makes and models of the other vehicles if we hadn't known what we were looking for."

Slade cursed under his breath. "Right. Snap that screen and send it to Mac. I'll have everyone plow through databases and see if they can find anyone in the area who owns a similar truck."

"A brown pickup in rural Tennessee." Chloe leaned back in her chair. Sweat beaded on her upper lip. She'd clearly pushed herself too far today. "That should cut down our search."

"And they might not even be from Tennessee." Stella snapped the image. "With nothing else to go on, that search could take a while. And we just don't have 'a while.'"

Slade's phone pinged, and he scowled at the screen. "It's from Martin. I've had him going over the Bisgards' financial records, personal and business. Doesn't look like there's much there. They took out a fifty-thousand-dollar bank loan five years ago to renovate the store. They haven't missed a payment, though, and there's only five grand left to pay. Their house is free and clear, and they don't appear to have any other debts."

"So, no trouble with loan sharks." Hagen sounded disappointed.

"Wouldn't want to make your life too easy, Hagen. Caleb's been checking out the store's employees. Other than Brenda Renelle and Troy Harvey, the Bisgards only employed two other people. Billy Joe Tompkin. He's seventy-two and has worked as the custodian for over twenty years. And Roxanne Jenham. Nineteen. They took her on just two months ago."

"Roxanne Jenham?" Stella reached for the pile of folders on the table next to her laptop. She searched for the most recent employees binder and pulled out an application form. "Here. Thought I recognized the name. Someone wrote something across the top of the form."

Ander peered over Stella's shoulder. "What does it say?"

"It says 'Go easy on her, Ron. I think she really needs this job.' The handwriting appears to be feminine, so I think it's safe to say it's Dee Dee's."

Hagen patted Stella on the other shoulder. "Guess you were right about those notations. Smart thinking."

Stella shuffled forward in her seat. If those boys got any closer, they'd be sitting on her lap. And if Hagen got any more patronizing, he'd get a smack in the mouth.

"Uh-huh, yeah. I'd like to know what made Dee Dee write that."

"Y'all found anything yet?"

Stella twisted in her seat. Chief Houston stood in the doorway, the top of his face just visible between Hagen and Ander.

"We're getting there." Slade rubbed his eyes. "I think. The question is whether we're getting there fast enough."

"Yep. Time's never on the side of the good guys, is it? How'd y'all get on with those interviews?"

Hagen turned sideways, allowing Houston to take a half-step into the room. "Drew a blank with Wayne Bisgard. Couldn't even get a good cup of tea out of him."

"And Kay Harvey was a…a handful." Ander added a small laugh.

"Oh, yeah. She's fifty-seven flavors of crazy, that one. Never thought of her as dangerous, though."

"Gerry Renelle might be." Hagen seemed thoughtful. "I don't think he kidnapped six people to get at his wife. That seems a little out of his wheelhouse. But he's lying about something. That guy worries me."

Chief Houston nodded. "Worries me too. We checked his alibi. Didn't pan out. According to his head nurse, Molly Martin, and a psychiatrist who has an office on Renelle's floor, a Dr. Horace Shannahan, Renelle wasn't at the hospital on Monday evening. Another coworker, John Hable, heard Renelle say he was going to strangle the life out of Darrel

Dowers for even thinking about dating his ex-wife. Said he sounded serious." Chief Houston handed Hagen a folder. "There's your search warrant."

Hagen took it. "I'll head that way as soon as we're done here."

"What about Kay Harvey?" Stella closed her laptop and dragged her chair forward. With Chief Houston standing in the doorway, the room was growing claustrophobic. "I'm not sure I agree with you about her not being dangerous. And I'd like a look in her basement, Troy's bedroom."

Slade pushed to his feet. "All right, we'll talk to Billy Joe Tompkin and Roxanne Jenham tomorrow. I doubt an elderly man or a teenage girl has anything to do with this, but they might have seen something while they were at the store. Dowers's body is still at the local morgue awaiting transport to the forensic center for autopsy and additional testing."

Stella frowned. "Still?"

Slade lifted a shoulder. "They're down a pathologist right now."

Tennessee was one of the few states with a county- or district-based medical examiner system. Due to how rural some counties were, they sometimes maintained coroners whose primary functions were to identify victims, notify next of kin, and determine if a death appeared to be by natural causes or foul play. If the latter was suspected, the coroner referred the decedent to one of five regional forensic centers, where an autopsy would take place. For this region, that center was located in Nashville.

Stella almost raised her hand but managed to keep it in place. She might still be a newbie, but she didn't have to act like one. "Sir, did forensics give us any indication of when the tests on the food might come back?"

Slade lifted a shoulder. "They're hoping for some preliminary findings tomorrow, but the full range of testing could take several weeks." The SSA squeezed between the agents until he was at the whiteboard. "Forensics picked up nothing from where Darrel Dowers's body was dumped, but they're still working on his clothes."

They all waited as Slade updated the board, knowing he'd be dishing out assignments next. They didn't have to wait long.

"Hagen, I want you to head to Gerry Renelle's now. Techs will be on their way."

Hagen nodded. "It'll be the highlight of my day."

"I'll come with you." Stella reached for her bag. "I came in your vehicle, remember?"

"Me too." Ander lifted a finger. "Guess I'll grab the gloves."

"Me too." Chloe started to rise out of her chair, but Slade held up a hand.

"You're going home and resting."

Her expression turned stormy. "But, sir—"

"No buts."

Stella squeezed out of the room after Hagen and Ander, happily leaving Slade to battle Chloe down.

Maybe they'd get lucky, and the search would drop some answers their way.

Or maybe they'd get unlucky, and the killer would drop another victim.

14

"Never been to a surgeon's house before. Think they have their own operating room in the basement? Kinda like a doctor's version of taking your work home with you?"

Ander sat in the passenger seat, his body half-turned toward Stella. He was grinning widely, pleased with his joke.

A glance in the rearview mirror told Hagen that Stella didn't think it was funny. Of course, she'd just survived a madman who'd used a hacksaw in place of a scalpel.

Crash and burn, my friend.

To be fair, Hagen usually found spending time with Ander a nice relief from the daily grind. Whenever they cracked open beers and watched a game, thoughts of work and the lingering memories of his father's murder pushed aside for a time. They wouldn't disappear, but they'd find a place in the background of his mind, far enough away to ignore them.

Now, though, Ander's presence was a disruption. To be fair, Ander couldn't know he wanted time alone with Stella in order to pursue his burning need to avenge his father's death. Ander was simply trying to get their current job done.

So, what was bothering him so much about Ander's presence?

Hagen knew the answer to that question. He and Ander often joked about women, but they had different attitudes. Hagen wasn't interested in anything serious. He couldn't even think about a long-term relationship while his father's murder still drove his thoughts. A partner, a wife, or even a girlfriend would have too big a claim on him. He needed to be free. At least for now.

For Ander, a long-term relationship was his current goal. It was what he'd been looking for since Kelsey left. On evenings at the bar, women sitting alone or in pairs would often eye him and blush. He'd sometimes flash a smile, but more often, he'd ignore them even when they were attractive and available. He wasn't looking for perfection, he insisted. Only someone he believed could be perfect for him.

The attention Ander currently gave Stella suggested that he believed he might have found it.

Hagen couldn't let that happen.

"I guess we'll see soon enough." Hagen pointed to a large, colonial-style house at the end of a rising drive at the top of the road.

It was very different from the small brick home Gerry Renelle's ex-wife Brenda lived in with their daughter, Angela.

Ander faced the front and let out a low whistle. "Damn, must be good money cutting people up. We're going to need a bigger search team."

Above the eight-foot double doors stretched three stained-glass gable windows. Hagen had to agree with Ander's comment this time. That was some entrance. This guy must think he lives in the Notre Dame Cathedral. The home seemed far too large for Gerry Renelle and his daughter. It was even too big, Hagen thought, to house Gerry's ego.

"Wow, look. A tennis court. Can you imagine having your own court to play on every day?"

Ander twisted in his seat again. "You play? I didn't know that. We should have a game sometime."

Stella's face reddened as she opened the car door. "I dabbled in college."

Hagen lifted an eyebrow. He'd read her background report. She'd played varsity tennis back in college and had been extremely good. Now that he'd spent some time with her, success in sports didn't surprise him. He couldn't see Stella ever giving up, not when she was learning to play, and not when she was five games down in the second set and facing match point. She'd find a way to turn the game around or die trying.

Ander stepped outside, leaned on the hood of the Explorer, and looked around. "This is a nice part of town. More open space than where Brenda lives."

"She's on the other side of town." Hagen headed toward a double set of stairs that led to the front door. "I doubt that's an accident. I suspect she tried to move away as far as the court's visitation rights would allow."

Warrant in hand, he pressed the doorbell. A deep *ba-bong* sounded from somewhere in the bowels of the house. Ander and Stella joined him as he waited.

When there was no answer, Hagen held his finger on the button. "He's probably upstairs. He has to call the elevator, find the keys to the golf buggy, drive through the living room, through the first dining room, past the second dining room, through the courtyard, and all the way down the hall before—"

The door opened. Renelle's face turned to thunder when he saw Hagen. "You again."

"Yep. And I've brought some friends."

"Agent, I told you at my wife's...at my ex-wife's house that I had absolutely no interest in talking to you. Now, if you don't mind, I have—"

"I also brought paperwork." He handed Renelle the packet. "A search warrant."

From thunder, Renelle's expression grew to a barely controlled rage. As he read through the documents, his jaw turned to stone, and a vein on his temple threatened to explode.

He pointed a long finger at Hagen. "Now, you listen to me. My daughter is here. She's been traumatized enough. The last thing she needs is a bunch of government goons trawling through her stuff and treating her father like some...some...criminal."

Hagen glanced at Ander and indicated with his head that he should go inside. With no hesitation, Ander pushed past Renelle, Stella on his heels. Hagen remained on the doorstep, ready to cuff the man if he resisted. If searching a house traumatized a kid, what did fourteen years of having an asshole as a father do?

Hagen stepped forward until the surgeon's finger almost touched his chest. "No, *you* listen to *me*. We're going to search your house. In a few minutes, a forensic team will be here to take away anything we believe might be helpful to our investigation. We're going to take what we want, and we're going to take as much time as we need because, if there's anything here that could lead us to your daughter's mother, we will find it."

Renelle's mouth opened and closed several times before a sound escaped. "I'm calling your supervisor. You don't know who you're dealing with. You won't have heard the last of this. By the time I'm done with you, the only thing you'll be investigating is uncollected dog poop."

"Sir." Anger stirred, but Hagen managed to keep his tone level. "Please step aside. We have the right to be here, and if you don't cooperate, I'll ask a police officer to detain you in the back of his cruiser. For your safety and ours. Do you understand?"

When the surgeon said nothing, Hagen stepped inside.

The hallway, with its shiny, checkerboard-patterned marble floor, was distracting enough for Hagen to ignore the man and get on with his job. To his right, Ander was pulling on a pair of blue latex gloves in the dining room. Off to his left, Stella was checking the contents of an ornate built-in cabinet in the living room beyond the hallway. Leaving Renelle behind, Hagen climbed the curved stairway to the second floor.

Somewhere downstairs, Renelle had found his voice again, clearly thinking he would have a better chance of pushing his fellow agents around. He was telling one of them they couldn't touch something they were no doubt touching.

Let them deal with the bastard.

At the top of the stairs, Hagen pulled on his latex gloves, deciding where to go first.

A marble table in front of him held a large crystal vase filled with fresh flowers. An oil painting hung above it, depicting some idyllic pastoral scene in which sheep grazed happily in front of a wooden watermill as fluffy, white clouds floated over rolling green hills. Even the gilded frame gleamed.

He wrinkled his nose. This place was way too pristine for comfort, as though a team of cleaners swept through it each day to turn the house into a factory for semiconductors. Homes were for families, and families were messy. This house wasn't a home.

Three doors were down the hallway to his left, while one stood on the right. Hagen turned right.

Bingo.

The bedroom had to be the largest and most ornate he'd ever seen, taking up this entire side of the house. A four-poster bed took center stage, each of its pillars made of dark oak with floral carvings. An ormolu writing desk had been pushed up against the window, its roll top open, the surface clean and empty. An armchair had won the best spot in front of a fireplace, perfect for late-night reading before bed. Sleeping in the room seemed odd. Hosting a ball would have been more fitting.

Hagen tried the writing desk first. The top drawer housed a neat pile of plain, white envelopes. The second drawer contained a box of ballpoint pens, paperclips, and plain paper.

Hagen moved over to the nightstand, where a hardback history of the Civil War was displayed next to an alarm clock, promising to send Renelle to sleep before waking him up. He pulled open the drawer, expecting to find a bottle of Ambien. What he saw instead?

Bingo.

On one side of the drawer was a stack of photographs of Brenda. Hagen picked them up and leafed through them. They must have been taken when she and Renelle had first met.

In one picture that looked like it had been taken on a college campus, Brenda reclined under a tree, a book open in front of her. In another, she wore a swimsuit, with her long, red curls pulled over one shoulder and a wide-brimmed sunhat covering much of her face.

In the next photo, she stood naked in front of the fireplace, one hand resting on the mantelpiece.

He placed the photographs back into the drawer. Conducting searches always felt intrusive, but few things felt more invasive than inspecting personal items that turned up in people's bedrooms.

Next to the photographs was a half-empty bottle of perfume. Hagen took it out and sniffed the nozzle. The scent was floral with a hint of vanilla and a touch of lavender. Brenda's favorite scent?

A pair of gold bands were nestled on a small piece of burgundy-colored silk. Hagen didn't need to pull them out to know what they were.

How long had the woman's panties been there? He didn't want to guess. The couple had divorced over five years ago, so Renelle must have been holding onto them since then. Hagen would have admired his persistence if it wasn't so creepy and obsessive.

He removed his phone and took a picture of the items. Forensics would be here soon. They'd bag all this up and take it away. They might be able to give an indication of whether Brenda had worn those panties recently too.

If she had, Gerry Renelle had some explaining to do.

15

Stella peered into the bottom of an ornate, porcelain box and wondered what it would be like to live in a house with more than one living room.

Since she currently resided in a studio loft, it was hard to imagine having a choice of places to nap or relax with a book. This house seemed to have a room for every mood.

On the other side of the hallway, Ander opened cupboards in a dining room that could only be used when Renelle hosted formal dinners. She seemed to be searching the room designated for entertaining the local gentry and resolving the issues of the hour over a fine brandy and some secretly smuggled Cuban cigars.

Where did Renelle go to put his feet up and watch the latest episode of The Bold and the Beautiful?

She closed the box, which contained nothing, not even dust. Footsteps sounded behind her on the marble floor. They were fast and light, too soft to be Hagen or Ander's, and too free of anger to belong to Renelle.

"Agent?"

Stella turned to find a young girl in the middle of the

doorway. Her mid-length, auburn hair was braided and pulled over her left shoulder. Her denim shorts were probably a little too short for Renelle's taste…which might have been why she was wearing them.

"You're Angela, right?"

She nodded.

Stella glanced at her hands. The blue latex gloves looked far too conspicuous. They seemed to turn the entire house into a crime scene and everyone in it into an accomplice. She snapped them off and stuffed them in her pocket.

"We're doing everything we can to find your mom, okay?" Though Stella was eager to pepper the girl with questions, the rules around interviewing juveniles couldn't be ignored. "If you know anything that might help us, even if it sounds silly, you can tell me. You never know what we might find useful."

Angela's green eyes were bright and intense as she played with the end of her braid. Her demeanor seemed both frustrated and hesitant. "There is something."

"Go on." Stella kept her posture casual, not wanting to startle the teenager, who struck her as skittish.

Angela glanced over her shoulder and lowered her voice. "It's about my dad."

Stella's stomach tightened. She glanced across the hallway. Renelle was in the dining room, arguing with Ander, who was ignoring him, asking to be led to the basement. Stella motioned for Angela to follow her and moved toward the window at the opposite end of the room.

Angela did so, and glanced back at the door again before leaning close. "It's like…he acts like he hates my mom. But he doesn't. I know he doesn't."

Stella's stomach eased. Was that it? Was the kid just defending her father? That was sweet but useless.

"How is your father's relationship with your mom now?"

Angela lifted her shoulders as though she could hide herself between them. "He's obsessed with her."

That wasn't the answer Stella had expected. "Obsessed? Why would you say that?"

Angela glanced over toward the door again. "I found a bunch of Mom's old stuff in his nightstand. There's, like, some pictures of her. And her perfume. And I think there's some of her old underwear in there too. Freaked me out."

Though she kept her expression carefully blank, excitement walked up Stella's spine. A fixation was one thing, though. Acting on it required something more.

"Right, that's—"

"And I've heard him sometimes crying after I've gone to bed. He thinks I can't hear him, but I can. He says her name, and he cries." Angela hugged herself, rubbing her arms. "Look, I know he can be mean. He shouts a lot, and he tries to control the whole world. That's why Mom left. But I think he still really loves her. I was worried that he might do something...you know, something bad. Because he can get so angry."

Be careful. Don't push too hard.

"Angela, has your dad ever hurt you? Or your mother?"

The girl shook her head. "No. He shouts a lot, but he's never hit me. And I'm sure he's never hit Mom either. I'd have known."

Some of the tension that had settled in Stella eased away. But would Angela have known? Parents kept a lot from their kids.

"Thank you, Angela. You've been a huge help. And you were right to tell me." When the young woman didn't appear to be convinced, Stella squeezed her arm. "I know it's asking a lot, but keep the faith, okay? We're doing everything we can to find your mom."

Angela headed out the door, and as soon as it clicked

shut, Stella raced up the steps. She reached the top just as Hagen emerged from the room on the right.

She skidded to a stop. "Hagen, we've got to check Renelle's nightstand. He's got—"

"I know. I've seen it. Look."

Hagen pulled out his phone and showed her the photos he'd taken of the bedside drawer. The sight of the images and the panties stuffed behind the perfume bottle stirred something dark in Stella's gut.

Hagen put his phone back in his pocket. "I've texted forensics and told them to bag everything when they arrive. I'm going to step outside and tell Slade what we found."

Stella followed him back down the stairs. As Hagen strode out of the front door, Ander came in from the kitchen, where the basement door presumably was. Praise be to God, Gerry Renelle sat alone in the dining room, and Stella couldn't help but wonder how Ander had managed such a feat.

Ander must have read the question in her eyes because he grinned. "Pulled out my phone and called Slade in front of him. Asked the boss to secure a warrant for obstruction. That set him down pretty quick."

She was impressed. "Good thinking." She glanced back the way Ander had come. "What did you find?"

"The basement's just a basement. He could hold about four hundred people hostage down there, but there's nothing but space and a gigantic television. I'll get a team to search the walls for any hidden spaces, but my gut says we won't have any luck. You find something?"

Stella took a deep breath. "Our friend's got a secret obsession."

"I take it we're not talking about a freezer full of mint chocolate chip ice cream?"

"No. More like a nightstand with Brenda's underwear and nude photos."

"Jeez." Ander turned toward Renelle, who caught his eye.

The surgeon paled. He glanced at the stairs and started to get up before sinking into the seat again. "Look, I know what you've found, okay? I know what it looks like. But you have to understand."

Stella followed Ander into the dining room. "What exactly do we have to understand?"

"It's just…oh god." Renelle dropped his face into his hands. "Look, I'm not a psychopath or a pervert, okay? I don't go around kidnapping people, and I could never, ever hurt my wife."

"Ex-wife," Stella reminded him. "And no one's accusing you of anything." Stella watched their suspect closely. Either he'd shrunk since she met him in the entryway, or the house had doubled in size. He appeared to have been deflated. "But if you want to explain your little collection, we're all ears."

Renelle scrubbed his face before dropping his hands. "Tell me something, Agents. Have you ever had something you loved just ripped away from you? Gone. Just like that."

Emotion hit her like a punch. "Yes."

"Me too." Ander's thick jaw was set, and a wave of sympathy passed over Stella. The agent covered up his pain well in general, but sometimes there was a flicker, like he'd been stung by something no one could see.

Renelle wiped a hand under his nose. "If that's the case, if you've both lost something you loved, then you'll understand how impossible it is to let go. It's not what it looks like. I just wanted some part of Brenda close to me. That's all."

Soft footsteps came from behind them, and Stella turned to find Angela standing in the doorway. "Is everything okay?"

Stella's heart broke for the girl. In the span of twenty-four hours, her world had been turned on its head. "Yeah. We were just telling your dad that we're going to be here for a while, and he might want to take you out for something to eat. Maybe pack a bag too. We're not sure how long this will take."

When Stella faced the surgeon again, gratitude shone in his eyes. He coughed into his hand and swiped at his face. "Yeah, honey. Let's go. I'm starving."

As father and daughter walked away, Stella met Ander's eyes. Behind him, the sun offered its last rays through the open door.

It was dinnertime now. How were the hostages fairing?

And how much time did they have left?

16

Stella stirred her dirty martini and pulled the olive off the cocktail stick with her teeth. The Sunrise Bar on McFerrin Avenue was only half full at ten after nine, but tonight must have been couples' night. Every other table seemed to be filled with pairs. Their hands touched in the bar's dim light. Their gazes connected across drinks.

Stella sighed away the envy. How much simpler life must be when you aren't focused on hunting down killers—either one who was about to kill again or one who had killed someone you loved. To live without that weight always on your shoulders must be…heaven. You could just switch directions at will and float off to a new adventure on another cloud or link up permanently with someone and settle down to a life of suburban normalcy.

Other people had that luxury.

She did not.

She pushed the thought out of her head and checked her watch. Mac was late again, but Stella didn't mind. She knew Mac. For all her accuracy and careful timekeeping in the office, she was much more relaxed outside it. She seemed to be able to draw a firm line between home and work, between nerdy Cyber Mac and relaxed Fun Mac. Now, Stella did let envy wash over her. She'd never been able to find that line.

The door opened, and Mac strode in. She waved at Stella and quickly pushed between the tables to join her.

"See you started early."

Stella pushed the other martini glass toward her. "Got yours."

"That's mine? I thought you were just lining them up."

Stella grinned. "It was a tough day, but not that tough. Not yet anyway."

Once the techs arrived at Gerry's house, Stella, Hagen, and Ander headed over to Brenda's for a similar search. They'd found nothing in the small house to suggest that Brenda Renelle had been a target of the kidnappers.

Mac slipped her bag over the back of the chair and sipped her drink. She leaned forward and lowered her voice until it barely made its way across the table. "Hear you guys are planning to bring the, um, surgeon in. You think it's him?"

Stella glanced around. She didn't usually talk shop in a public place, but the bar's clients seemed more interested in each other than in Stella and Mac, the country music was loud enough, and their voices weren't carrying. Still, she was glad Mac had avoided using Gerry Renelle's name.

She cradled her drink and spoke quietly, "Maybe. Once forensics is finished, we'll bring him down to the station and see what he says. Honestly, I'm not sure it's him. Where is he keeping them? The only one he seems to care about is his ex." She took a sip of her martini, letting it swirl around her mouth. "Should get the search warrant for the bible-thumping mother tomorrow too. Though, frankly, I'm not sure I want to know what we'll find in that house."

Mac laughed and stirred her drink. "Let's hope it's one of our missing, and you can wrap this up tomorrow."

"It feels like tomorrow is already too late." Stella sighed, momentarily hating herself for sitting in this bar while people's lives were at stake. But there was nothing they could do tonight. "There's the custodian we need to talk to. Chief Houston spoke to him already, and he's expecting us. One of us will go down there tomorrow. And there's that new girl who works in the grocery store. No one's managed to reach her, but we'll pay her a visit tomorrow. See if she saw anything. I'm not sure where we'll land a break."

"Maybe another body will drop, this one full of clues."

Stella didn't smile. "That could happen anyway." She stabbed the end of the cocktail stick into the table. "Let's talk about something else."

"Sure." Mac sipped her drink. "How was the drive with Hagen and Ander today? Lady's been in the casino five minutes and already hits the jackpot."

Stella's cheeks warmed. It wasn't the martini. "Ha. Funny. If spending half an hour in a car with those two is the jackpot, what's the booby prize?"

"Pa-lease. I see the way Ander looks at you. He sees you, like, he's…Thor and you're his hammer. I've never seen him look at another woman that way. I'll tell you that."

Stella's cheeks grew even warmer. She wasn't sure she liked where this conversation was going or that Mac had even started it. Maybe talking about kidnapping and murder was better. "You're crazy. The only thing Ander is interested in is his kid and his hair conditioner."

Mac pulled her blond ponytail over her shoulder and played with the ends. "Whatever he's putting on his head, I want it. If I had half that volume, I'd be twice as happy."

"Wouldn't we all? Anyway, Ander's not an issue. Hagen might be."

"Uh-oh. Going for the emotionally unavailable one. *Tsk-*

tsk. Ah, well. It's good for me." Mac batted her lashes. "Maybe I'll just have to help mend Ander's poor, broken heart."

"That's not what I meant." Stella ran a finger up the side of her glass. "Hagen overheard us talking about Uncle Joel. Matthew Johnson. He offered to go with me to Atlanta to find his family."

"Seriously?" Mac put down her drink. "That's strange. What did you say?"

"Nothing. I mean, I can't go anywhere until we've cracked this case anyway, so his offer doesn't matter for now."

"But will you take him with you?"

"I dunno. Like he said, another pair of eyes could be helpful. And while he might be a bit intense, he is an excellent agent. He's focused. It could be good to have someone to bounce ideas off."

"Sounds like you should take him, then." Mac gave a sly wink over the rim of her glass.

Stella flipped her the fastest bird in history. "Yeah, maybe. But this is personal, you know? I really appreciate your help, Mac. You've been so great. I'm just not sure how much I want to involve someone else in my affairs."

"Huh. Sounds like you've got some thinking to do while you're chasing down a multiple-person kidnapper, child snatcher, and killer."

Stella drained her glass. "Yeah, fair point. I think I'll ride in with Chloe and Slade tomorrow. Put some space between me and those two. If I can clear my head and we can crack this case, I can jump off that other bridge when I get to it."

"Good idea."

"As we were driving back, Slade called to tell us about the warrants. He also told us we need to think outside the box on this one. He reckons that in a small town, where everyone knows everyone, someone had to have seen or heard something. I'm not so sure. All I know is five people are being held somewhere, and if we don't find them soon, at least one of them is likely to follow Darrel Dowers to the morgue."

Mac squeezed Stella's hand. "We'll get him. Just because you can't see the answers yet doesn't mean they aren't out there. They're out there, and you will find them. Both the answers that lead you to this kidnapper and the ones that take you to your father's killer."

Stella took Mac's hand between hers, savoring this unexpected but lovely friendship. "Don't worry. I'm not giving up. Quitting's not in my blood."

"That's the spirit." Mac pulled back and lifted her empty glass. "And in that spirit, I'll grab another round."

17

H agen led the way up the brick steps of the Everglades Home for the Elderly, adjusting his tie and collar. His suit wasn't uncomfortable, but watching Chloe adjust her sling made him itchy for some reason he couldn't explain.

Chloe whistled in appreciation. "Not a bad place to live out your last years. Being a custodian must pay better than I thought. Good for him."

She was right. And wrong.

Stretching over a city block, the home, with white rocking chairs on the veranda and flower-bedecked balconies, was beautiful. Ivy covered the brick-red walls, and a bright-white banner declared *Visitors Always Welcome!*

"He doesn't live here," Hagen corrected. "This is the poor man's second place of employment."

With no new warrants issued overnight, Hagen and Chloe had been dispatched to interview Billy Joe Tompkin, the custodian for Bisgard's Best. Stella and Ander had been tasked with locating Roxanne Jenham. His run of bad luck getting Stella one-on-one continued.

They had been lucky in a different way, though. No new

bodies had been dumped overnight. That was especially lucky for Hagen because he was *almost* prepared to bet his Corvette that he'd be assigned to visit the M.E. if the time came.

A woman in nurse's scrubs greeted them with a smile at the front desk. "How can I help you folks?"

Hagen flashed his ID. "Special Agent Hagen Yates. Can you tell us where we can find Billy Joe Tompkin?"

The woman's smile disappeared. "Billy Joe? Whatcha want him for?"

"We just need to speak to him, ma'am." Hagen gave her his best *there's nothing to worry about* smile. "Can you help us with that?"

"Well…I don't know." She ran her hands down her scrubs before twisting them together. Having agents appear at her desk must not be part of her regular routine. "He's workin'."

Chloe leaned an elbow on the counter, her expression hard as stone. "So are we. And if *you* want to keep working, you need to tell us where we can find him."

Damn.

Chloe had been in a foul mood since the moment she slid into the Explorer, but it wasn't like the agent to take her moods out on innocent citizens. Was her injury worse? Was she hiding her pain behind a hateful exterior? Hagen didn't know, but he needed to run interference before their request turned into WWIII.

"What Agent Foster is trying to say is…please."

Hands twisting even harder, the receptionist returned her focus to Hagen. "Well, I'm guessin' he's in the dining room 'bout now. Down that way." She giggled. "Good luck talkin' to him."

Chloe's dark expression turned darker. "What does that mean?"

The receptionist swallowed hard and rolled her chair

back several inches. "Well, Billy Joe's deaf as a post. We got residents older than him that can hear better, and this place ain't nothin' more than God's waitin' room."

Terrific.

"Which way is the dining room?"

She pointed down a hallway. "Go to the end and hang a right."

"Thank you."

"Visitors welcome, my ass," Chloe grumbled as she stalked down the hall.

He might catch hell, but it had to be done. "Do me a favor and turn the attitude down a notch."

She whirled, all the fires of hell glowing in her eyes as she glared at him. "What did you just say?"

Sweat dampened his armpits, but he didn't let the discomfort show on his face. "I said that you need to turn your attitude down a notch. Or ten. Maybe even twenty." He waved a hand to a group of little old ladies with walkers coming down the hall. "Those residents are going to think the Prince of Darkness is coming for them."

Hagen could practically hear all the things she wanted to say spinning around in her mind.

Finally, she bared her teeth in a forced grin. "Is this better?"

Damn, the woman was scary.

"Not even a little bit."

She worked her jaw, her tongue running over her teeth. She tried again. This time, her widened mouth more closely resembled a smile. "Will this do?"

The clacking of the walkers was getting closer. "Try it one more time."

Exhaling, she closed her eyes. When she opened them again, a genuine smile appeared.

He clapped. "Now you won't scare small children. Let's go."

As they passed the women, Chloe gushed out a friendly, "Good morning, ladies. Gonna be a beautiful day, isn't it?"

Hagen shot her a thumbs-up and got a finger poke in the ribs as a reward.

In the dining room, tables were pushed against one wall, with chairs piled next to them. The floor was covered in cornflakes and oatmeal. Puddles of milk, coffee, and orange juice created little ponds between all the dried food, turning most of it into a spongey mess. It was like a post-breakfast war zone in here. Wayne Bisgard would have been right at home.

Hagen paused in the doorway. "Looks like a frat house."

"Milk and orange juice on the floor?" Chloe pushed him aside with her good arm. "Don't know what kind of frat house you were in. Anyway, this isn't the result of a party. It's what breakfast looks like when you struggle to feed yourself. Very few of us get a pretty ending, Hagen. Plus, it's how my kitchen looked this morning." She gestured at her sling.

An older man in a blue boiler suit swiped a gray mop across the floor, blending tea with milk with mushy cereal. His face was lined and covered in a gray fuzz. The mustache decorating his upper lip was whiter than the milk he was cleaning up.

Chloe strode over to him. "Billy Joe Tompkin?"

The man didn't react. Hagen pulled out his ID and flashed it in the man's line of sight, trying his best not to scare him. Billy Joe stopped, leaned on his mop, and squinted at the card.

"I don't know what you're showing me, son," Billy Joe shouted. "Hold it up. I can't see too well."

Hagen did as requested but, apparently, it wasn't close enough.

Billy Joe reached out and pulled it even closer until the badge was little more than an inch from his face.

"Oh. FBI. Yeah, the chief said you was comin'. I'm Billy Joe Tompkin. Work at Bisgard's Best when I'm not keeping this place running."

Hagen liked the man right away and hated that someone of his years had to work so hard. He waved to a chair. "Let's sit down. We need to ask you a few questions about the Bisgards."

"What can I do for you?" The bellow nearly knocked Hagen back a step. "You probably want to know about the Bisgards, don't you?"

Hagen glanced at Chloe. She shrugged.

"That's right." Hagen raised his voice several decibels. "Have you—"

"Terrible business. I don't know what the world's comin' to. Such a lovely couple. They don't deserve none of this trouble." Billy Joe pounded a fist over his heart. "Tears me right up, what's been happenin' to 'em. And that poor Brenda and young Troy. And that little baby. Like family, they are. No, they don't deserve none of this. Not one of them."

Hagen leaned closer to the man's ear. "Have you seen anything odd or out of place around the store in recent weeks?"

Billy Joe frowned. His forehead, already a field of plowed lines, became a mountain range. He thought and thought while Hagen waited. What was he searching for in there?

Finally, Billy Joe shook his head, his rheumy eyes filling with tears. "I'm sorry, son. Did you ask me something? You'll have to speak up. I can't hear too well."

"I was just…" Hagen leaned in until his mouth was almost touching the man's ear. "Did you notice anything strange at the store recently?"

Billy Joe pulled back. "No need to shout, son. I'm only a

little deaf in one ear. And a little hard of hearin' in the other."
He cackled. "Was there anything strange at the store? No,
everything was the same as always. They took on that new
girl a couple of months ago. Roxie. Apart from that, nothing
special."

"Roxie? What do you know about her?"

"What do I know about Roxie? Is that what you asked?"

Hagen nodded.

"Well, is it? You're going to have to speak up, son. I can't
hear you."

Hagen closed his eyes for a second. When he opened
them, Chloe was grinning. He pushed on. "Yes, sir. That's
what I asked."

"Oh, Roxie's nice enough. Kinda friendly. Eager to please,
y'know? Like she was grateful for the opportunity. Dee Dee
loves her."

Chloe cupped her hand around her mouth. "Why's that?"

Billy Joe must have been able to hear her higher-pitched
voice better because he didn't hesitate. "Not too sure. Think
it was because Roxie had some kind of rough background. I
don't know the details. You'll have to ask Dee Dee." His face
fell into a puddle of wrinkles. "Oh, you can't, can you? When
you find her, you can ask her."

"We will." Chloe lifted a boot, shaking orange juice off the
bottom. "You didn't talk much to Roxie yourself?"

"Me? No. I wasn't too crazy about her, if I'm honest. Saw
her once…more than once it was. Though, I don't recall how
many times."

"Saw her where?"

Billy Joe frowned at Hagen. "Huh?"

Chloe took over. "Roxie. You said you saw her somewhere. A few times?"

Billy Joe leaned on his mop. "I did? Oh, yes. I did. That's
right. Out in the parking lot, it was. Right at the back there,

behind the garbage bins. Roxie was with some fellow. Probably why she was so far back. Security cameras don't reach that far, y'see."

Chloe took half a step backward and a prune squelched under the bottom of her boot. She sighed. "What were they doing?"

"Makin' out is what they were doing. Like a couple of lovestruck teenagers. She was a bit old for that kind of behavior, y'ask me. Could have just gone back to her place. Or his."

Hagen nodded. "Can you describe him?"

When Billy Joe held a hand up to his ear, Chloe repeated the question.

"Describe him, y'say? Naw. It was dark every time, and my eyesight ain't all that. 'Specially at that distance."

"What about his car? Did you see what he drove?"

"Couldn't say for sure. Truck of some sort. Couldn't tell if it was a Chevy or a Ford. Maroon maybe, or brown. Something like that."

A shot of adrenaline hit Hagen's system and he could tell it'd done the same to his partner. "Do you remember if the truck bed had a cover?"

"Did the truck bed have a cover? Let's see now." Billy Joe rubbed his chin. "My memory's not what it used to be, but yeah, I think it might have. That important?"

Hagen nodded as Chloe said, "Maybe. Think you might recognize it if we showed you some pictures?"

"Well…I'll surely try."

18

M ain Street in Stonevale was a lovely mix of brick buildings that appeared to be mostly empty. Though it was already midmorning, parking spaces were plentiful. An occasional car drove down the road, but no pedestrians moved along the sidewalk. With only a handful of businesses open, there were few reasons for anyone to visit the quaint area.

One store sold charity goods. Two were liquor stores, and a third offered payday loans. Most of the remaining businesses, mainly antique stores, were either boarded up or only open on the weekends.

Stella hated to see older parts of a town go under. "Not much, is it?"

"Feels like we're a long way from Gerry Renelle." Ander nodded toward the payday loan operation. "Application form lists that place as Roxie's address. No wonder she was desperate."

Stella followed Ander to the back of the building. She'd been relieved when Slade had partnered Hagen with Chloe that morning. At least, she'd have a little more time to debate letting him help her or not. If she didn't have to think about his offer at all until this case was cracked, she'd be happy.

She wasn't sure Mac was right about the way Ander looked at her. He'd flirted shamelessly with witnesses to get more details out of them. She also wasn't sure all that muscle and hair was really her thing. And, besides, for most of the short drive from the police station to Main Street, he'd talked about nothing but his son. If he was trying to show her what a good father he was to woo her, he was definitely barking up the wrong tree.

Ander led the way up the metal stairs behind the building until they reached the apartment's front door. There was no number or name. If the door had once been white, those days were a long way behind it. The wood was now covered with marks and scratches. Wooden squares had been nailed over holes, and the door handle hung loose.

Stella caught up with Ander just as he knocked.

The door swung open. He glanced at Stella before pushing the door wider.

"Hello! Roxie?" No answer. The place was dark, the curtains drawn, and the lights off. "Roxie, you in there?"

Still no answer.

"What do you think?" Ander's hand rested on his holster.

"She hasn't been answering her phone. Door's left open. Works with the Bisgards." Stella paused. "She might be another victim. I think we've got cause."

She stepped inside.

In the gloom, she made out an old armchair in the corner of the living room. A tear ran across the front of the cushion, and one leg was braced with a piece of wood. It was the only furniture she could see. The walls were bare, and there were no plants or even a television to take Roxie's mind off the emptiness of the space.

Click.

Ander had a finger on the light switch. He tried again. *Click. Click.*

Nothing happened. The bulb must have blown. Or the light switch. Or perhaps Roxie hadn't paid the electricity bill. If this was even her current residence.

Stella opened the fridge. The bulb inside worked, so there was power. Three deli containers marked *Bisgard's Best* took up space on the shelves, but the fridge contained nothing else, not even a sticky ketchup bottle or the out-of-date jar of mayonnaise Stella had seen in nearly every fridge she'd ever opened.

Ander stood in the middle of the room, his nose in the air. "You smell that?"

Stella closed the fridge and inhaled deeply. There was a faint odor of old carpet and a hint of burnt wood that drifted through the apartment door, but nothing else. Nothing that indicated rot or unwashed clothes or anything more dangerous.

"I can't smell anything."

Ander nodded. "Strange, right? You ever been in a place like this and found it didn't stink?"

"True. It's like Roxie barely lived here. She might have just moved in, I guess."

Something crunched under Ander's foot, and his nose wrinkled as he kicked to flick a smashed potato chip off. "Do we have the rental agreement or anything?"

Stella snorted. "Does this place look like they use agreements?" She stepped into the apartment's only bedroom. An air mattress was on the floor with a thin sheet and blanket thrown to one side next to a half-empty soda bottle. Stella opened the closet door. Empty. Not even a hanger dangled from the closet rod.

Ander snapped on a pair of latex gloves and picked up the soda. When he twisted the top, the bottle released a loud *pssshtt*, and bubbles rose through the bright-red liquid. "Only half flat. Whoever opened that didn't do it very long ago."

Stella pulled an evidence bag from her pocket. "Bag it. Since we're only working on the theory that this is Roxie's apartment, we need some proof. Not sure we've got a good enough reason for forensics to come down, but we could get them to run prints. See if anything comes up."

Stella's phone vibrated in her pocket. She pulled it out. Hagen.

"Yes?"

"Stella, you at Roxie's with Ander?"

"That's right. What do you need?"

"Put me on speaker. You both need to hear this."

Stella frowned and pressed the speaker button. "We're here. What's going on?"

"Chloe and I are on our way back from speaking to Billy Joe Tompkin. He says Roxie was seeing a guy. No description, but get this…he drives a maroon or brown truck with a covered bed."

Finally, they had something. The wave of relief that flowed through Stella was followed by a burst of energy. Now they had two things to search for. Roxie. And the truck.

Ander moved closer to Stella until their shoulders touched. "That's great news. Listen. Roxie's not here. She couldn't be gone more than a couple of days, though, because an open soda bottle hasn't yet gone flat."

"Timing works."

That's exactly what Stella had been thinking. "She could also be a hostage. We're bagging the soda bottle for prints."

"Okay. Meet us back at the station. Let's see if Mac can track down another address for Roxie and see if her prints are in the system."

Her phone beeped. "Hang on a second, Hagen. Slade is

calling." She took the call. "Boss, you're on speaker. Looks like we've got—"

"Whatever you've got, get your asses over to Stonevale Park now. You can tell me there."

Dread became a weight in her chest. "What's in Stonevale Park?"

After what felt like ages but would have been just a second or two, Slade's voice echoed through the apartment again. "Ronald Bisgard's body."

19

"**I**'m next."

Troy's voice was flat, as though he were listening to someone else speaking from far away. Hearing the words out loud made everything feel so much better. Fear drifted away. It would be over soon.

He would kneel. There'd be a loud bang. Then nothing.

Would it hurt? He didn't think Darrel had suffered. Or Ron. They hadn't moved after they'd fallen. They hadn't even twitched.

Dead before they hit the floor. He'd heard that line in movies, and he desperately hoped it was true.

Maybe everything just went black at that point. When it was his turn, maybe he'd just float up to heaven and be free of all this guilt.

Or maybe his mother was right, and all that time he spent with the Bisgards meant he'd be heading straight to hell. Troy no longer cared. Whatever the devil had in store for him couldn't possibly be worse than where he was now.

"No. Troy, you can't."

Brenda gripped the bars of her cage, tears running down

her cheeks in rivers. She looked so different. Whenever she was at work, her red hair was neatly arranged, her makeup light and fresh. Now, her hair was clumped around a pale and puffy face. Had Troy run into her outside this prison, he wasn't sure he'd have recognized her.

"Brenda, I gotta do this. You can't take this away from me."

"You're too young. You've got your whole life ahead of you."

That's what he was afraid of.

"I ain't got nothing good ahead of me. Not now. Not after what I've done. I just want to die. Let me die, Brenda. You gotta let me go."

"She's right, Troy." Dee Dee sat against the wall, little Ashton asleep in her arms. "You'll get over this. I know you will. You're strong. And Ron…he wouldn't want you to die. He wouldn't."

"So, he'd want Brenda to die?" Rage strengthened his voice. "Is that what you're saying? He'd want her to leave her daughter?"

Dee Dee lifted a trembling hand to her lips. "You know that isn't true. It's just…he loved you. You were like a son to him."

A flame rose from somewhere deep in Troy's chest. It burst behind his eyes and exploded into a thousand pieces. When the words came out of his mouth, they shattered in the air and threw shrapnel between the bars.

"Then why did he make me kill him, huh? Why did he make me do it? Why?"

As if the questions had released all the emotion in the world, Troy broke down. His shoulders shook uncontrollably. Great streams poured from his eyes. He couldn't remember ever crying like this. Not when his father died. Not even the month after, when it had finally sunk in that his dad wouldn't be coming home. Even then, his tears had been more restrained, as though somewhere there was still some hope that it wasn't true.

Now, he had no hope at all.

"He…" Dee Dee's words caught in her throat. She stopped, hugged Ashton closer, and started again. "He knew you were strong. That was why he did it, why he asked you. He trusted you to make it quick."

Troy squeezed the bars until the metal dug into his fingers. "Is that what it means to be strong? To kill someone you love? Then I don't want to be strong. I want to be weak. I want to be nothing. I just want to die."

He released the bars and dropped to the floor, curling into a fetal position.

Rrring.

Troy didn't even need to look at the clock to know it was noon.

He didn't react. The noise was too far away. He was only vaguely aware of the door to the room opening, the footsteps approaching, a voice asking the same question as before. "Who's next?"

"I am." Brenda's voice was clear and firm.

He jumped to his feet. "No, no. It's me. I'm next."

Ignoring Troy, the woman in the ski mask unlocked Brenda's cage. It was Two. She glanced over her shoulder. "You can wait."

Troy sank to the floor. His suffering would never end. It was all he deserved.

As despair filled his every cell, Brenda stepped into the corridor. She dropped to her knees but held her back straight.

Dee Dee screamed as Three yanked Ashton out of her arms and held a gun to his little head. The boy didn't cry. He'd already learned that crying did no good.

Poor kid.

"Brenda." Dee Dee reached through the bars, touching nothing but air. "I'm so sorry, I…"

"Tell Angela I love her." Brenda's voice was strong, the sobbing over. "Tell her I…I'll be watching her. I'll always be there. Tell her that."

"I will."

One's voice was sharp, like broken glass against gravel. "Who's going to send Brenda to heaven? Or wherever she's gonna end up. Let's hope you've been a good girl, Brenda, because it's judgment time." He cackled. "You up again, Troy? Come on out, killer."

One pulled the revolver out of his pocket, flipped open the chamber, and inserted a single round. Even though Troy hadn't answered, Two unlocked his cage and opened the door.

Troy scrambled to the back wall and pulled his knees to his chest. "I can't. I can't do it again. Please don't make me."

"Come on, killer. If it's not you, it's gotta beeeee…" One faked a drumroll. "Dee Dee."

Three laughed as if that was the funniest thing he'd ever heard. "What do you think, Troy? You gonna let Dee Dee kill her friend in front of her own kid? Or should I just go ahead and kill the child now?" Ashton whimpered as the gun moved from his cheek to his temple.

Dee Dee shook the bars. "No, no."

One lifted the gun. "We can't do this all day. Brenda's waiting. She's got an appointment with her maker. You don't want to make her late, do you?"

There was no winning here.

Defeated, Troy found himself crawling out of his cage. His body seemed to be moving of its own accord. One knee landed on a small pool of dried blood, and he couldn't tell whether it was Darrel's or Ron's. In the corridor, he extended his right hand.

"That's my boy." One dropped the weapon into Troy's palm. "Now remember, killer. No funny ideas. You have one bullet. We have enough for all of you."

Troy said nothing. He gripped the gun and turned around. Brenda's shoulders shook but she didn't make a sound. Not wanting her to suffer anymore, Troy lifted the gun and pulled the trigger.

Bang.

Even as the sound still echoed around the room, Brenda dropped face-first onto the concrete. A dark-red puddle grew around her.

When will my turn come?

20

I couldn't take my eyes off the monitor. Troy's reaction was truly remarkable. Everything I'd hoped to see. Mesmerizing.

That he was breaking was clear. He barely talked, hardly moved. When One gave him the revolver, his hand didn't tremble. He didn't even wait for Brenda to say a prayer or wipe her tears. He just took the gun, lifted his arm, and...*boom*. A second later, he drifted back into his cell.

This time, my hypothesis that Brenda would be the next fatality was accurate.

Troy had volunteered but had been denied, which was also interesting. I hadn't expected Brenda to volunteer so readily, though. And I surely hadn't expected her to die so quietly.

Humans were truly unpredictable.

While my three servants dragged the body away, I studied Troy. He could have been a zombie, some sort of half-dead, half-living creature. He had pushed away all feeling, all sense of life.

In a way, he reminded me of...me.

That was where the resemblance ended, though.

I had many happy years in front of me while Troy faced only suffering, guilt, and certain death.

It was interesting that I'd devised this experiment in part to study my own emotional response. In an ironic twist, I was growing more pleased by the hour that I possessed no emotion at all.

Someone had once told me there was a reason to go on, that life was filled with things worth living for. Perhaps Troy needed to be told something similar.

I stood on the edge of Stallion Bridge. The water rushed into the darkness fifty feet below me, and I wanted to know what the drop would be like. Maybe I would feel the joy of flight during my last few seconds. That might be interesting. Would I need to take in a lungful of water and feel my capillaries flood? Would the impact knock me out instantly, so I passed out from flight to blackness without even noticing? How quickly would it take to die?

I just wanted to know.

As I teetered on the edge, the tips of my shoes extending beyond the steel girder, headlights lit up the bridge. A car slowed down and pulled up behind me. The door opened, and a man in his late twenties or early thirties stepped out. His wedding ring glinted in the bright beams.

"Hey." He stepped over the barrier until he was almost on the edge with me, one hand wrapped around the steel girder above. "Come on, pal. I know you're feeling bad right now, but there's nothing you can't get through. Not with God's love."

Love? How did that feel?

"I don't feel bad," I told him honestly. "I don't feel anything. I want very much to feel something."

Why didn't he just drive on? What did he care if I jumped? Whether I existed or went extinct?

"I understand that numbness. You have to fight through it. You have so much to live for."

I did?

"What do I have to live for?"

"Everything, man. Everything. Think of your family."

"I don't have a family. Just a mom."

"Then think of...think of all the adventures ahead of you, all the amazing things you can see and experience. I know...I'm sure...that things look bleak right now, but God loves you, and He wants you to live."

I didn't understand the concept, but realized I very much wanted to.

"Does He? Why would God care about me?"

He stared at me, clearly stunned at my question. "God cares about everyone, man. He loves us all, sinner or saint, good or bad. He loves us all."

That was interesting.

"Sinners too?"

"Absolutely. How about you come with me? I'll buy you a coffee, and we can talk it all through. I promise you'll feel so much better."

As he extended an arm, I looked down. In the darkness below, the water in the river caught flashes of moonlight and shimmered white as it washed under the bridge.

What would it be like to meet those flashes head-on?

What would it be like to see someone else *meet those flashes head-on? That might be interesting.*

The man reached closer. "Come on, friend. Take my hand. Please."

"Okay."

His palm was warm, and his fingers strong as he intertwined them with mine. "That's good. Let's—"

His cry of shock and anguish wasn't even very loud when I pulled and twisted his hand. A single jerk caused him to lose his grip on the girder. As he fell, his eyes, wide as plates, locked into mine.

At that moment, I realized that he was almost right. I didn't feel better. He'd broken that promise. I did feel something, though, just a hint of fascination, even some excitement, until the splash swallowed him whole, and the water carried him away.

Troy was trying to shut down his emotions just as I'd been trying to rev mine up. We were on opposite trajectories. Which intrigued me.

Could I help him eliminate emotions entirely? First, I'd have to reassure him that nothing he'd done was in any way important. How old were the people he had shot? Late forties? Early fifties? They couldn't have had more than thirty years to live, perhaps no more than twenty.

And how many of those years would have been useful? The last five or ten would've been spent drooling into their cups at some home for seniors, forgotten by everyone they had known —except as a reminder of the unappealing fate awaiting us all.

No, Troy had done nothing bad by saving them from that fate. He might have even done them a favor.

I wanted to tell him he didn't *need* to feel regret about that, or anger, or even peace.

Something stirred inside me. Maybe admiration? Envy? Sympathy? I didn't know.

How fascinating.

The door opened. Without a knock. Again.

It was a good thing my pistol wasn't in my immediate reach.

Refusing to be distracted until I was ready, I watched Troy on the screen for a second longer. He remained curled at the back of his cage. Still. Unmoving.

I spun the chair around. "Yes?"

Two stood in the doorway. She'd pulled up her ski mask to reveal pockmarked cheeks and those nasty scars around her meth-ravaged mouth.

"Put your mask back on."

She did so. That was better.

"I think they're going to catch me." Her wringing fingers were as annoying as her high-pitched voice. "I think they will. You gotta help me."

This again. Tedious. "They won't catch you. Trust me."

"They will. I know they will. I'm the only one who worked at that stupid store who isn't in one of those cages, apart from that deaf old janitor. We should have taken him. I said we should have."

I shook my head. I wouldn't even need to write my hypothesis for how that would've turned out. Of course, he would have been the first to be shot. An old man? Half-blind, half-deaf, half-dead already. A waste of time.

"Did you do what I asked you to do?"

Two nodded. "Yeah."

"You did. You found a job at the store, didn't you?"

She nodded again, more confidently this time.

"And you won Dee Dee's trust. When she mentioned that she was looking for someone to help with deliveries and small tasks like that, you were ready with a recommendation, and we were ready with the drugs. Has everything not happened exactly as I told you it would?"

"Yeah. Yeah, that's true. But—"

"But nothing. You are no longer living at the address you gave the Bisgards, and you never have to go back to Stonevale again. Once I provide you with your new identification, no law enforcement agencies will ever find you. So, for pity's sake, stop being so hysterical."

Two stiffened. The outline of her mousy, little face seemed to curl in on itself. "Hysterical? I'm not being hysterical. You'd be worried, too, if you'd done any of the dirty work instead of sitting in here on your ass all day watching us clean up your mess."

Now, that was an interesting burst of anger, even if it was predictable.

"Watch your tone, young lady. Otherwise, I'll take you back to that crack den I dragged you out of, and you can go back to turning tricks for your next hit. Is that what you want?"

She glared at me, her eyes like slits through the holes of the mask. Did she believe any of her thoughts or emotions had any effect on me? She turned on her heel, leaving the door open.

Perhaps I should return her to the crack den I found her in, leaving her to smoke herself to death. It was only a matter of time. Not yet, though.

I needed her. For now, at least.

For my sanity and hers, though, she needed to calm down. Law enforcement would never catch her. I'd make sure of that.

———————

21

By the time Stella and Ander reached Stonevale Park, Hagen and Chloe were already standing under a grove of tulip poplars. The grass was immaculately green, the sun bright and hot, and sprinklers shot streams of water off in the distance. It was far too beautiful a day to be looking at a dead body.

Ronald Bisgard lay at the bottom of a small culvert. His face was half-buried in mud. Stella couldn't make out details, but his naked skin was pale against the grass.

"Shot in the back," Hagen answered the unasked question hovering in the air. "Like Darrel."

Slade and Chief Houston stood near the culvert, speaking with the medical examiner. Crime scene techs were just arriving. Stella didn't envy any of them their jobs.

"The M.E. doesn't look more than sixteen," Stella murmured.

Chloe slowly rotated her left shoulder, at least as far as the restrictive sling allowed. She was sweating, and probably not just from the heat. Her black clothing wasn't doing her any favors in the afternoon sun. "I was thinking younger."

"Bisgard looks terrible." Ander leaned against the tree trunk. "He looked better in his photo."

"They always do, don't they?" Hagen seemed unphased by the death and the heat. There wasn't a single sweat stain anywhere on his person. Stella envied his seemingly strange ability to control his sweat glands. "What did you find at Roxanne's place?"

Ander flashed him a half-grin. "Soda."

"Hm." Hagen stepped toward the caution tape as if a closer look would reveal the bigger picture he was missing. "So you said."

"Didn't look like she was there long either." Stella stood in the sunlight, hoping the rays of sun would bypass her skin and soothe the cold sensation icing her insides. "An air mattress on the floor, no signs of any furniture other than a chair, and nothing left behind but half a bottle. I'm sure that wasn't a permanent address."

Chloe chewed on the thumbnail of her right hand. "You think she's a hostage too?"

Stella had been considering that very question on the ride to the park. "I'm not sure. Either that or she could be connected to the kidnapping somehow. The timing is too much of a coincidence."

Chloe spit out a sliver of nail. "Then we just have to find her."

Hagen rubbed his temples. "Or her boyfriend's truck. A brown pickup with a covered bed was seen in the parking lot of Bisgard's Best. We should be able to find at least one of them."

Slade's voice sounded from behind Stella's shoulder. "I've asked Mac to look for Roxanne Jenham's previous known addresses, as well as anything else she can dig up on her. Excuse me." He pushed past Stella, stopping under the shade.

Following Slade, Chief Houston slipped under the

caution tape and joined them. "Thank you all for making it out here." The poor man looked exhausted.

Slade didn't look much better. "Chloe, Darrel Dowers's body is still here at the local morgue, and the plan is for the M.E. to take both him and Bisgard to the Nashville forensic center for autopsy."

Stella gritted her teeth. She still couldn't believe Dowers's autopsy hadn't been completed yet, which might provide a fountain of evidence for them to follow. This wasn't the movies, though. While most medical examiners strove for a twenty-four-hour turnaround, some rural areas like this didn't have the technology or staffing to work at that pace.

"I want you to follow the M.E. to the local morgue to get some preliminary answers on both our victims. From there, they'll move on to Nashville. The forensic center promised autopsies on both later today." He paused. "Take Hagen with you."

Hagen closed his eyes, and Stella almost laughed. He was notorious for disliking the M.E.'s office, which was why Slade probably assigned that particular duty to him.

Chief Houston turned to Hagen. "When you get to the local morgue, be careful what you say. This whole thing's taking off now. The press has been sniffing around over there, trying to get someone to leak information." He indicated the small collection of people across the park with a slight nod. A couple had cameras, and three more wrote in small notepads. "And the phones have been ringing off the hook at the office, people saying they saw all kinds of stuff."

Ander pushed away from the tree. "Any useful tips?"

"Oh, sure. Half the town thinks they saw the Bisgards being bundled into government vans, while the other half thinks aliens zapped them up. You fellows want to get to work on those reports?"

Ander offered a crooked smile. "I think we can rule out

government vans. Whoever did this has been pretty efficient so far."

"You fellows just be careful what you say out there. Public's getting antsy enough as it is. I'll see if I can rustle up a press statement later, but don't be surprised if you meet some angry folks. They're getting worried."

Stella's pocket buzzed, and she reached for her phone. "It's Mac. I'll put her on speaker." She tapped the screen and held the device out. "Mac, everyone's here. What did you find?"

"It took some digging, but I think I've found an address for Roxanne Jenham. It's not in her name, but she slipped up and used a debit card to pay a water bill that was normally paid with cash. It's a trailer out in the woods near Murfreesboro. I'll text you the details. The previous tenant moved out about six months ago, so she could have been there that long. I'm sending the landlord's info too."

Chief Houston pulled out his cell phone. "I'll get to work on the search warrant. You fellows get yourselves over there."

Slade tossed Ander keys to his Expedition. "You and Stella find that trailer, sit on it until the warrant comes through. Chloe. The M.E. is all yours. Hagen, you're with Chloe. Go."

———

22

Hagen rested an elbow on the reception desk at the local morgue, the temporary holding place for Ronald Bisgard and, now, Darrel Dowers. As Slade requested, they needed to learn anything they could from the county medical examiner before the bodies were transported to Nashville.

For an older building, the place was cleaner than he'd expected. The walls were bright white, and the smell of formaldehyde was only faintly annoying. But the best part, which *almost* made up for visiting this place of death, was the air-conditioning.

The receptionist, a cute blond with deep dimples, beamed at him. She was far too perky for this environment. "Dr. Penzotti will be out shortly." She twirled a curl with her index finger. "So, you're an FBI agent, huh?"

Hagen's smile was brief. He didn't want to encourage any flirting. "Yes."

Chloe sat in a chair against the opposite wall. "I'm an FBI agent too."

The receptionist's grin faded. "That's nice." She picked up

a pen and returned to her sudoku. After filling in a square, she glanced up at Hagen and smiled again.

Hagen pushed away from the desk. He really wasn't in the mood. Not today.

For a brief, shining moment, when Slade had assigned Chloe to this grisly task, he thought his luck might have changed, and he'd be heading off with Stella to check out a trailer in the woods.

Of course not.

Today was no better than yesterday. Ander was still working with Stella, and Hagen would soon be standing next to the cold remains of a murder victim. No, two murder victims, he reminded himself.

The double doors at the end of the reception area opened. "Sorry to keep you waiting. Dr. Eric Penzotti."

With his smooth cheeks and black-rimmed glasses, he looked younger than Hagen, young enough to make him wonder whether the M.E. had finished medical school. Hell, he looked young enough that Hagen wondered whether he'd finished high school, despite the white coat hanging loosely from his shoulders.

After handshakes and introductions, Dr. Penzotti led them toward the dreaded double doors and into a room cold enough to freeze beer. "Protective clothing is there."

Hagen handed Chloe some gear before slipping into his own. He shivered. "Cold in here."

Penzotti pulled on a second pair of gloves. "Wouldn't want it any warmer than this. They don't complain, but heat doesn't do them any favors either."

Hagen suppressed a shudder, and this one had nothing to do with the temperature of the room. Because he no longer had a choice, he turned his attention to the two steel tables. Darrel Dowers lay on his left. He had a white sheet draped over his body up to his shoulders.

To his right was Ronald Bisgard. He had just arrived. The black body bag was unzipped. The man was mercifully clothed, but his shirt and trousers were covered in mud and bloodstains. A rugged tear across the front of his t-shirt exposed part of his belly.

Penzotti moved to stand in front of Darrel. "Let's start with this one. I estimate time of death to be between two to nine a.m. Thursday morning." He lowered the sheet, revealing what could only be described as a crater in the man's chest. "I feel safe to say this is cause of death. The manner of death is homicide."

No shit.

Chloe stepped closer. "You can't get anything closer than that, timewise?"

Penzotti shook his head. "I'd probably edge closer to eight a.m. based on rigor and livor mortis, but I wouldn't wager my mortgage on it. At that point, the differences in musculature and blood loss are more difficult to determine without a deeper dive into the body."

Chloe pointed at the large hole in the left side of Darrel's chest. "The exit wound is massive."

"Yes, it is." Penzotti leaned forward and placed both hands under Darrel's left shoulder. He tilted the body toward him. "Can you see the entry wound on his back? There's stippling from the blast, so it was close range. Guess they weren't taking chances."

Chloe crouched down for a closer look. She held onto Hagen's forearm for balance since she only had one useful arm. After she peered at the wound, inspecting it carefully, she glanced up at him. "You're not looking."

Mentally cursing, Hagen dropped to his haunches. The wound was bigger than he'd expected. The skin and muscle were torn away, leaving a hole almost large enough to put his fist through.

His stomach twisted.

He stood up and breathed out slowly. Chloe's good hand fell away.

"You okay?" Chloe looked up at him again.

Hagen frowned. "Of course. I'm fine. The wound's big. I'd think a shotgun at close range, but I can't see any pellet wounds."

"No." Penzotti lowered Darrel's shoulder. "I had to do a bit of digging to come up with a bullet that could do that kind of damage. The closest I could come was a .454 Casull. I've never seen one of those before, so if your ballistics people ever find the round, I'd like to know if I'm right."

Hagen looked away from the body, relieved when the tension in his guts eased. "You ever heard of one of those, Chloe?"

"Yeah. My dad used to talk about them. One of his friends liked to use them to shoot down trees. He was an idiot. Those are expensive rounds. Actually, my dad's friends were all idiots."

"Hmm." Hearing someone say something less than perfect about their parents always sounded strange to Hagen, disrespectful. But he knew that not everyone was raised in a loving home either. He pushed Chloe's comment out of his head. "Strange choice, even if you're not shooting a tree."

"Yeah. Why not just stick to regular ammo?"

Hagen took a step back. The distance from the body helped him think more clearly. "I'm guessing our unsub was after the extra damage. They didn't want the victim to survive, even if nothing major was hit. Like you said. No chances."

Penzotti took a step back and mimed holding a gun, aiming down. "Judging by the height of the entry and exit wounds, I'd say he was shot while kneeling. If your murderer wanted to hit something major, I don't think they could have missed."

"I see. Did you get any DNA off the clothes?"

"They've already been bagged and sent for testing, but nothing obvious yet. Could be weeks before you get those results, I'm afraid. I checked the toxicology reports on Darrel Dowers before you came, though. We found traces of Valium, Ambien, and ketamine in his system. My guess is that they used the Valium to knock him out and the Ambien and the ketamine to keep him out, at least for a while."

Hagen searched his memory. "We didn't find any pills at the scene."

"More than one way to slip someone a Mickey." Chloe leaned closer to the exit wound. Her hand drifted toward her shoulder. She snapped it back as though she had touched a hot stove. "Drugs could have been in the food that night. That would explain how they were all knocked out at the same time."

Penzotti peeled off the top layer of gloves before lowering his glasses to polish them with the end of his white coat. "I understand a child was also taken. A two-year-old. That's more problematic if the drug is administered through food. Sedating a child that age usually requires some precision. The kidnapper wouldn't have known whether the child was receiving a safe dosage."

Hagen gritted his teeth. "To be honest, Dr. Penzotti, I don't think our kidnapper gave a rat's ass whether the child lived or died."

Chloe moved past Darrel Dowers to stand closer to the corpse of Ronald Bisgard. "What about this one?"

Penzotti turned and put his glasses back on. "First impressions suggest a similar cause of death, and I guardedly estimate time of death between eighteen and twenty-eight hours ago. Manner of death is, of course, homicide."

After snapping on a fresh pair of gloves, he lifted Ronald Bisgard's shoulder, twisting the man free of the body bag for a moment. The body made a thin *crrrk* as the sticky, dried blood separated from the plastic. Hagen ignored the groaning in his stomach and approached the body for a closer look. A large hole in the back of the man's t-shirt revealed the ends of his ribs and the white edge of a vertebra. He took two steps back.

"You okay there?" Chloe seemed amused, based on the half-smile on her face. "Looking a bit pale."

Hagen forced a small smile. "I'm good. Thanks. I'm guessing we'll find the same drug cocktail in his system as in Darrel Dowers's."

Penzotti lowered the body. Taking a long pair of tweezers from a tray next to the table, he lifted the edges of the hole in the front of Ronald Bisgard's t-shirt. Blood and mud had combined to leave a black streak across his chest. He released the material and peeled off the top layer of gloves again. How many pairs did the man go through per day?

"Maybe. But my first impression is that they weren't killed at the same time, so drug traces might be different. Won't know for another twenty-four to forty-eight hours, and the full autopsy report will take at least six weeks for each of them. At first glance, I stand by my assertion that the same weapon was used on both men, shot from a similar position."

"Any idea how long he might have been dumped in that culvert?"

"Not yet. Like I said, we've only just met."

Hagen knew medical examiners hated to provide estimates, but he needed to push. "Can you guess?"

Penzotti removed his glasses again. They added about five years to his age, which turned him into a middle schooler without them. "I can always guess. If I had to, I would say there was little difference between them, perhaps no more than a few hours. Judging by the state of the body, I'd say Mr. Bisgard was only dumped recently, perhaps as late as last night. Considering where he was found, I would have expected to see much more water damage, animal bites, fly larvae, that sort of thing. I'd guess they were both dropped off yesterday, less than eight hours apart, if that."

Chloe pushed her free hand into her pocket. "Okay, so we've got two bodies shot at point-blank range by a gun that could fell a tree. They were both shot within two-to-eight hours of each other, and it's likely the victims were drugged before they were killed. As soon as you get more, Doctor, please let us know."

The M.E. slipped his glasses back on. "I will."

Hagen led Chloe out of the room. When they reached the reception area, he stopped. Warmth flooded back into his limbs. "Two down within hours of each other? And if the kid was dosed with all those drugs, he could be dead too. I'm starting to think they're all dead already."

Chloe narrowed her eyes. "You can't think like that. We'll find them."

Hagen slapped a hand against the wall. "Yeah. We'll find them too late."

The receptionist looked up from her sudoku. "You okay, Agent?"

He lifted an apologetic hand but didn't speak.

What was the point? If they couldn't save anyone, what the hell were they doing?

23

Stella leaned on the hood of the Expedition, then jerked back when the metal burned through her slacks.

Beside her, Ander chuckled.

She ignored him and focused on the trailer in a clearing on the side of the road. The small structure's exterior had once been white, but mud and mold had spread up the sides. Stella wasn't sure where the mobile home ended and the ground began.

"Not much, is it?" Ander squinted in the sunlight. "I wasn't really expecting a penthouse. Dee Dee wrote on her application that Roxanne was desperate. That looks pretty desperate to me."

It sure did. The trailer reminded her of some meth houses she'd come across during her time with the East Nasty PD. "After seeing this, I'm thinking that tiny apartment must've looked like The Ritz to her."

Stella drew closer to the rusty home, one hand resting on her holster. She was almost certain she wouldn't need her weapon. But almost wasn't enough.

"Lonely too." She nodded toward the trees. "Nearest

neighbor must be at least half a mile away. No cars come down here. I don't think this place could be more remote."

Ander reached the window first, and Stella was glad he was the one attempting to peer through a thick layer of grime. Pulling away, he shook his head. "Can't see shit. Pretty handy if you've got something to hide."

"Or if you're the one trying to hide." Stella moved to the right side of the door and pounded on the center of the grungy entrance. "Roxanne Jenham! This is Special Agent Stella Knox of the FBI." She waited for a response. When there wasn't one, she repeated the knock-and-announce process. "Ms. Jenham? You in there? This is the FBI. Open up."

Silence. There was no hint of movement beyond the door, no sound of footsteps or a mad scramble to hide evidence. Stella waited for what seemed like an eternity.

She flipped the catch off her holster and pulled her weapon. She tried the door handle. Locked. Ander took up position on the other side of the door. "That's a good sign. At least it's not abandoned like the other place."

"Roxanne Jenham, this is Special Agent Stella Knox of the FBI. We've got a search warrant." She directed this statement to the locked door and listened. No sign of life behind it. "We are entering the premises!"

Ander stepped back, lifted his foot, and kicked his boot at a point just below the door handle. The second the door burst open, Stella raced inside. "FBI!"

The place was empty, and it only took them a minute to clear the rooms.

Stella re-holstered her gun and scanned the interior. A mattress sprawled below a dust-covered window at the end of the trailer. Gray sheets and a worn blanket were piled at the bottom of it. Dirty plates filled the sink and took up space along most of the filthy, dilapidated laminate counter-top. Someone had been eating here.

A yellow paper towel holder was nailed under the cupboards. But it was empty, broken, with one end snapped off. The roof buckled. Scuff marks tore up the floor, which didn't look like it had seen soap and water in a decade. But, again, it was evident someone had been here fairly recently.

Stella pulled on her latex gloves and flicked a switch by the door. A single light in the middle of the ceiling came on, casting a dim, amber glow over the gloomy interior. She pulled the faucet lever up, and a stream of water poured over the dishes, releasing a smell of old food and nasty drainpipes.

Ander pulled on a pair of gloves, his curls nearly brushing the low ceiling. "Still functional. Someone's been keeping this thing going." He opened the cupboard under the sink and dragged out the garbage can. A box of takeout food spilled onto the floor, its remains still wet. "More than half a bottle of soda in here. Same generic brand as the apartment."

Stella lifted some clothes from a pile on the floor. Both the torn t-shirt and the pair of size two jeans with holes in the knees and dirty brown marks at the bottom of the legs reeked of body odor and old Chinese food.

A burst of white light filled the space as Ander photographed the garbage can. "Smile." Another flash had Stella blinking as he took a picture of the bed and the jeans Stella was holding up.

"Thanks." Stella dropped them onto the mattress.

"One for the yearbook." Ander grinned and lowered the phone. "Want to wait and see if she turns up?"

"No point. She sees our vehicle outside, and she won't come anywhere near here." Stella picked up another t-shirt. She wrinkled her nose and dropped it. Roxie must have worn them for a month at a time to get that smell so deeply embedded.

"Fair enough. Let's see what we can find and get out of here."

Stella checked the pockets of the clothes and lifted the mattress before checking the floor and baseboards for any hiding places. As Ander photographed the contents of the filthy trailer, she rummaged through the bits of string, random cables, and rubber bands stuffed into the cutlery drawer.

Stella pulled out a spoon. The bowl was bent back almost to the handle. A white residue had settled into the bottom of it, and the back was covered in soot. "Look at this."

She held it out to Ander, who took a photo. "Guess we know why she was desperate."

She dropped the spoon back into the drawer for the crime scene techs to take care of later. "How long do you think she's been gone?" Stella closed the drawer and looked around. She very nearly reached for her gold stud before stopping her dirty gloves from touching her skin.

"Don't know. Could be a few hours. Could be a few days. You think maybe we have one more kidnapping victim?"

Stella shrugged. "I honestly don't know. It's strange and sad." Finally, she sighed. "I'm done here."

"Me too."

Stella followed Ander out of the trailer and back into the afternoon sun. She took a deep breath of fresh air and pulled off her gloves. "Can you imagine living like that?"

Ander peeled off his gloves and stuffed them in a separate evidence bag, holding it out for her to do the same. "No. I kinda hope I'd have the sense to get help long before I reached that stage. Or that I'd have friends who'd force that help on me. What do you want to do now?"

Stella twisted her ear stud. They needed to find Roxanne. She was their best lead. "I'll call the chief, have someone come and stake the place out for a few hours.

We're pretty close to Murfreesboro, and Roxanne's got a habit to fund."

"You think she's got herself another job in town?"

"Bisgard's Best isn't handing out any hours, so she's got to be doing something. Let's get someone out here, grab a bite to eat, and circle back."

24

Roxie Jenham slipped quietly off the road and down into the brush before the cops could see her. Their black SUV parked near her trailer was about as hard to miss as a polar bear in Starbucks.

As she crouched behind the trunk of a young oak tree, she trembled, but she didn't know whether it was from nerves or withdrawal. One thing she did know for certain was that she was glad she'd told Benny to drop her off at the bottom of the hill. She always made him leave her there, even though it meant walking for a good half-mile to her trailer.

Safety precaution. Couldn't be too careful, not while this whole insane experiment was going on. The mess that man was making. He was sure to attract attention and bring the Feds down on everyone's heads. And there they were… searching her home.

Benny thought she was crazy. He actually trusted that psycho.

She didn't understand how anyone could trust someone who manipulated people into killing each other. The blond-haired, blue-eyed "scientist" gave her the heebie-jeebies. He was like ice. No emotion. He also thought he was superior to all of them. But he didn't understand.

Smart. That's what she was.

Teachers hadn't seen it, and neither had her ma or pa, but Roxie always knew she had more gray matter than the average bear. She wouldn't have survived this long otherwise. The junk might have burned off a few of those cells by now, but she still knew what she was about. No way they were going to catch her.

Too bad, Feds. If you can't see me, you can't catch me.

Roxie crouched lower. She'd just wait there in the trees until the Feds had enough and got lost. Couldn't be too long now, surely. Not much else to do out here in these woods. She swatted a mosquito away.

The woman yelled Roxie's name just before the other agent with the curly mop head lifted a foot and kicked in the door.

Roxie slapped her hand to her face to stifle her gasp. She dug her fingers into her own cheek, even as anger burst in her chest.

What the hell, dude? You can't just go and kick my door in, you government goon.

Roxie dropped lower, ignoring the cramp in her hamstring, and waited. The light came on inside. She was a good fifty feet away. Too far to hear anything. A soft wind, which did little to cool the heat, rustled in the branches around her.

The dude passed in front of the window. A white flash lit the trailer, then another.

Roxie punched the tree with the side of her fist.

Damn you, pigs.

But she didn't move to stop them. She just waited behind the tree, peering between the branches until the agents came back out. They huddled there for a moment. One of them, the woman, walked away from the trailer, her phone to her ear. Roxie strained to hear what she was saying but only caught a few words. She heard her own name. She was sure of that. And something about "watch" and "grab her."

Roxie snarled. *Grab me? Fat chance.*

The curly-haired agent frowned. He jogged toward the road, toward the tree line where Roxie hid.

No, no.

Her heart thumped in her chest. Had she spoken out loud? Benny said she talked to herself sometimes. Well, so what if she did? Only way to engage in an intelligent conversation in that place was to talk to herself.

She ducked lower until she was almost lying on the ground and could barely see over the top of the tree roots.

The Fed approached the edge of the road. She watched his boots inch closer and closer before they stopped. Roxie peered through the bushes. The Fed was tall, and he shielded his eyes against the sun as he stared into the woods.

Roxie breathed out slowly, quietly, not daring to move. Something crawled up her leg. She clenched her jaw and tensed her muscles but didn't budge. She wouldn't.

The woman's voice came from back by the trailer. "He'll be here soon. Let's go."

"Right."

The Fed lowered his hand. He turned, walked away, and they both climbed back into the SUV and left.

Roxie exhaled and slapped her ankle, squishing the bug into her skin. With a glance down the road to make sure it was clear, she stood and ran to the trailer. She knew it was a dangerous move, but she needed to see what they'd done. Her door hung from its hinges, a deep dent in the front next to the handle.

"Damn you, Feds. You're going to pay for that."

She peered inside. The place was a mess. Relief surged

through her. The place was always a mess. Maybe they hadn't rifled through her stuff after all. But, no, her jeans were on the bed even though she'd left them on the floor. The cutlery drawer was halfway open, the one with her cook spoon inside.

Leave. Get out of here.

Trusting her gut, she raced back into the woods, pulling out her phone as she ran.

"Benny, get your ass back here now. The Feds've been here. They're all over me."

"What? Where are you?"

Tripping over roots and getting scraped from branches, she explained what had happened and what she needed him to do. She didn't stop running until she reached the corner. A ditch ran along one side, and she crouched at the bottom of it, her sneakers buried in the mud and grass. There was no sign of the Feds, but there was also no sign of Benny. She crept forward slowly.

Where are you, you little—

The sound of an engine caused her to freeze in place, and she didn't dare breathe until the familiar brown truck came around the curve. Benny had slowed down and was peering into the woods to find her.

Even he couldn't spot her hiding place, and she was right under his nose.

She scrambled up the side of the ditch, yanked open the passenger door, and dove onto the seat.

"Drive, you idiot. Drive."

Nothing.

Benny's forehead was knitted, highlighting the scar cutting through his eyebrow, a souvenir from the time he'd headbutted the bedroom mirror. He'd been so high he didn't even feel it.

"Where we going?"

"Just go, will you? Quick, before they come back."

When the urgency of the situation finally kicked in, Benny hit the gas. The wheels spun as the truck sped off.

"Where are we going?" he asked again.

Roxie sat low in the seat, her eyes scanning for any vehicle that looked like it might be a Fed. "Christ, Benny. I don't know. Can't you think of something?"

"The Feds are after you, not me."

Roxie glared at him. "What's that supposed to mean? If they're after me, they're after you too. Let's just get back. Dr. S. will know what to do."

Benny didn't look so certain, but he did as she instructed. After what felt like forever to Roxie, being slouched so uncomfortably in the seat, he turned off the road and continued until they reached the block of run-down one-story buildings where they kept the captives.

The street was empty, just as it was supposed to be. The whole area was scheduled to be flattened since the neighborhood had been rezoned for industrial use. That was what Roxie had heard. She didn't know if it were true, but the place was certainly a pit. Bricks were crumbling, and those that remained looked like little more than mold and graffiti were holding them together. The bars on the windows of the building they were using were coated with rust.

Because she was worried the Feds might have found this place, too, she had Benny stop a few buildings away from the back entrance. Roxie was out of the truck before he'd turned off the engine and began jogging, staying low until she reached the door. Once inside, she exhaled a long breath but stayed on her tiptoes as she headed toward the observation room, the place where the boss watched those people like a pervert.

What a freak!

All Dr. S. did was sit with his notebook and monitor,

watching those people kill each other. He just didn't care. None of what was happening in those cages moved him at all. She often tried not to care, but she could never reach his level.

Her philosophy was simple. Life was shit, and then you died. In the moments between the beginning and the end, she had to take care of herself.

At least the drugs made waiting for the Grim Reaper a little bit easier. And the stuff the freak gave her was good.

So good.

Dr. S.'s voice echoed from the room down the corridor. "Will you please just shut up for one minute with your constant whining?" As usual, the man sounded bored.

Three was complaining…again. He was always complaining. It drove her crazy too. She wasn't sure he was capable of getting through to the boss, who was never shaken, but that guy could make a saint suicidal.

Roxie lifted a finger to her lips when Benny came down the hallway. He slowed, then listened with her.

"I agree with you. I don't think her suspicions are in any way grounded, but her nervousness is indeed a concern. She could crack under pressure, and I am right on the verge of a scientific breakthrough. She is becoming a liability."

Roxie stiffened. There could only be one "she."

"A liability, eh?" That was Three. "I know what to do with liabilities."

Despite the fear making her shiver, Roxie rolled her eyes. Three didn't know what to do with his shoelaces.

"You do indeed, my friend. So do it. She can't endanger my experiment if she's dead, can she?"

A chill ran down Roxie's spine.

He was going to kill her. He was really going to do it. She had to get out of there now.

Afraid the doctor could hear the beating of her heart, she

began to back away. Benny went with her, equally quiet. Once the door was closed behind her, she ran back to the truck.

"Go, go, go!"

Benny slammed the gears into reverse and punched the gas. "Where to? Where should we go?"

"Dunno. Anywhere." Pressing her fingers to her temples, she forced herself to think. "Let's get back to the trailer real quick. I'll grab my stuff, and we'll head north to my sister's place. We'll be out of here before those psychos even know we're gone. They'll never find us."

She checked the rearview mirror.

And neither will the Feds.

25

S tella winced as hot chocolate burned the roof of her mouth. Trusting a vending machine was always a bad idea and trusting a vending machine in a gas station was even worse. The drink tasted like semi-sweet mud mixed with foam from a fire extinguisher.

She drank it anyway.

The sun was finally drifting low in the west, and it was actually nice outside.

Ander leaned next to her against the SUV, a half-eaten granola bar in his hand. Stella envied his choice. To go into a store full of chocolate, potato chips, and candy and come out with nothing but oats and honey was a genuine act of self-discipline. She certainly couldn't do it.

She lifted her cup to take another sip just as her phone rang.

Ander swallowed a dry mouthful of oats. "You need to get a ringtone. Something to get you moving, you know?" He wiggled his shoulders. She assumed he was dancing.

"Nope, really don't." Stella fished her phone from her back pocket. "Agent Knox."

The voice on the other end was young and excited. Stella was sure that, on any other day, the speaker would have been at least an octave lower. "Agent, this is Officer Scott from the Stonevale Police Station."

"Go on, Officer Scott."

"Uh, so, er…the chief sent me into the woods to keep an eye on that trailer. I found a neat spot where no one can see me, and I'm watching it real good."

Stella mentally counted to three. "That's great. Is there anything to report?"

"Uh-huh."

Stella lowered her cup. "Scott?"

"Yes, ma'am?"

Stella blinked. She had to remind herself that she was once a newbie too.

"*What* is there to report?"

"Oh, er…people. A couple of folks turned up. A man and a woman. They're in the trailer right now."

Stella was already moving, tossing her cup into the closest garbage can. "We're on our way."

Ander swallowed what was left of the granola bar and leapt into the driver's seat. Moments later, they were racing out of the gas station and back down the road toward the trailer.

Once they hit the correct road, Ander slowed down. Off to the side, Stella saw the Stonevale police car in the lengthening shadows of the trees. Officer Scott, a man in his early twenties who didn't seem old enough to grow peach fuzz, gave her a thumbs-up as they passed. It took effort not to roll her eyes.

"There." Stella pointed to the corner where the road met the dirt lane.

A pickup with a covered bed was parked there. The paint was rust brown. Though, it was hard to say where the rust ended and the brown began. Stella's heart thrummed in her chest.

Ander pulled up behind it as Stella reached for her phone.

"Mac. I need you to run a plate for me. Quick as you can." She read out the numbers.

"On it." Mac was as calm and efficient as ever.

Ander had already dialed Slade. "Sir? Looks like we've got activity at the trailer. We're about to go in." He listened to the response before hanging up.

He turned to Stella just as Mac came back on the line. "Unless your brown truck is actually a green Honda Civic, those aren't its plates. Looks like they're stolen. Driver's probably hiding something."

"Perfect. Thanks, Mac."

She reached for the door handle. "Let's not spook them."

Ander nodded and climbed out of the car. "Slade says we're good to bring Roxanne in. He also says they've got the arrest warrant for Gerry Renelle. Chief Houston is heading down there now to bring him in."

"Good." Stella eased the door closed. "Maybe we're about to crack this thing."

She dialed the last number that had called her. "Officer Scott, I want you to keep watch on the brown truck. Box it in. I don't want anyone driving off, okay?"

"Yes, ma'am."

She disconnected the call. "Let's go."

Stella jogged toward the trailer, keeping as close to the tree line as possible. The sun threw deep shadows across the path. Ander padded softly behind her.

Beyond the gray curtains and the grime on the windows, she could see shadows shifting about. Young Officer Scott was right. Roxie was there. Stella took a deep breath to calm the adrenaline surge.

Creeping around the front of the trailer, Stella nodded for Ander to cover the back.

The door was closed, the dent Ander had made clearly visible under the handle. Stella pulled her weapon. The weight felt heavy in her hand. She raised her fist and beat on the door.

"Roxanne Jenham? FBI. Open up."

"Shit."

She heard a woman's voice, thick with panic.

Then the woman yelled, "Go!"

"We're coming in."

Stella grabbed the door handle and pushed. The door didn't budge. She tried again. The door was stuck, the damage they had caused earlier jamming it in place. Stella clenched her teeth, lifted a boot, and kicked. The door swung back. An instant later, she was up the step and into the trailer.

The room was empty. Drawers were open, and the pile of clothes on the floor was gone, as were the cartons of food in the cupboard above the sink.

Ander's footsteps sounded from the back. "What the heck? Where are they?"

Stella looked around. The side window swung gently on its hinges. Through the dirt that covered the glass, she could just make out two figures sprinting toward the trees. "There! Tree line. Go round."

In one movement, Stella was out of the door and racing after the pair. "FBI! Stop!"

They didn't slow.

Nuts.

Picking up speed, Stella sprinted toward the trees, holstering her weapon as she moved.

They ran hard, but Roxie's companion outpaced her by a

good half-yard with each stride. He disappeared into the trees. So much for chivalry.

As Ander went after the man, Stella shouted again. "Roxie, stop!"

The woman turned and almost instantly dropped from view.

Where the hell did she go?

Roxie popped up from where she'd fallen, and Stella ran harder, narrowing the distance down to five yards, then three. At one, Stella dove. Roxie went down hard, her body cushioning Stella's landing.

Down but not out, the girl tried to fight. "Get off me."

Breathing hard, Stella drove a knee into her suspect's spine. With one hand on her head, she yanked an arm behind the young woman's back, torquing it hard toward her shoulder blades. The girl howled but stopped resisting enough that Stella could release the handcuffs connected to her holster. A minute later, both wrists were secured, and Stella had enough breath to speak.

"Roxanne Jenham, you're under arrest—"

"Fuck you."

Ignoring the outburst, Stella continued the Miranda rights. "Do you understand each of these rights I've explained to you?"

"Go to hell, Fed," Roxie snarled.

"I'll take that as a yes."

Stella dragged Roxie, her head on a swivel, looking and listening for any sign of Ander and his suspect.

Nothing. Shit.

Ander was big, and he was fast, but the other guy had a big lead. Not that it mattered. He was probably circling back around, heading for the truck where the officer was waiting for him.

They had them both.

Stella shoved Roxie toward the trail they'd just created. If one hand hadn't been grasping the cuffs while the other was clamped down on her suspect's shoulder, Stella would have punched the air in celebration. This could be it. The crack in the case they needed. Roxie had to know something. The sooner she got these two back to the station and into interrogation rooms, the better.

As she reached the end of the woods, she slowed. There was the Expedition, but where was the truck?

Shit.

Officer Scott was on the ground, rubbing the back of his head, a thick log on the ground beside him. The Stonevale black-and-white sat off to the side. He hadn't boxed the truck in after all.

Ander bounded through the trees as Stella approached. The officer turned and lowered his hand. Blood covered his palm and matted his sandy hair. "I'm sorry, Agents. I didn't see him coming."

When Roxie chuckled, Stella led her toward the cruiser. "Do you need an ambulance?"

The officer shook his head, then winced and staggered before righting himself. "I'm fine."

"No, you're not." She picked a set of keys up from the ground and tossed them to Ander. "He'll drive. We'll have an EMT meet us at the station to check you out."

"It won't do you no good." Roxie laughed harder. "I don't know nothin' about nothin'."

Stella pushed Roxie into the rear of the police car. "Just sit there and relax. We'll get to know each other better soon."

As she slammed the door shut, her phone rang. It was Slade. She braced herself, preparing to get reamed for letting the second suspect escape. "We got Roxie Jenham, but the guy she was with got away."

"Okay." Slade's voice was flat and even. "Get her back to the station quick as you can. But Stella?"

"Yes."

"Gerry Renelle is dead. Chief Houston found him hanging from the top of his stairway."

26

R oxie rested her arms on the table and scratched the back of her hand, one then the other. The withdrawal was hitting her fast. Her mouth was as dry as sandpaper. No matter how much she smacked her lips and worked her tongue, she just couldn't work up any saliva.

She'd been talking with the Feds for an hour already. Or, rather, they'd been talking, making assumptions about her. They'd read a few files, looked at a couple of places she'd lived, and thought they knew her.

"Want some more water?" That was Knox, her name was. "Uh-huh."

Knox pushed her chair out, left the room, and came back with a plastic cup filled with cold water.

Roxie gulped it down. The chill of the liquid helped for a few minutes. Soon, though, her mouth was bone-dry again.

The other agent, the one with the curly, blond hair, folded his hands on the table and stared at her from close range. "Where are they, Roxie? Where are you keeping the Bisgards?"

His scare tactics didn't work at all. She even liked him a

little better than Knox, but that could be because he hadn't tackled her.

Roxie's leg jiggled under the table. She was so damn tired.

If there was one good thing about working for Dr. S.—and there had been only one good thing—it was that he kept his side of the bargain. He made sure that she always had a good supply. Made all that crap worthwhile. As long as it lasted.

That was over now.

Bastard wanted to kill her.

She'd heard him with her own ears. Was that a new development, or had they been planning that all along?

Three. Out of them all, how had that bastard become the winner of Dr. S.'s trust?

She could turn the freak in now, tell these agents everything she knew. Would serve him right. He'd probably get life without parole. Might even get death with a bit of luck. A lethal injection right in the arm. He wouldn't be the first to go that way. What he really deserved was being shot through the chest with an elephant gun.

The thought made her smile.

"Come on, Roxie. Help us and we'll help you."

What if he got away, though? Benny had gotten away, and Dr. S. was much smarter than Benny ever hoped to be. He probably knew she'd been arrested by now. He was probably taking precautions. Hell, he'd probably cut his "experiment" short. The Bisgards—however many were left—were probably dead already.

She shuddered, and not from withdrawal.

Roxie's memory wasn't all that great anymore, but she could certainly remember what he'd said when he'd walked up to her in that abandoned building.

"Work for me, and I'll give you all the meth your body can demand. You can smoke yourself to death or inject yourself into

oblivion. I really don't care, but as long as you work for me, I'll make sure you never have to look for another fix again."

It had been like finding Father Christmas in a heroin den with a sack full of drugs for all the naughty children. Whatever work this lunatic was offering, she'd do it—that's what she told herself.

Would she have taken that offer if she'd really known what the work entailed?

The thought made her pause. She wanted to believe that she would have told him to get lost. She'd never wanted to kidnap anyone. She certainly didn't want to kill anyone.

Who was she kidding?

It wasn't like she'd had to kill anyone herself. They'd done that to each other, hadn't they? 'Course she'd have taken the job. That's what the drugs told her to do.

It was what Dr. S. said next that she remembered most, what he'd done after she agreed.

He took out his phone and showed her some pictures. Of her parents' home. Of a woman—her ma—buying groceries. That man with the protruding belly, photographed through the living room window watching television, was her pa.

Her blood ran cold. How did he know who her ma and pa were?

Then he flicked the screen, and there was her sister, sitting outside a café with her boyfriend. The next picture was sis dropping her kid off at school.

"You bastard, you—"

Dr. S. shoved her so hard that her shoulders and head smacked into the wall. "Work for me, and you get all the drugs you want. Betray me, breathe a word of what I do to anyone, and I'll butcher everyone you ever loved."

Even now, just remembering his voice sent a shiver down Roxie's spine. He'd been so calm, like he wasn't threatening her, merely explaining the facts of life. She didn't doubt for a minute he'd meant what he said.

His threat almost didn't work. He could butcher her parents if he wanted. She hadn't seen them since they'd kicked her out to fend for herself when she was just fifteen. She didn't give a damn what happened to them.

But her sister? She'd always lived right. She didn't deserve to die. And her little nephew…

"Get lost, Fed."

Knox leaned across the table. She'd sounded mean when she'd slapped on the handcuffs. Her voice was a lot softer now. She wanted something. She was playing nice. Unlike Dr. S., Knox seemed to understand emotions and how they worked. "Help us, Roxie, and we can help you. It's the best chance you've got."

Help her? They couldn't help her. Even if the Feds managed to protect her sister, they'd throw away the key for what Roxie had done. She was no murderer, but they'd think she was. At the very least, they'd charge her as an accessory or something. To murder. And kidnapping.

Worse…she was guilty. She wasn't too far gone to know that.

Still, she had to protect herself. Protect her sister. "Don't know what you're talking about, Fed. I ain't done nothing."

How long could they hold her? Twenty-four hours? Forty-eight? Roxie wasn't sure, but whatever it was, she could keep her mouth shut that long. Might even be kinda nice. A proper bed, some hot meals. After she got out, she'd find Benny. They'd get her sister, and they'd disappear. No one would ever find them.

Knox twisted at her ear.

Nice gold stud she had in it. Might even get a quick payday for those if they were real gold.

"Roxie, we're going to find them. You know that. If you help us find them faster, then we can help you. We know you worked for the Bisgards, and we know you're involved in their kidnapping. I don't think you know how much trouble you're in."

That made her laugh. *Lady, it's you who doesn't know how much trouble I'm in. You've got no idea.*

The other agent scowled. "You think this is funny? We've got two bodies…"

Three, but you ain't got one of them yet.

"We've got four people still missing."

That's three again. Guess neither of us was ever much good with numbers.

"Now, you need to tell us where they are."

I do that, Agent Ander, and my sister gets the same thing the others got.

Roxie fixed her eyes on Knox's. "Can you show me to my cell now? I'm tired."

27

S tella led the young woman into the cell and waited while Officer Scott dug in his pocket for the key. Did Roxie grin when she saw the officer's bandaged head? It looked like she did. Stella had never seen anyone so content with being held in a jail cell overnight.

The door clanged shut.

"You okay, Officer? Head not too sore?"

Scott couldn't meet Stella's gaze as he rubbed his bandage. "Yeah, I'll be fine. Chief says I was good and lucky."

Curiosity got the better of Stella. "Because the guy in the brown truck might have shot you?"

"Naw, because he reckons I was saved by having a thick skull."

Though there wasn't much to laugh about right now, Stella forced herself not to release a chuckle at his comment.

They'd grilled Roxie for hours. Every question they'd asked had been met with silence or the occasional smug grin. Either Roxie was smarter than she looked, or she was as scared. Stella wasn't sure which.

Chloe stood at the entrance to the police station with Slade. They'd been waiting on her.

"You ready?" Chloe asked.

After rubbing her neck, Stella nodded. "Yeah. We'll pick it up tomorrow. Maybe a night in the cell will make her more cooperative."

Slade led them to the Expedition. "I wouldn't be surprised if it's the thought of release that does that. Whoever's behind this will assume she talked, especially if we let her go without any charges."

Chloe took the passenger seat and wrestled the seat belt one-handed. "Sounds like a good reason to let her go. Every corpse we get brings us new clues. I'd rather it was hers than Dee Dee Bisgard's. Or her kid's."

Stella climbed into the back seat and looked out the window. She didn't want them to find any corpse, even Roxie's. The young woman struck Stella as troubled, not evil.

Slade pulled out and onto Route 41. The streetlights flickered through the glass.

"We might have to let her go whether we want to or not. Working for the Bisgards isn't a crime, nor is *not* being kidnapped. We don't know what that truck was doing on the road by their house that night. We've got nothing to hold her for."

Chloe looked over her shoulder. "Maybe we don't need anything. If Gerry Renelle was our man, this thing's as good as done. We just have to find the Bisgards. Or what's left of them."

"What was the story with Renelle? Do we know why he did it?"

Slade glanced at her in the rearview mirror. "I got off the phone with Chief Houston just before we left. Looks like the daughter had a nasty blowout with him this afternoon.

Called her father a liar and a bunch of other names not fit for polite company. She found him."

"That poor girl."

Slade nodded. "Looks like Renelle lost the woman he loved and thought he was losing his daughter too."

So awful. Stella slumped in the seat. "Guess that would do it."

"Yeah. He tried to make up for it in the end. Left his daughter every dime he had and a note. Said he was sorry for being so hateful and hoped she'd be able to find happiness now that he's gone. Also left a note for his ex, telling her that she was the love of his life."

"What a piece of…" Chloe frowned. "If he were really sorry, he would have just changed. It would have taken time, and it would have taken effort, but he could have done it. Guess it's much easier to just off yourself and make others feel bad. The lazy, selfish coward."

Slade turned up the air-conditioning. The night was still warm, and Chloe wasn't making it any cooler.

"Guess you don't believe in that *don't speak ill of the dead* nonsense, huh, Chloe?"

"No. The guy was an asshole when he was alive. He was still an asshole in death. So, he remains an asshole in the afterlife."

Stella leaned against the door and rested her head on her hand. "Any chance the suicide was staged?" It was terrible to wish for murder, she knew. But Stella hated to think that Angela might end up blaming herself for her father's death. Murder might ease that guilt, at least a little.

"M.E. will let us know if anything suspicious comes up in autopsy."

"What about Angela? Her father's dead. Her mother's missing. Who's looking after her now?"

Slade cleared his throat. "Her grandparents are with her.

She'll stay with them until we find her mom. The sooner we find her alive, the better."

The space fell silent. Stella exhaled slowly.

The situation must be unbearable for the girl. Not knowing where her mother was or whether she was still breathing. Her father's suicide must have doubled the pressure on her emotional fragility. And the note only made it worse.

Stella hadn't suffered the dual blows of her father and brother's death simultaneously. And she had never felt either death was her fault. Her brother's illness was fate, rotten luck, life's constant unfairness, but there'd been no one to blame. Someone was at fault for her father's death, and she was going to catch them. But it wasn't her. She had just been a kid when he died.

Angela wasn't that lucky. She would always believe that her arguments and accusations caused her father's death. It wasn't true. His suicide was a tragic event that had nothing to do with her. Her mother would tell her that.

If her mother were still alive.

Stella remained silent until Slade pulled into the HQ garage.

"Get some rest, you two. We've got an early start tomorrow."

"Yeah, I'll try."

Stella climbed into her 4Runner and drove home. The streets of Nashville were clear this time of night. She made it back to her door, safe and sound.

As she fished her key out of her bag, her hand landed on her phone. She pulled it out and called Mac. Sure, the time was past midnight, but Mac enjoyed late-night chats.

"Hey, Stella. Still awake?"

Though the sound of laughter and loud music in the

background made her hard to hear, Mac's voice was as bright and chirpy as Stella expected.

"Yeah, just got home."

"Seriously? Wow. Want to join us? I'm with a couple of college friends. We're trying out a new bar in East Nasty. It's hopping."

Stella sighed. She wasn't in the mood. Not for laughter and drinks and a bar. She'd just wanted a chat.

"No. I'm good. Thanks. I'll speak to you tomorrow."

"Hey, Stella. Just a sec."

Stella waited. At the end of the line, a door creaked open and thudded shut. The noise died down. Mac's voice came through again, clearer this time. "I'm outside now. You okay?"

"Yeah, just a rough day. Thinking about that poor kid losing her father like that."

"Right. Slade told me. Made me think of you too. Listen, I got a message from my contact at the Memphis Field Office. She dug up an address for Matthew Johnson's family in Atlanta."

Instantly awake, Stella gripped her phone tighter. "Seriously? That's awesome."

"Isn't it? See, the day wasn't a complete nightmare."

"Thanks, Mac. Go back in and have a drink on me. I'll speak to you tomorrow."

As the line went dead, Stella leaned against the wall. That really was good news. After they wrapped this case up, she wouldn't be heading off on a blind hunt. She knew exactly where she needed to go next.

28

The next morning, Hagen pushed open the door of the tiny Stonevale Police Station interview room. Roxie Jenham sat on one side of the table, her head resting on her arms.

Hagen took the seat opposite and glanced at the camera fixed to the ceiling in the corner of the room. Stella was on the other side of that camera, watching the interview on a monitor in Chief Houston's office. The plan was for him to begin, to break Roxie down. Stella would come in later to pick up the pieces.

Hagen provided the time, date, and other relevant information for the recording before offering Roxie a tight smile. "Morning, Roxie. Sleep well?"

Roxie tilted her head so that her chin instead of her ear was on her arms. "What do you think?"

"I'd have thought the police cell would be more comfortable than your old trailer. It wasn't?"

Roxie pushed herself straight in her chair. Her eyes were unfocused and barely open. The fatigue of withdrawal had apparently already started. Headaches, dehydration, and anxiety were all on deck. They didn't have long before they'd need to get her medical attention. He made a mental note to monitor her progress.

Hagen rested his elbows on the table. There was room now since Roxie wasn't sleeping on it. "Feeling rough, huh? When was your last fix?"

Roxie folded her arms and said nothing.

"All right, then. Roxie, we know you've been in trouble before. Left home at fifteen, arrested twice on drug charges and once for petty theft. But, see, you're not being investigated for possession of a few pills or swiping a bottle of... what was it? Tequila? From a liquor store. Not this time. You're being investigated for kidnapping. And murder. There are currently forty-four people in federal prison waiting to be executed. The way things are looking, Roxie, you're going to be forty-five."

Roxie's eyes widened. The fatigue that came with withdrawal was still there, but the shock of her predicament had slapped her more fully awake. She remained silent, though, her arms folded on her chest.

"Why did you run when my colleagues found you in your trailer?"

Roxie clenched her jaw.

Hagen pushed on. "We've got two dead bodies, both with huge holes in their chests. That's two murders we've got you for. Anything more you want to tell us?"

A tear welled at the corner of her left eye.

Hagen gentled his approach. His questions were clearly getting through. "Look, Roxie, you're not a hardened mafioso with a record as long as your arm. You're a young addict who is into something much bigger than you. That something is scary enough to keep you quiet. We understand. If you tell me, we can help you."

She bit her lower lip as though forcing herself not to talk.

He shifted in his seat, leaning away from her to give her as much space as possible in the cramped room. "You've been working at Bisgard's Best for about three months. Is that right?"

Roxie cleared her throat. "Yeah. Well, two."

"Good." He shifted gears again. "What about your other job? How long have you been doing that?"

Roxie frowned. "What other job?"

"Oh, come on, Roxie. You can't yank my chain. I'm not one of your johns."

Her teary-eyed expression was swallowed by red-hot rage. "Who the hell do you think you are accusing me of something like that?"

Hagen looked up at the camera. Stella needed to get ready. Roxie was getting angry. Anger was a loss of control, and once she was out of control, she could say anything.

"Don't get coy. I'm not passing judgment. You're not the first junkie who's had to do what she had to do to get her next fix. But you were seen. Out in the back lot, turning tricks after your shift."

Roxie's cheeks, which had been ghostly pale throughout the interview, grew more scarlet by the second. She whipped a finger out of her folded arms and jabbed it at Hagen's face. "That's a load of bull. I've been a lot of things in my time but I ain't never been no hooker. I don't know who told you that, but they're lying."

Hagen sighed. "We have a witness. The custodian. He saw you out there getting real heavy with some guy." He lifted his hands as if he *possibly* doubted the witness statement. "Maybe he got it wrong. Maybe that was your boyfriend out there, and you just couldn't wait until you got back to that romantic little trailer of yours out in the woods. But Billy Joe is pretty sure he saw money change hands."

Roxie slammed a hand on the table.

There she goes.

Roxie leaned forward and glared. "I never had sex in that parking lot. I'm a lot of things, but I'm not slutty trash. Billy Joe is a blind, old idiot, and Benny is not my boyfriend."

She fell back in her chair and smacked a hand across her mouth.

Benny. Now we're getting somewhere.

"So, Benny owns the brown truck, does he? Where can we find him?"

Roxie crossed her arms over her chest again. She looked over his head at a spot somewhere behind him on the wall.

Hagen softened his voice. "Were the kidnappings Benny's idea?"

Roxie didn't move, didn't even blink.

"Did he make you help him?"

Silence.

He leaned forward and lowered his voice. "Did he hurt you, Roxie? Are you frightened of him? We can—"

"Benny? Hurt *me*?" Roxie's dark pupils bored into him. "That fool ever tried anything, I'd knock him halfway into next week. You're such an idiot, Fed. It's not *Benny* I'm scared of." Eyes wide, Roxie pushed her chair back and put both her hands over her mouth.

Gotcha. Almost.

"No? Then who?"

He glanced at the camera and gave a slight nod. "Come on now, Roxie. Who's frightening you?"

The door opened and Stella came in, concern written on her face. "Sorry for intruding, but I just heard what you said. That's terrible." She dragged the remaining chair to the table, sitting close to the young woman.

Hagen waited. He'd pushed and twisted. Now, Stella would give Roxie an easy landing.

"Listen to me, Roxie." Her voice was soft. "We can help

you. I can see that you're scared and I'm sure Benny's scared too. Whoever has done this to you, to both of you, doesn't deserve your silence. We can protect you."

Roxie sniffed and wiped a tear from her cheek. "You can't. You don't know, you just don't know."

"Tell me what I don't know."

Another tear fell. "You can't protect me. That's what you don't know."

"Yes. We can. You're not the first person who's bitten off more than they can chew and needs help. We *can* keep you safe."

Roxie bit her bottom lip. Her eyes drifted from Stella to Hagen and back again. "It's not…it's not just me and Benny. It's my sister too. He said he'd hurt her. And he will. I know he will."

Stella placed a hand on Roxie's arm. "That's not a problem. You tell us where she is. We can protect your sister. We'll send someone out right away. We can protect all three of you. Benny, your sister, you."

"I want proof first." Though clearly still frightened, Roxie straightened her back and stuck out her chin. "You show me that my sister's safe, and my nephew, and I'll tell you what you need to know."

Stella glanced at Hagen, who nodded. She pushed her notebook and a pen to Roxie. "Just write down your sister's address, and we'll get someone out to them right now."

For a long moment, Hagen thought Roxie would reconsider. He let out a breath when the girl grabbed the pen and scribbled an address. "I don't know about Benny. He's staying up at a motel somewhere on the edge of Murfreesboro. I ain't never been there, so I don't rightly know which one." She slid the pad of paper back across the table. Her tears had dried up, and the color had drained from her face. She was calm and peaked as hell again. "You gotta understand. This whole thing. It's not my fault. And it's not Benny's either."

Hagen ripped out the page and read the address. "Whose fault is it?"

Roxie folded her arms, her nails digging into her skin. "When I know my sister's safe. Not a minute before."

"You realize whoever put you up to this probably already thinks you're talking to us?"

Her face hardened, her body quivering. "Then you better save my sister. Now."

Hagen folded the page and placed a hand on Stella's shoulder. "You put her back in the cell. I'll pass this on to the chief. See you in the parking lot."

He left the room and headed for Chief Houston's office. The chief sat behind his desk, a folder resting in his lap. A screen was tuned to the camera in the interview room. "Looks like you're getting somewhere."

"Slowly." Hagen gave him the note. "You'll find Roxie's sister at this address. She and her son need protective custody."

Chief Houston took the sheet of paper and unfolded it. He stroked his mustache. "Uh-huh. She ain't going to give you an address for where they're keeping those hostages. You know that, right?

Hagen nodded. "We need to protect her sister, anyway."

"Okay. And while we're doing that, what exactly are you and that lady agent gonna be doing?"

Hagen stopped in the doorway and turned around. "While you're tracking down a junkie's sister, Chief, Stella and I are going to go out and find ourselves a sleazy motel."

29

I waited for One to dole out the breakfast to my remaining captives and finish cleaning out their buckets. That was one advantage of the subjects' numbers shrinking. My experiment might not yet have yielded the results I'd hoped for, but the smell was improving.

While I never actively liked or disliked people as a whole, One was changing all that. I disliked that guy. Something arrogant in the way he moved. And his attitude.

But he wasn't my most significant problem right now.

Two wasn't here. And I had a sneaking suspicion her absence was not due to her imminent demise, since I doubted the dolt I'd asked to eliminate her had completed that task so quickly. Had she been arrested? Had she run for the hills? She was my problem.

And Three, once again, had proven himself useless.

Like right now. He just slouched half asleep on the sofa in the corridor, waiting to be given an order. His face was gray, and he had been unusually quiet all morning. He wouldn't tell me what was wrong. Even if I cared enough to ask him, he'd lie. Addicts always lied, and I didn't have the time or the patience to squeeze the truth out of him. I just needed him to keep the experiment going.

"Three. I want to talk to you."

Three rolled out of the couch with so much effort it was as if he'd been glued to it. Then he proceeded to shuffle down the corridor, barely lifting his feet. He was skidding. Skid. It finally made sense. That's what he told me his name was when I first met him.

"Shut the door."

Three turned and shuffled back and closed it with a swipe of his hand. It slammed shut.

"Did you do what I asked you to do?"

He stared at me, frowning. "What did you ask me to do?"

I sighed. I might as well have recruited three monkeys. They would have been more intelligent and worked twice as fast. They also would have been missed by others, so that wouldn't have worked.

"Did I not ask you to deal with our friend?"

The frown deepened. But despite it, his dull eyes and gray skin made him appear featureless, like a rock. "Who's our friend?"

"Number Two, you gormless toad. Roxie. Did you kill her or not?"

He chuckled and picked at a scab. "Oh, when you said 'friend,' you confused me. No. No, I didn't do that. No."

A flicker of something—rage maybe?—burned in my chest. There was definitely *something* there. Perhaps it was irritation or disappointment. Or maybe it was just the churro I had picked up for breakfast on my way to this place. Oily food could play such havoc with my intestines.

"Why didn't you do what I told you to do?" I pushed the three fountain pens on my desk into a line, the sharp points directed at Three.

"She wasn't there. Couldn't do it if she wasn't there, could I?"

The greaser had dark patches under his eyes. He looked drugged out, sallow, and gaunt. I doubted he would notice if Two were standing in front of him at this very moment.

"She wasn't in her trailer? Interesting. How long did you wait for her?"

Three shook his head. "Oh no, I didn't wait for her. I just saw she wasn't there, and I went home." He scratched a spot behind his ear. "I suppose I could have waited for her. But if you wanted me to wait for her, you should have said. You didn't say nothing about me waiting out there for her."

I closed my eyes. I had hoped to feel something from this experiment. Fear mostly. Perhaps some sympathy. Even mild concern would have been something of a victory. Frustration and exasperation were two emotions I'd experienced in the past, and to feel them now because of my "assistants" instead of my subjects was…exasperating.

"Come with me, Three. We're going for a ride."

Glancing at my watch, I considered my next steps. Yes. I would have plenty of time to see to this next bit of the plan personally. I led him out of my office and out to the parking lot, stopping only to tell One he was in charge while we were gone. He looked up at me with wide, vacant eyes.

I really should have used monkeys.

And bananas were cheaper than meth. Next time.

With Three in the passenger seat, I drove away from the old dog kennels and out toward the woods where Roxie kept her trailer. She thought I didn't know where it was. She really believed that asking Benny to drop her off at the corner of the road each day prevented anyone from knowing where she lived.

As if I hadn't done my research long before all this started. I'd planned this experiment for years, prepared

everything. I certainly wouldn't leave something as important as one of my assistants' addresses out, would I?

I turned off the main road and drove slowly toward the
hovel where Roxie lived.

I assumed we'd find her spaced out in her trailer. Perhaps,
Three would get lucky, and she overdosed, and his job would
be complete. It made no difference to me. One more junkie
misjudging the trip and taking a one-way ticket to oblivion
solved my problem just fine. But, if she was just too high to
move, finishing her off would be easy enough, even for a half
human chimp like Three.

To ease the annoyance chiming through me from being
away from my subjects, I hummed "Maurerische Trauer-
musik in C minor," one of Mozart's least appreciated works,
to soothe my nerves. I'd just reached the crescendo, my
favorite part, when I turned a curve and slammed on the
brakes.

Three thrust forward, the seat belt stopping his head
from smacking into the dashboard. "Whoa, man. What's up?"

Could the chimp not see? I pointed to the line of yellow
police tape running around the trailer. It flapped in the
morning breeze. "What's up? When you were here last night,
was any of that tape here?"

Skid shrugged. "I dunno, man. It was pretty dark last
night."

Not trusting a single word coming from his mouth, I eyed
him carefully. "Were you high?"

The expression on his face told the story. "Nothing major.
I wasn't on, like, an LSD trip or something. Or smack.
Nothing like that. Just a bit of weed. And my meth. Gotta
have my meth, y'know."

Annoyed at him for breaking the rules and at myself for
hiring him in the first place, I scanned the woods for signs of
police officers. There didn't seem to be any, and the absence

of police vehicles suggested they were finished for now—although they would undoubtedly be back.

"And you didn't think this was something worth mentioning? Maybe last night? Certainly, this morning?"

Three shrugged again. He was like an example of reverse human development, as though after having descended from a chimp-like ancestor and developed language, he changed his mind and turned back.

"Three, when I took you on, I offered you a deal. I would give you food and pay for your lodging. I would make sure you received one drug. Every day, you would get the exact amount of methamphetamine you needed to avoid withdrawal. But you could not use any other drugs because, if you did, you would be utterly useless to me. Didn't I tell you that?"

"Uh, yeah, but like I said. It was just some weed. A bit of weed doesn't count. It don't do nothing. I mean, jeez, I had a big blunt while I was out there cleaning the buckets, and you didn't notice nothing, so that's proof right there."

That was, indeed, all the proof I needed.

"Open the window."

He looked at me. "Huh?"

"Open. The. Window."

As soon as the window had fully receded, I pulled a gun from my pocket, lifted the muzzle to his temple, and pulled the trigger.

The mess was remarkable. Most of the contents of his head sprayed through the open window as I had hoped, but much of it also splattered against the headrest and leaked out onto the seat. Interesting that someone with so few brains had so much gray matter in his skull.

Good thing this wasn't my regular vehicle.

Was there any guilt at what I had done? Any regrets?

No and no. There was a mild irritation at the thought of

having to clean my car, but killing this particular creature was on par with swatting a mosquito. It put some goo on my hand, but nothing that wouldn't wash off.

I opened the door and shoved him out.

Now, I would have to find some other junkie to help me. How irritating.

30

"No, ma'am. Ain't no one here called Benny, Benjamin, or Ben."

Stella sighed as the receptionist's voice rang through the speakers in the Explorer. "What about a guest driving a brown 1973 Ford F350? It might have a covered bed. Tennessee license plates. Have you seen one of those in your parking lot, or do you have a record?"

"Sorry, ma'am."

Stella thanked the woman and disconnected the call before searching the map on the GPS. They were still twenty minutes away from Murfreesboro.

"How many's that?" Hagen asked.

Stella scanned the list of local motels she'd pulled off her phone. "That's the eighth one without a Benny or a brown truck. You'd have thought they'd be more common around here."

"I'm kinda surprised that motels still stand in this era, period."

"You really lived a sheltered life, didn't you?" Stella dialed the next place on the list. "Motel Seven? This is Agent Knox of the FBI. Can you tell me if you have a guest by the name of Benny staying with you?"

"Benny? Benny who?"

"I'm afraid we don't know that. He drives a brown 1973 Ford F350 with a covered bed."

"Naw, we ain't got no one like that. But you meet Benny, you tell him we got free cable and Wi-Fi, and rooms available now for just—"

"Okay, thanks." Stella hung up. "Let's try this one. Luxury Suites Motel. Huh. What do you think makes them luxurious?"

Hagen raised an eyebrow. "I'm guessing that will be the hot tub, private swimming pool, and butler service."

"Jeez, you and I really do live in different worlds. I was thinking more of running water and a free, secondhand bar of soap." She drummed her fingers on her thigh as the phone rang through the speakers. "Luxury Suites Motel? This is Agent Knox of the FBI." She rattled off the same question she'd asked a dozen times before.

The woman's voice was curt, her answer quick. "No one here by that name. Anything else I can help you with?"

"You sure about that? Can you check again?"

"Hun, we only got three guests staying here. None of them is called Benny."

Stella sighed. "What about the brown Ford F350?"

"With a covered bed? Yeah, Lenny's got one of those. Been staying here a few months now."

Stella smiled. "Does *Lenny* have a last name?"

"Let me look." Keys clicked. "Duggle. Lenny Duggle."

"Thank you." Disconnecting the call, Stella drummed her hands on the dash in celebration. "Broad Street. Go."

Hagen shifted lanes and punched the gas. "Lenny, huh? Something tells me Benny isn't the brains behind this operation."

Stella grinned. "Ten bucks his last name is Muggle…no, Chuggle…no, Ruggle."

Hagen lifted an eyebrow. "That your final answer?"

"Yep."

He offered his fist, and she bumped it.

Ten minutes later, Hagen pulled the Explorer into the parking lot of the Luxury Suites Motel. A Nissan Sentra with a rusted blue body and dented gray doors was parked next to the lobby entrance. The rest of the lot was empty.

Stella stepped out of the vehicle. "No truck. Guess Benny's not at home today."

Hagen hopped out and locked the doors. "Lenny."

The woman behind the reception desk wore an unfortunate striped t-shirt that did her plump arms no favors. She glanced up from her phone, two fingers scratching her head.

Stella pulled out her badge. "Agent Knox, FBI, ma'am. We just spoke. We believe the guest who owns the F350 might be in danger. I'm going to need the keys to Lenny's room."

The receptionist snorted. "Now, honey, I don't care if you're the FBI or just fell out of a UFO. You know I can't do that. You want me to give you the keys to a guest's room. You need to go back to your office and come back here with a warrant."

Hagen leaned an elbow on the counter. "We will, but it's going to take time, and if that man's lying in a puddle of his own blood and dies while we're getting a warrant, I hope you can live with yourself."

The receptionist paused the show she was watching on her phone and crossed her arms. "You're free to go knock on his door. Room 217. Otherwise, warrant."

Irritation erupted from the back of Stella's neck like steam from a boiling kettle. The receptionist was only doing her job. But, right now, that job could get someone killed.

Once they were outside, Hagen whirled on Stella. "You

think I had a sheltered life? My dad might not have been a police sergeant like yours, but he was a lawyer for some of the sleaziest, most disgusting, and immoral people in the state."

Had he really been pissed about that for this long?

She held up a hand. Unlike most officers of the law, she didn't detest defense attorneys. Well, not most of them anyway. "Your dad was just doing his job by making sure we do our jobs. Because of defense attorneys, we dot our *i's* and cross our *t's* so the bad guys don't walk. They hold us accountable. There's nothing wrong with that."

Hagen's stony features softened. "Yeah. Okay. Now, let's do our job."

She followed him to a set of cracked concrete stairs that led to the second floor. The curtains on the window of room 217 were drawn, but the door was open several inches.

Stella and Hagen exchanged a glance. Without a word, they drew their weapons.

"Benny?" Stella called through the door. "This is the FBI. We're here to check on you. We understand there was a threat to your safety. Please answer or we're coming in."

A loud crash was the response.

Stella burst inside, her gaze raking over every corner of the room. "FBI!"

An angry, ululating bark greeted her. A raccoon, the size of a dachshund, stood on its hind legs on the ratty couch near the partially opened window. It gripped part of a Styrofoam container in its tiny paws. Before Stella could think of what to do, the raccoon skittered out the window, taking the shredded container with it.

Surprisingly, neither Stella nor Hagen moved.

"Did that just happen?" Hagen turned to her wide-eyed.

Stella, remaining frozen for one second more, couldn't quite answer. With a shake of her head, she recovered and put her weapon back in its holster. "Yeah…yeah…that just happened."

"Had a vision from *Elf* of that coon attacking Will Ferrell in Central Park."

Stella smiled. It was one of her favorite movies. "Me too."

With the front curtains drawn, the place was dark. Hagen flipped the light switch on.

The room was a mess. The bed was unmade. Cans of soda littered the floor. The air stank of stale food, dirty laundry, and the sour, vinegary stench of old meth. No sign of Benny, dead or otherwise.

"Think he got in through the window?" Hagen stepped over the trash and detritus to look out the glass. Tree branches scratched against the rear of the building.

"The raccoon? Probably. But why was the door open?" Stella turned to the door and closed it, but it drifted back a few inches. The latch was busted. "So much for security." She took in the disaster of a room. "And I guess housekeeping isn't a luxury at the Luxury Suites Motel."

"Lucky for us." Hagen tipped the trash can under the table toward him with his foot. "Look."

Stella peered at about half a dozen empty pill bottles. Hagen moved the can so that they rolled to reveal their labels.

"Valium. Ambien. Even a couple of bottles of ketamine in there. That's exactly what the M.E. said might have been used to knock out the Bisgards and their friends."

Stella vibrated with excitement. They weren't yet at the heart of the evil that had struck that family, but they were getting near it.

"It's always darkest before the light," her father would whisper, wrapping his arm around her shoulders. From anyone else, that advice would have been hopeful and optimistic, but Stella's father had been a cop. He knew that before you saw

the light at the end of a case, you had to meet the darkness that created it first.

They were getting close. She felt it in her gut. That little burst of adrenaline told her they would soon be within touching distance.

Stella stepped into the bathroom. A dirty towel was draped across the side of the bathtub. The lid of the toilet was up and the bowl was stuffed with toilet paper. The floor was littered with empty food cartons, identical to the one their furry friend had stolen. Bits of dried potato and chicken still clung to the grease-stained cardboard.

Stella crouched in front of a box to read the label. *The Roadside Drop-In. Murfreesboro's favorite diner.*

"Hagen? Come and take a look at this."

Hagen stood in the doorway, his well-built frame blocking the meager light that was coming in from the room. He flicked the light on with an elbow so as not to taint the scene. A fluorescent tube above the sink flickered to life.

"This look like the food at the Bisgards' to you?"

He knelt next to her, leaning so close she could smell his Old Spice. Hagen smelled clean and untouched by their surroundings. His body heat was comforting. "It sure does. Doesn't look as tasty on the bathroom floor…"

No, it didn't.

Stella's mind whirled to create a connection. She'd left her tablet in the Explorer, so she couldn't pull up the list of evidence found at the Bisgards'. But…

"What if they catered their meal that night? It makes sense. Maybe Dee Dee didn't want to cook for so many people because she had Ashton and a full-time job." She closed her eyes, trying to imagine it. "Maybe Benny was pretending to be their caterer or food delivery person. He bought the food from the diner, laced it with drugs here, and repacked it into boxes to take to their house.

Hagen nodded along. "He delivers the food in his brown 1973 Ford F350. Which is why it was on the footage that night."

And that was when Stella's theory lost steam. "Kinda late, no? The truck arrived after everyone else was already there."

Hagen stood and stepped back into the main room. "This place look like it's being rented by someone who's good at being timely? If he'd turned up when he was supposed to, I'd start thinking we were looking at the wrong guy."

"Fair point. But that also means he's not working alone. I don't think he's the one paying for this motel, and he wouldn't have been able to move six unconscious people by himself, even if one of them was a kid."

Hagen nodded. "Let's get out of here and call it in before we contaminate the scene any more than we already have."

Stella shifted position, noticing a brown paper bag that had been crumpled into a loose ball. There were some black marks that looked like writing. "Hold up." Pulling on a glove, she smoothed out the bag and smiled at the name written there. She was right. "Look at this."

Hagen whistled. "*Ben*. Looks like Benny might have been late after all. Let's let the others know."

Stella followed him through the front door, leaving it open a few inches, just like they'd found it. She stood against the railing, looking out over the parking lot, and waited for Hagen to finish talking to Chief Houston.

The street that ran past the motel was empty. She hadn't heard a single car or truck in all the time they had been there. Whoever had chosen this place had picked it well.

Hagen slipped the phone into his pocket. "The chief's sending a uniform to watch the place while they get the search warrant."

"Not the youthful Officer Scott, I hope."

Hagen shrugged. "It's what he's got. Let's hope Benny

doesn't come back while he's here. Scott'll end up with another bump on his skull to match the first."

"You think Roxie helped move the Bisgards and their friends once Benny's food had done its job?"

Hagen scratched his chin, looking thoughtful. He nodded slowly. "I mean, sure. She's not exactly a mountain of muscle, though, is she?"

"Right." Stella twisted her ear stud. An idea was forming. "Maybe whoever organized this thing, that guy she's so scared of, maybe he was with them that night. *Maybe* he helped pick up the food and drove with them to the Bisgards'."

Hagen finished her thought. "And, maybe, not even a small maybe, that roadside diner would remember an order this large and have a security camera on the premises." Hagen tapped a knuckle twice on the balcony's steel railing.

Stella took over. "We could get Mac to run face recognition to figure out who else is involved in this."

Hagen held out a fist. "Smart thinking."

Stella bumped it. "Let's just hope for a camera."

A police car pulled into the parking lot, drawing her attention. It was, indeed, Officer Scott. Hagen chuckled and shook his head. "Oof. Let's hope he's ready for Benny this time. Let's go. We've got a date at a diner."

31

T ick tock. Tick tock.

That damn clock in front of Troy's cage just wouldn't shut up, ticking all day and all night long.

Now, as the time stretched toward eight a.m., the ticking gnawed at Troy's brain, each click sounding off one more second from his life.

He would be the next to die. Final answer.

There were only three of them left now. It was Dee Dee, Ashton, and he. Nobody was going to murder Ashton. Nobody. Hadn't they put themselves through all of this— chosen to die and volunteered to kill—so that at least the boy would survive this horror?

Troy wouldn't shoot a child. Neither would Dee Dee. That meant either he or the woman who'd been like a second mother to him would be next. There was no one else left. He wouldn't let the next victim be Dee Dee. He wasn't saving Ashton just to leave the kid an orphan.

It had to be him. He so wanted the next victim to be him.

Please, let me die. Just let me go.

He uncurled himself from the corner of his cell. His joints were sore. Hunger twisted his stomach. The air stank with the coppery scent of dried blood and the heavier stink of their unemptied buckets.

Tick faster. Please tick faster.

Troy shuffled across the floor to the bars of the cage.

"Dee…?" His throat was dry, and his voice faded away.

Hours had passed since he'd last spoken. Answering Dee Dee's cries for help meant forcing himself out of the hole in the back of his mind where he'd been hiding. It meant coming back to this horror. Far better to remain where he was, numb and blind and distant from everything.

He coughed, hoping to clear all the emotion clogging his throat. "Dee Dee. We've only got half an hour left. You have to do it."

"Troy." Her voice was weak but immediate. "I…I can't. Don't make me. Please don't."

"You have to. I won't shoot you. It's not right. Ron, he… he'd…it wouldn't be what he wanted. He wanted you to live, you and Ashton."

Dee Dee knelt in front of her bars. Her fingers gripped the steel. Behind her, Ashton scratched on the concrete wall of their cell using a piece of masonry he'd found on the floor.

"Troy, you're like…you know you've always been…"

"I know. You don't have to say it. You and Ron were the parents I'd always wanted. You know, my mom never…"

He couldn't continue. He was leaving his mom now. This wasn't the time to speak badly of her. Wasn't she about to suffer enough? His chest burned as he imagined her agony when she received the news. He pushed the image away.

Just talk. Persuade Dee Dee. That's all you have to do now.

"You've got to be both mom and dad for Ashton now, y'hear me? That's who we're doing this for. He's already lost his dad. I won't take his mom from him. I won't. You two have to make it out of here alive. He has to grow up and put all of this behind him. He'll need you to help him do that."

Dee Dee pressed her hands to her face but didn't argue. That was something. She wouldn't refuse. She was going to be okay, or as okay as possible.

Troy jerked his head up. "Dee Dee?"

"Hm?"

"Listen to me. You listening? It's important now."

"Yeah, I'm listening, honey."

He waited until she dropped her hands and met his gaze. "When you've done it, after you've fired the gun, you gotta forget. You have to just wipe it out of your head."

A sob, broken and choppy, escaped her lips and she shuddered.

Ashton stopped scraping at the wall and tugged on his mother's sweat-stained shirt.

She pulled him into her lap. "How? I don't know if I can live with myself if I have to—"

"You will! You just block it off. It's like…it's like building a wall in your brain. All that stuff goes on the other side of the wall. Everything you see, everything you hear. You put it back there, and you never look at it. Even when you close your eyes, and the bricks come down, you turn away, y'hear me? You never go there. You'll be okay. It's just the once. You can do it."

Dee Dee hugged Ashton closer. Her shoulders shook, but she nodded.

Relieved, Troy pushed away from the bars. A weight fell from his chest and brought the closest thing to peace he'd experienced since waking up in this caged, concrete hell.

There wouldn't be much longer to go now. Just…seventeen more minutes, and he would follow Brenda and Ron and Darrel. He'd be free of these thoughts. He wouldn't hear the bang echoing in his head every time a door slammed somewhere in the building.

The wall he had tried to build in his own mind to protect him from the three murders he'd committed had crumbled into rubble. The pictures he'd stuffed behind it, of Ron's exploding chest and Darrel's limp body and Brenda's blood-soaked hair glued to the back of her neck, were constants in his mind's eye. Everything he looked at—the bars, the concrete floor, Dee Dee, Ashton—brought one of those memories boomeranging around his head. They wouldn't stop.

Soon, he'd make them stop. Dee Dee would blow them all away.

Thank you, Dee Dee.

Troy closed his eyes. Sleep was on its way, at last. A real sleep.

Rrring.

Finally. Troy opened his eyes. In her cage, Dee Dee cried. The door at the end of the room swung open.

One came in. Troy vaguely wondered what his real name was. *Surely, there had to be a human being behind that ski mask.*

One stomped to the alarm clock and turned it off. He stood there for a moment, scratching the back of his neck, his eyes darting between the cages.

Troy waited. The other two would be here soon. They usually came together. One, Two, and Three, like some kind of unholy trinity. Troy put his temple to the bars, feeling the cool metal on his skin as he waited.

The door at the end of the room was open, but no one else came through.

He frowned. This was new. Had two of them bailed on the "experiment"? Maybe they had been caught by police.

Maybe their absence was something…good? So many maybes.

"Where are…" Troy propped himself up against the bars. A small flare of hope pushed him upward. "Where are the other two?"

One stopped scratching and glared at Troy. "Shut up. You shut your mouth, all right?" His voice was shriller than usual. Sharper. Nervous?

A strange calm washed over Troy. He'd never been so at ease, so relaxed. One couldn't do anything to him that he hadn't done already…or would be done soon.

"They're not here, are they? They've left you."

One took half a step forward, a finger outstretched. "Now, you listen to me, you little—"

Troy smiled.

Yes, he actually smiled at his tormentor. After so many days in the cage, Troy imagined his smile looked fearsome and out of place. From the way One had stopped in his tracks, Troy was right.

"So, you're in charge now, huh? They made you the boss. That's nice, man. Congratulations. You should really celebrate your promotion." He stuck his hands between the bars and gave a small round of applause.

One moved toward Troy's cage, the finger still leading the way. "Uh-huh. That's right. I'm the boss today, so you better—"

"That doesn't seem fair, them leaving you with all this responsibility. I wouldn't take it if I were you. I mean, they've just gone and left you all the work, haven't they?"

One scratched the back of his neck again before readjusting his ski mask. "You don't know anything, kid."

"They get caught?"

"Shut up," One snarled.

Troy felt that cursed bit of hope surge again. His guess might have been close. He decided to push a little further. "Uh-oh. They're gone. Maybe caught. And you have to do everything by yourself. Now, how can you do that? You can't hold a gun to the boy's head and control both of us. Heck, there's two of us and one of you. It's not fair. It's dumb is what it is." He lowered his voice. "Dangerous too."

One stepped back from the cage and dragged his gun from his waistband. "Now, don't you get no funny ideas, boy."

Troy lifted his hands. "I'm not armed." The smile felt natural on his lips. "Not until you arm me, and then it'll just be you and me with guns."

One hesitated. He clearly hadn't considered the ramifications of being the sole perpetrator. Even if he pulled Ashton from his mother's arms and held a gun to the kid's head, he didn't have the same amount of leverage over Troy as he did when Two and Three had been there.

Very slowly, One placed the gun back in his waistband and took another step away from Troy's cage. One's hesitation saddened Troy a little. He must look like the murderer he was.

Troy glanced down the corridor, but he didn't see or hear anyone else coming. One was truly on his own.

The top of Ashton's head was just visible inside the depths of Dee Dee's arms. His pale little hands barely reached around Dee Dee's back.

His own life didn't matter, but he couldn't gamble with Ashton's. He needed to convince One to stall the execution.

Could he do it? Did he want to?

Yes.

That little flame of hope burned brighter as Troy realized something important. He didn't want to die. Not by Dee Dee's hand, anyway. That sweet woman didn't want to kill him in front of her son. If the other two members of the unholy trinity had been caught, then he needed to keep One hesitant.

"When it was three of you, well, that was different." He pressed his face into the bars, feeling it smush and distort his features. Good. "I only had one round, and y'all had three loaded guns between you. But if it's just you and me, and I've got a gun, that's a whole different story, isn't it?"

"I don't know." Hands held up in a defensive position, One took another step back. "Yeah, no. You're right. Shut up. I gotta think."

Where in the hell had the mad scientist found these guys? They all seemed so lost and *slow*.

One stepped back even farther. He was almost at the other end of the corridor. "Yeah, this is a two-man job, this is. At least two. I can't do it by myself."

"'Course you can't." Troy pulled back from the bars, trying to sound reasonable. "No one would expect you to. Not if they've got any sense."

One paced to the door, turned around, and stomped to the other end of the room. His sneakers made a ripping sound as they marched across the dark, sticky patches where Darrel, Ron, and Brenda's blood had mixed and dried.

He came back to Troy's cage. "What am I gonna do, man? I can't do nothing. He'll kill me if I screw up this stupid experiment of his. I'll be down there on the floor next, with that damn gun at my back. You gotta help me, man. What do I do?"

Troy thought of One kneeling on the floor, the blood on the concrete sticking to the knees of his dirty, black pants. That man, the one in the white coat, would stand behind him, stretch out that big gun…and *bang*.

What would happen next? With One gone and the others missing in action, what would stop that lunatic from finishing them all off? After killing One, Troy would be next. He wouldn't stop there, though. He'd also turn the gun on Dee Dee and Ashton.

Troy's smile fell. He needed a better plan than stalling outright. Maybe he could turn One against the mad scientist. Maybe he could sow chaos in their ranks.

He gripped the bars again, his fingers finding their space around the steel. "Why would you want to work for that guy anyhow? He gives you an impossible task and then threatens to kill you if you don't manage it? What kind of lunatic does that?"

One lifted his gun and pointed the muzzle at Troy's head. "Just shut up. You just keep your mouth shut, all right? I do what I gotta do. You don't understand me."

Troy shifted his head closer to the gun. A lifetime ago, when all this had started, the sight of that weapon aimed in his direction would have been enough to make him piss his pants. Now, it had no effect on him at all. If he felt anything, it was a small, warm comfort.

It could all end now.

Across the way, Ashton hiccupped.

No, Troy decided. Dying now wasn't the right choice. "All I'm saying, man, is that your boss isn't being fair to you. It's just not right what he's doing."

The gun lowered. "No, it's not. It's not fair at all. How can he expect me to do everything by myself?"

"Maybe he doesn't." Troy let go of the bars and paced to the back of the cell. "Maybe you just misunderstood what he wanted. Or he didn't speak clearly. He couldn't have meant for you to make us kill each other right now, not by yourself. He probably just wanted you to watch us and make sure we didn't escape. That's probably what he meant you to do."

"Yeah…" He stepped back from the cage. "Yeah, he wouldn't have—"

"And you don't want to make a mistake, do you? What would he do to you if you screwed up his...his experiment?"

One's head jerked up. "Aw, man, if I screwed this up, he'd have me hanging by my guts. He'd do a number on me like you wouldn't believe. But he ain't here, and I can't contact him. I don't know what to do."

That was interesting information. No leader. No assistants. There was a kink in the experiment.

"I'll tell you what you should do." Troy lowered his voice, like he was sharing a secret. "You should let us help you get rid of him."

For a precious tiny second, Troy thought that One was considering that plan.

Eyes widening, he lifted the gun again. "You're trying to trick me."

Troy lifted his hands. "No, I'm not. If you don't like that option, then another one is that you wait. You protect yourself first. Do nothing until he gets back, and if he asks why Dee Dee and I are still here, you explain that the other two didn't turn up. It's not your fault. It's all down to them."

One's head went up and down faster and faster as the idea settled into his thick skull. "That's right. I think I'll wait. It ain't my fault I'm the only one here." He tucked his gun back into his waistband and ran from the room.

Exhausted by the game, Troy leaned against the wall and slipped down to the floor.

His stomach tingled. Was that hunger? Or hope? If One waited long enough...

He looked across the corridor to where Dee Dee cradled Ashton against her, the little boy's pale fingers tangled indelibly in his mother's brown hair. Dee Dee had to swivel to make eye contact with him.

Meeting his gaze, she smiled.

Troy tried to smile back. He really did. But he'd killed

Ron, Brenda, and Darrel. He was a murderer, and he would never forgive himself for that. But maybe he could save Dee Dee and Ashton somehow.

If he did, maybe that could bring some kind of redemption.

The smell of burnt oil and fried potatoes hit Hagen's nostrils as soon as he pulled into the parking lot behind The Roadside Drop-In.

Hagen turned off the engine. The humid air smelled of grease. "Diner food. How do people eat that stuff? Their arteries must look like a clogged toilet."

Stella slid back her seat belt. "I never knew a clogged toilet could smell so tasty. Kinda making me hungry. You couldn't go for a plate of fries right now?"

"No." Hagen lifted an eyebrow. He did a covert examination of her slim frame as she climbed out of the car. With her athletic figure, Stella looked more like the *salads and protein shakes* sort than someone who splurged on burgers and fries. "Really? You like this stuff?" He climbed out too.

"Hell, yeah. I eat whatever I can get my hands on." She met him at the front of the Explorer. "I don't understand how people find time to cook. Or have the patience for it. All that washing and chopping and seasoning when you can get perfectly good takeout for half the effort in half the time and bypass the cleanup afterward."

Hagen started toward the diner's entrance, shaking his head. "So, you really don't care what you eat?"

"Of course, I care. It's gotta be tasty. If it is, in it goes. If it's tasty with a dollop of mayo, in it goes faster."

Hagen gagged a little in his throat.

Forcing the bile back down, he pulled open the diner door. It swung easily. Hagen was met by the clatter of crockery and the smell of fried onions and overcooked meat mixed with stale coffee that literally made him choke.

Recovering, he looked behind him. "Stella, when we're done here, I'm going to cook you a meal. It will be healthy, made by these very hands, and it will be the best damn meal you've ever eaten."

Stella pursed her lips. "Will it come with fries?"

"No."

"Well, then it won't be the best damn meal I've ever eaten."

"Challenge accepted."

A waitress approached. Hagen put her age at somewhere in her forties. The lunchtime crowd had yet to settle in, but too much head-scratching with a pen had already given her hairstyle a new wave above her right ear.

"Table for two, is it?" She gestured toward a line of empty booths that looked out over the empty road. "You can take a seat anywhere. I'll be along in just a second."

Hagen glanced at her name tag and pulled out his ID.

"We're from the FBI. Got a few questions for you, Jill, and perhaps some other members of the staff, if that's okay. Were you working here on Wednesday? Around late afternoon or evening?"

Jill sighed and put a hand on her hip. "Didn't think I'd get a good tip out of you two. Told Errol back there on the hot plate as soon as you came in, bet those two aren't tippers. See if I wasn't right."

Hagen opened his mouth to answer, but Stella stepped forward, cutting him off. "That's amazing. You really know how to size up a person. Agent Yates is, in fact, a questionable tipper since he doesn't believe in eating outside the home."

His mouth dropped open. "Hey—"

"But, Jill, this is really important. Were you working here on Wednesday afternoon or evening?"

"Now, where else would I be?" Jill tossed a glance back at the kitchen. "I always get the Wednesday night shift. That's just how it is. 'Course I was here."

"Since you're so good at assessing people, do you remember if someone came in and picked up a takeout order? It would have been big enough for at least five people."

"A takeout order for five?" Jill scratched her head with the end of her pen. "Yeah, I remember that. Was kinda weird."

While Hagen didn't appreciate Stella throwing him under the bus, he couldn't complain about the results. "Weird how?"

"Came in around six, but he called it in, like, the day before or some such. Don't know where he thought he was. If it's on the menu, you don't need to call ahead here. Errol will just heat it up and toss it in a box for you."

Hagen glanced at Stella, his instincts confirmed. That was the kind of food you got at places like this. Prepared, reheated, and indigestible.

She just nodded. "Do you remember who picked up the order?"

"Not really, hun. I was kinda busy."

Stella turned on her bright, charming smile. He almost forgave her for insulting him, even though the smile was for the waitress. "Did the guy tip well?"

"Ha!" Jill snort-laughed, jolting the pen stuck over her ear loose. "Takeout pickups? They're worse than out-of-towners like you. No tip at all from them."

Hagen clenched his jaw.

Stella pressed on. "So, you don't remember anything? What he looked like? Who he was with?"

Jill shook her head. "Like I said, he was weird. But if weird's a crime, you'll have to lock up everyone who comes in here." She cast her eyes over Hagen and Stella, who were both dressed a little too formally for this crowd. "And throw yourselves in with them. But I remember the name on the order was Ben. Or Benji. Or something like that."

Now they were getting somewhere. "You got a security camera here?"

"Right behind ya, hun." She pointed over Hagen's shoulder to a camera above the door. The lens was well positioned and would have been able to take in the entire restaurant, including everyone who came in, picked up their takeout orders, and left. Relief swept through Hagen.

Jill grinned at him. "You've been on *Candid Camera* this whole time. What do you think of that?"

"I think we're going to have to see that footage as soon as possible."

Her face fell. "Can't do that without talking to my boss. And he ain't here."

"Then call him."

Jill rolled her eyes. "I don't think I—"

Stella reached for the woman's hand. "Please. This is very important."

The woman softened and fished her phone from her apron pocket. "Like I ain't got nothing better to do than call the owner. If he fires me for this, I'll sue."

The ring at the end of the line was loud enough for Hagen to hear it, even as Jill pressed the phone to her ear. He shoved his hands in his pockets. There were only a few diners in the restaurant. Two had tucked hungrily into their meal. A third diner sat at the counter, his thighs spilling over the edge of the barstool like a half-inflated kiddie pool, as he waited on food.

Hagen wanted to tell her that no, she didn't have anything better to do, certainly nothing better than helping them figure out who had ordered the food that had drugged the Bisgards and their friends.

The ringing stopped. A man's voice escaped from the gap between the phone and Jill's ear. "Jill? What the hell's happened there now?"

"Gotta couple FBI agents want to look at camera stuff."

"FBI? What the hell? Is this about that potato salad lawsuit? We settled that—"

"No, sir." Hagen stepped forward and spoke loud enough to be heard. "We're following the track of a suspect in an unrelated case."

Jill held her phone between them but didn't tap the speaker button. She didn't need to. "Nothing about potato salad?"

"No, sir."

"Show 'em the tapes, Jill. And don't bother me again during *Wheel* reruns." A series of beeps indicated the boss had hung up.

Jill's face was as sour as a lemon. "Come with me."

She led them around the counter, through a pair of swinging doors, and into the kitchen, where a single cook stood over a hot plate. Grease stains fingerprinted the front of his hat. Hagen nodded a greeting but didn't get one in return.

It didn't matter.

The office was at the back of the kitchen. The front wall of the room had painted plywood that reached only a yard high. Glass, extending all the way to the ceiling, made up the remainder of the wall. A chair and desk faced the door so that anyone sitting in the room could keep an eye on what happened in the kitchen.

Jill moved the mouse on the desk until the screen came to life. A couple of clicks brought a top-down view of the diner, the wide-angle lens making the counter look wider and farther from the door than it really was.

"You two can cope from here? I was never much good with this technology stuff." Jill took her pen and notepad from the pocket of her apron and held them up. "This and this. It's all I needed since I was sixteen."

Stella slipped into the office chair. "Yeah, we're good. We'll shout if we need anything." She smiled. "Thanks, Jill. You've been a big help."

"Uh-huh." Jill left the office, giving the cook a big ostentatious shrug as she returned to the dining area.

Hagen closed the door and quickly realized that it made no difference. The windows gave them no privacy at all. The cook rested his back on the kitchen counter, eyes fixed on him.

As Hagen came around the desk, Stella angled the screen. "Here, this is the footage from last week. Here we go. I'll start at five in the afternoon in case Jill's memory isn't great."

Hagen scowled at the screen. "Surely not. How could Jill's memory be anything but perfect? She just writes everything down with her pen and paper."

Stella poked him with her elbow. "You could have been nicer. She's just doing her job."

"So am I. So are you. What have you got?"

Stella fast-forwarded the footage. Diners speed-walked to tables. Jill and another server raced with plates balanced carefully on their arms. Their legs moved like pistons, but the dishes never fell. Through the window behind the counter, the cook shook a skillet and flicked his spatula like a juggler keen to finish his set and head for home.

"There." Hagen tapped the back of Stella's chair, but she'd already hit pause. A man in baggy cargo pants and a black baseball cap shuffled to the counter. Jill rushed him box after box of takeout food, placing them in a couple paper sacks. "Can you zoom in on those boxes?"

Stella stopped the video and did as he'd asked. The containers were the standard kind found in most restaurants across the country. A label stuck to the top said *The Roadside Drop-In. Murfreesboro's favorite diner.*

"What's that?" She zoomed in on one of the paper bags. A name was written in big black letters.

She was right. Hagen squinted at the name. "Ben."

Stella leaned back in the seat. It creaked loudly. He stopped the chair with his thigh before the whole thing tilted her onto the floor. She barely noticed. "That's him. It's got to be."

"He's alone, though. Keep going."

Hagen bit his bottom lip. The screen showed only the back of Benny's cap, his black hair underneath tousled and greasy enough to shine.

Someone else entered the restaurant, a short man with a line of gray hair just above his ears and a weak attempt at a comb-over.

Hagen leaned forward, pushing Stella's chair toward the screen as well. "This could be him."

The man stopped just past the door. He stood there for a moment before turning left and joining a party of three who welcomed him with a slap on the shoulder.

Hagen exhaled. Both he and Stella fell back, disappointed. Stella let the footage keep running in real time.

A new figure passed under the camera. This man was taller than the last, his gray hair neatly parted. He walked straight to the counter and stopped next to Benny, both arms resting on the counter's surface.

"Here we go," Hagen murmured.

Benny and the other man appeared to exchange words. The new guy raised a thumb.

Hagen lifted an eyebrow. "What I wouldn't give to hear what they said."

Stella leaned closer to the monitor. "Could be just another customer. They might just be talking about the quality of the fries."

He snorted.

Benny tucked a handful of napkins into the paper bag. The stranger stood next to him, his back straight, until Jill came out of the kitchen and gave him a bag of takeout. He slid a bill across the counter before turning and disappearing under the camera.

A flame of frustration lit in Hagen's chest. "Dammit."

Benny picked up the first bag that he'd placed on the floor and left the restaurant. His face remained hidden by the peak of his black cap.

Stella stopped the video. "Well, we've got Ben picking things up and drug bottles in his room."

Hagen slammed a fist onto the desk, letting his frustration out. A sharp pain shot up his arm, but it felt satisfying. "But is this goofball smart enough to carry out a crime like this?" That was the question he couldn't get past.

Stella twirled in the rickety rolling chair. "I'm not so sure. I've got an idea. Let's get back to the police station. Now."

33

"I can break Roxie." Stella stared straight down the road as she spoke, her voice as hard as asphalt. "She knows. Somewhere inside that drug-addled head of hers is the location where Troy Harvey, Brenda Renelle, Dee Dee Bisgard, and little Ashton are being held. We just need to pry it out of her."

Hagen gunned the engine, and, for the first time, Stella wished they were in his shiny, red Corvette.

"That's it? That's your plan? You're going to break Roxie?"

Stella nodded. *Wasn't that obvious?*

"And you think you can do that?"

"Yes."

Hagen gripped the top of the steering wheel. "Christ, Stella. I hope you know what you're doing because we'll have to release her soon. If you've got nothing, she'll just disappear. You know how hard it can be to track down a junkie. No address, no credit cards, no phone. We won't see her again until they find her rotting, overdosed corpse in some hovel in Oregon somewhere. By which time, all the captives will have long been wiped from this Earth. She's the only lead we've got."

"I know." Stella swallowed. Hagen wasn't helping her confidence. She knew the stakes. If she couldn't crack Roxie, she couldn't see how they were going to crack this case or save the remaining captives.

Hagen brought the SUV to a screeching halt outside the Stonevale Police Station. He killed the engine and swiveled toward her. "Here we are. Let's see what you got."

Stella said nothing. She strode into the station. Officer Scott sat, head still bandaged, behind the desk. He looked up as they came in. She stopped short, surprised to see him.

"Hey, Agents. If you're looking for the other FBI folks, they just went out for lunch with your boss. Nice that he does that."

Stella blinked at him. "If you're *here*, who's watching the motel room?"

The officer shifted in his chair. "We got a rookie out there keeping watch. She's real nice. She promised to call if she sees anything."

Stella exhaled slowly. Benny was out on the prowl somewhere, and all they had watching his room was a rookie who was rookier than the rookie in front of her? She hoped the replacement would do a better job of stopping him than Officer Scott had, but she couldn't risk it. She'd call Slade and get someone with more experience to take over.

"And Roxie's sister?"

"Police up in Oregon say they picked her up with her kid and her partner. They're holding them in a safe house somewhere, though they didn't tell me where."

She held out a hand. "We don't need to know where they're holding them. Just bring Roxie into the interview room for me. Cuff her to the table, then bring her a coffee. Make it strong."

"Uh." The officer looked over his shoulder toward the chief's office. "Yeah…I just…"

Stella sighed. "If you need to clear it with your boss, then do it. But do it fast. And don't say a word about her sister. Got it?"

Nodding, the officer pushed himself out of the chair and practically leapt the five feet between his desk and the chief's office. He came out a moment later, jogged down the short corridor to retrieve Roxie, and guided her to the interview room.

"Did you cuff her, Officer?" Stella asked when he emerged a second later.

Officer Scott stopped. He lifted a hand to his head, spun around, and headed straight back into the room.

Hagen lifted an eyebrow. "Just can't get good help these days, huh?"

Stella tried to appear generous and graceful. "He did just get a knock on the nut. Can't blame him if it's slowed him down a bit."

"Slowed him down? If he'd had any speed to begin with, Benny would be the one wearing the bandage, and we wouldn't be chasing our behinds looking for him."

That thought struck home and lit a small, angry flame in Stella's chest. If they'd taken both Roxie and Benny, this would have been so much easier.

They could have played one against the other. The first one to crack got immunity. They'd race to talk, and the FBI would have the case cracked in half an hour.

The officer emerged from the interview room. "She's cuffed now, Agent Knox."

"Good." She extended her hand. "Key, please. To the handcuffs."

"Oh, sure." The officer dropped a small silver key in Stella's hand. He remained standing in front of her.

Stella inhaled deeply. "Coffee, Officer Scott?"

"Thanks, sure. Milk and two sugars, please." He froze when he saw the frown on her face. "Oh, you mean for…" The officer pointed over his shoulder to the interview room.

She nodded.

"Yeah, right away."

He poured a Styrofoam cup of coffee from the pot in the corner and took it to the interview room before returning to his desk. "She's ready for you now."

"Thank you." Stella took the seat by the door. Now, she would wait.

Hagen lifted his watch and tapped the face. "We don't have much time, you know. The clock's against us. While she's sitting in that room by herself enjoying her coffee and dreaming about her meth cabin in Oregon, our killer could be butchering the last of the Bisgards."

Irritation burned behind Stella's eyes. "I know."

Hagen lifted his hands and paced in front of the officer's desk. "Just saying. You call the shots."

"I am."

"Just hope you know what you're doing."

Stella knew she needed to take a page out of Hagen's book. He seemed to know exactly which button to push to trigger a reaction.

But she wanted to give Roxie time. Let her settle in, get some caffeine in her to take the edge off her withdrawal, then let the wait make her impatient and keen to be interviewed. They had little time, but the time they did have worked differently in that room.

Stella stretched her legs. The minute hand on the clock above the officer's desk ticked around from twelve thirty to twelve thirty-five and twelve forty. Stella waited until it had reached twelve forty-five before standing.

Hagen pushed away from the wall. "We're on the move?"

Stella stopped at the edge of the corridor. "*I'm* on the move. If I need you, I'll shout."

Hagen advanced until he stood in front of her. "Now, just a second, Stella. You've only been in this unit for five minutes. You think you can just walk in there and get what we need by yourself?"

Stella clenched her jaw. "You haven't been in this unit much longer. Listen to me. If both of us are in there, she'll just see a wall of Feds and clam up. I need her to see me as a friend, not a Fed. I need her to trust me."

"But—"

Stella leaned forward. She lowered her voice until it carried no farther than Hagen's ears, even in the tiny police station. "You want to come with me to Atlanta? You want to help me track down my father's killers? I need to see that *you* can trust me. I can do this."

She locked her gaze with his and waited. Only a few seconds ticked by before Hagen nodded and moved out of her way.

Stella straightened her spine. Her father had been an advocate of "fake it 'til you make it." She had said she could do this. Now she needed to believe it. Then deliver results. She strode into the interview room.

Roxie sat at the table. Her hair was a mess, her eyes red. Tears had left trails down her cheeks through the dirt caking her face. The coffee cup by her arm was already half empty despite the difficulty that Roxie must have faced drinking with both hands cuffed to a metal loop.

Stella stormed to the table. "Dammit, I told them not to do that. Here." She pulled a key out of her pocket and unlocked the cuffs.

Roxie yanked her arms back and rubbed her wrists, her fingers trembling. "You should fire that officer. He's an idiot, is what he is. I know my rights. He had no business doing something like that."

"You're not wrong." Stella pulled out the chair opposite the young woman and sat down. "But then again, your friend Benny hit him over the head with a log, so maybe we'll just call it even, eh?"

Roxie opened her mouth, clearly intent on continuing her tirade, but stopped. Instead, her lips twitched, and she offered a small, tired smile instead.

Stella lowered her eyes. Roxie's smile revealed two missing front teeth, and most of what remained was stained brown and black.

Roxie didn't seem to care. "Yeah, let's do that. You found Benny? You got him safe, right?"

Stella shook her head. "No, I'm afraid not. We located his motel room, but he wasn't there. We've got an officer on watch, but there's been no sign of him. I have to tell you, Roxie. It doesn't look good. The place was a mess. I'm worried about him."

"Aw, man. You gotta find him." Face flushing red, panic filled Roxie's eyes, followed quickly by tears. Her lower lip trembled. Controlling her emotions was obviously becoming a struggle. "Benny's dead, isn't he? I know he is. It's not right."

"If Benny's alive, I'll find him." Making promises was risky. Stella tried to avoid the word "promise," but she needed Roxie to believe her sincerity and stay calm.

Roxie was doing the opposite, nearly hysterical now. "He killed Benny, and he's gonna go for my sister next. He said he would. You gotta find her, Fed. You gotta keep her safe."

No way in hell was Stella going to tell her that her sister and nephew were safe yet.

"I'll find your sister, too, but it might take time. I can't be sure that I'll find out where she is before the madman who used you gets to her. The easiest way to protect her is to tell us *who* is going after her. We can't protect her against the world. But we *can* protect her against a specific threat."

"Please. She's the only one who was ever good to me, the only one who cares. All she wants to do is live her life. She's smarter than me. Real smart. She got outta that damn place some people call home, and now I'm just…"

Roxie lifted her hand to her forehead and sobbed quietly. Hiccups racked her body.

Stella took her wrist and leaned closer. "You love your sister, don't you?"

Roxie nodded.

"You're lucky to have her, and she's lucky to have you too. Roxie, listen to me. I know what it's like to lose a sibling, to lose someone you love."

"You do?" Roxie lowered her arm. She didn't pull it out of Stella's grip.

"I do, and I can tell you it doesn't matter how much you smoke or inject or stuff up your nose. Nothing will ever numb that pain. It will always be there like a sharp fragment of glass digging into your chest last thing before you go to sleep, first thing after you wake up, and cutting into your skin every moment in between. When you just want to pick up the phone and talk, you'll remember your sister's gone. When you hear a song she loved, that glass will stab right through you again. Just when you think you're used to the pain, it will come and leave you weeping on the bathroom floor."

Roxie stared, her reddened eyes wide open. "That's harsh."

"That's reality. It's what it's like to lose a sibling. If something happens to your sister, it will hurt even worse because you'll always know that *you* could have prevented it. You had the information that would have saved her, and you kept it to yourself."

Roxie bit her lip. A tear ran down her cheek, cutting a new, clearer line through the dirt on her face. "But he'll kill me. I know he will. There's no way he'll believe I didn't squeal."

Stella kept her hand on Roxie's arm, providing her an anchor with the contact. "If that's true, then you've got nothing to lose. Look, Roxie. You're safe here, in protective custody. The best way we can *keep* both her and you alive and safe is to find whoever's killing these people and find him now."

Terror came alive on the girl's expression. "I can't! He'll find out. I know he will."

Stella squeezed Roxie's arm. "It's okay to be scared. Whoever did this to you is very scary. He took advantage of you. You're an addict, and that's not your fault. You're not a bad person. You didn't intend for all this to happen, did you?"

Roxie shook her head.

"Of course, you didn't. You just got in over your head. The drugs will do that. They'll drop you right down, so when someone comes along offering to pick you up, you can only leap at the chance. You didn't know what you were getting yourself into, did you?"

"No. Uh-uh. If I'd known he was a monster… Jesus, the things he does, that he tells us to do." She shivered. "He doesn't feel bad about anything. I'm not sure he's even human. It's like he climbed out of a crypt all cold and half dead. I only went with him because I figured I couldn't take one more night on the street. If I'd known how scary he was, I'd have stayed right in that old meth house. That place ain't half as scary as that dude."

Stella gripped Roxie's arm tighter. "Of course, you would. I know you're not cruel like him. Who is he? What's his name?"

Roxie wiped at a tear running down her cheek. Mostly,

she succeeded only in smearing dirt across her face. "He says his name is Horace. Didn't give us his last name, but he wanted us to call him Dr. S."

A wave of excitement rippled through Stella. She had a name. Not a complete last name, but it was more than she had five minutes ago. She was making progress. She just needed to push further, dig deeper.

"And who's 'us'? There's you and Benny. Who else?"

Roxie sniffed. "Just me and Benny and this horrible old meth head called Skid. Dr. S. just calls us One, Two, and Three like he's being funny or something. It's not funny at all. Me and Benny aren't just numbers. We're people."

"Of course, you are. I can see that." Stella licked her lips. Roxie was opening up. She was talking. Now to pry the gap even wider. "Where is this doctor, Roxie? Where does he do all this? I can't keep you and your sister safe if I don't know where he is. I need to find him and put him behind bars."

Roxie sniffed again. She reached for the cup and took a slug of the remaining coffee. It must have been cold already, but Roxie didn't seem to mind. "He's…there's an old dog kennel on the edge of Murfreesboro, just off Compton Road. That's where he keeps them. Where he gets us to make them shoot each other for his experiment."

Stella's guts twisted. She couldn't have heard correctly. "*They* shoot each other? Who shoots each other?"

"That's what he does. I told you, he's sick. He makes us, me and Benny and Skid, hold a gun to the kid's head. Then one of them has to kill another one to stop us from killing the little boy. It's the sickest thing I ever saw. If I'd known he was going to do that, I would never have gone near him."

She explained how the doctor had installed her at Bisgard's Best and told her to make friends with Dee Dee. The next time the Bisgards had friends over for dinner, all she had to do was recommend her friend Benny as a delivery person.

Through tears and while wiping a runny nose on the back of her arm, Roxie swore that she thought it was just a scam. "Honest. I thought they pocket a load of cash, buy some cheap diner food, and keep the difference. If I'd known what he'd do next, I'd never have done it."

A brief wave of empathy for the girl hit Stella but drained away in a blink. Roxie really hadn't known what she was getting herself into in the beginning. "They? Who's they?"

The young woman lifted a shoulder. "Dr. S. Benny, I guess."

Stella withdrew her arm from the table. Her fingers shook. She was aware of her breath, of an anger that was rising from her chest and up her spine and boiling over into her brain.

"Thank you for telling me this, Roxie. It'll be all right now."

She leapt to her feet, yanked open the door, and ran into the police station's reception room.

He was making them kill each other. This country didn't have a hole deep enough to throw this man in.

Hagen stepped from the chief's office, his expression as excited as she felt. "You did good."

Stella didn't have time to congratulate herself. "You heard?"

"Yeah. The old dog kennels on Compton Road."

"Let's go." She pulled out her phone, preparing to call Slade as she strode to the door. But as Hagen pulled it open, she stopped and turned around. "I need you to do something."

Officer Scott rose to his feet. "Sure. What?"

"Take Roxie back to the cell. And charge her as an accessory to murder."

My car looked like a mobile abattoir. I could hardly drive it on a public road in that state. The police would stop me, and I didn't want to be stopped. Not now, when I was so close.

Two hours I spent at the end of a secluded wooded road, picking bits of skull out of the upholstery and scrubbing brain matter off the dashboard. By the time I was done, the hour was past noon, and I had missed the day's main event.

At the hospital, I had a colleague who was a baseball enthusiast. If a game took place while he was on duty, he would record it and insist that no one tell him the score so that he could enjoy watching the match at the end of his shift.

I didn't understand.

It seemed ludicrous that anyone would cheer on a team… or cry when their side lost…or feel a need to celebrate when their team won. In my understanding, it made no difference whether one group of people scored more points than another.

On days my colleague worked when his team was playing,

I would leave the psych ward, seek him out, and tell him the result just to watch his reaction.

His howls of despair were fascinating. Even the one time he punched me was intriguing. So much emotion over something so trivial.

Driving back to the old dog pound, I identified with him for the first time. I, too, had missed a live performance. But I would watch the recording and discover who had chosen to kill and who had chosen to be killed. Perhaps it would be a useful comparison to juxtapose a "live" experience with a "recorded" one.

Necessary questions would also be answered. Would Troy step up again? Would he take the gun and murder the woman who had become something of a substitute mother for him? Or would he volunteer to die instead, forcing a mother to kill in front of her child?

A flutter of anticipation rippled through my stomach. What a wonderful feeling.

I had a preference. I didn't want Troy to die. He had been so interesting to watch. Observing Troy was like seeing someone become me. He had grown numb, closed up, and turned into a viewer of the world, not a participant in it.

If he was dead when I returned, would I feel sadness?

Such an intriguing thought. My experiment was about to reach its most important moment. An emotion, a real, powerful emotion, could be just a few minutes away.

I put my foot down and drove faster.

What I felt when I arrived, that old, familiar sense of mild irritation, returned. Benny waited in my observation room. He sat in my chair, swiveling first one way and then the next, like a child in a playground. He didn't hear me come in, and he didn't see me standing in the doorway.

"Get out of my chair. Now."

He moved so fast that he fell and landed on the floor.

What a reaction. Fascinating. Such a display of fear was inspired simply by the raising of my voice. And by the threat that laid beneath it. I had inserted a tone of authority in my command. Apparently, I'd struck just the correct tenor.

His skittish emotion remained even as he climbed to his feet and righted the chair. He fiddled with his hands and shifted his weight from one foot to the other. He looked like a schoolboy brought to the principal for smoking in the bathroom. I was sure that my own reaction was little different from that of a principal. I sighed and wanted to do nothing more than throw One out of my sight.

"Is it done?" I demanded.

He scratched at a scab on his jawline. "Is…is what done?"

How sorely he tried my patience. "The experiment. Has the next stage taken place as scheduled?"

One ran a hand over his mouth.

"Now, the thing is, y'see, I was here all by myself. I didn't think you expected me to do it all on my lonesome. I mean, how would I hold the kid and unlock the cage at the same time? And what would stop the dude from killing me as soon as he got the gun? Huh? Nothing, that's what." One lifted his chin, some of the meekness leaving him. "I figured you just wanted me to watch them good and make sure that they didn't try to get out or nothing. I did that. They're still here. They ain't gone nowhere."

I closed my eyes. So, I wouldn't be watching the recording of Troy either killing someone like some sort of machine or dying like an unwanted puppy. I had nothing. Worse, I had no way of feeling anything. The anticipation turned to anger. A warm fire in my chest.

"So, you're saying that my experiment did not take place today, that everyone who was alive this morning is still alive now?"

One jabbed his finger in my direction. "What you should

be askin' is where's Skid got to? Done a runner is what he's done. *He's* the one who screwed this up for you. Want me to go track him down? I'll go git him now. I'll find him."

As he started to turn toward the door, I lifted my hand. "Stop. Here's what I want you to do. Go to the cages and keep an eye on my subjects. I will come along and join you in a moment."

One grinned and nodded vigorously, like one of those toy bobbleheads people placed in their cars for amusement. "Ha ha, y'see. I told you this was a two-man job. The two of us, we'll get it done. I'll see you in there, man, um, sir."

He stepped past me, leaving as much room as possible between us in the smallish office.

As One reached the doorway to my observation room, I turned, pulled the gun out of my pocket, pointed it at the back of his head, and pulled the trigger.

Boom.

I really should have thought twice about setting off that gun in a room that small. The blast echoed off the walls, ringing in my ears. I couldn't even hear the thump of One's body hitting the floor or the splat as the contents of his head sprayed into the corridor.

Another mess to clean up.

I stepped over the body. The back of my heel landed on the edge of a puddle of blood, causing me to slip a little. Glancing back, I noticed that my shoe left wide, sticky crescents on the floor as I marched toward the pens.

Perhaps this turn of events was for the best. Observation may not be the most effective way of generating an emotional response. While I had committed up-close and personal murders before, now that I would be facing someone who had earned my respect rather than my contempt, perhaps I would feel something in the next few moments.

A heavy odor of blood and sweat and urine and feces struck me before I reached the cages. My helpers had not been very fastidious in their duties. I should have known they wouldn't be. I covered my nose with my hand. But, as I stood in the doorway, the stink still found its way through.

Forcing my thoughts away from the smell, I focused on the only three things that mattered.

There they were.

Dee Dee Bisgard, the little boy huddled at the back of their cage, and Troy, dear Troy, leaning against his bars, his eyes open. He was sitting near a puddle of dried blood, but he didn't seem to care. Nothing could reach him. Dee Dee jumped and hugged the child closer when she saw me, but Troy barely moved. He just glanced in my direction and released a flicker of a smile before looking away.

What had I done? Was there really nothing left of him in there?

I couldn't wait to find out.

"Who will take the killer shot today?"

Silence. I turned toward Troy. Was he really going to kill a mother in front of her child?

I hadn't predicted this.

"Come. I won't ask a third time. Who will take the killer shot?"

"Me. I…I will."

The trembling answer came from Dee Dee's cage. Tears glistened in her eyes. Though judging by their redness, they were certainly not the first today.

A change. How interesting.

I faced my star subject. "Is that right, Troy? You have resigned from your position? You've had enough killing?"

He placed both hands on the bars and pulled himself to his feet, his gaze not leaving mine. "Let's get on with it. You're wasting my time."

So, this was how today would go. Troy would die. My dear Troy, the man I had turned into a version of myself—cold, unfeeling, and dead beneath the skin. I would watch Dee Dee blow a large hole in his back, and I would see him fall to the ground as his life disappeared.

Surely, now, as I watch Troy die, I will finally feel something.

"Out you come then, boy."

After unlocking the cage and opening the door, I didn't even pull out my gun. He wouldn't do anything. He didn't care whether he lived or died. I was sure, in fact, that given a choice, he would have preferred the second option. What was the point of living when you felt nothing?

I truly understood.

"Down, boy. On your knees."

He dropped to the ground, his knees sinking into the sticky, stained floor. Head lowered, he could have waited there all day.

"Now you."

I unlocked the door to Dee Dee's cage. She let go of her son, turned him to face the wall, and pushed him into the corner. "Stay there, honey. Don't look, okay. Don't turn around until I say so. Do you promise?"

The boy nodded and did as he was told. Someone else might have felt sorry for the child. He looked as though he were being punished for bad behavior, forced to stand in the corner for interrupting the class. I appreciated the irony. He was the only one in the room who had done nothing that warranted punishment.

When she didn't move, I grabbed Dee Dee's arm and pulled the sobbing woman into the corridor. "That's enough. Stand here. Turn around."

I dragged her behind Troy until she stood over him. She wiped her nose with her arm and shook so hard she could barely stand still as tears cascaded down her cheeks. If Troy had been more than half a yard away, I'd be worried she'd miss.

This would be the moment. After all these years of wondering and waiting. After all these months of planning and all these days of watching, my experiment was about to yield its results.

In a moment, I would feel...something. Sadness, maybe. Or regret?

Who knew?

I pulled the gun from my waistband, waiting for some wonderful or even brutal sensation to flood my every cell.

Nothing.

Something was wrong. Surely, I should be feeling something by now. Something more than anticipation, some excitement, *something*.

Still nothing.

Troy no longer cared whether he lived or died and, I realized, neither did I.

There was no fear, no remorse, no sense of impending misery.

There was nothing, the same nothing that had dogged my entire life.

In a brutal moment of clarity, I realized the truth. My experiment had failed.

My mind whirled as I turned away. Had I held my captives too long? Or not held them long enough? I had come so close. I was sure I was almost there. Perhaps, I just needed to work with Troy more. Use him as a substitute for myself.

Maybe I needed to make him kill more people with greater savagery, people even closer to him. His mother, perhaps.

He was now completely broken. I was sure of that. Broken by me.

But what if I could fix what I had shattered inside him? What if I could trigger emotion in him once more? Would I then unlock the key and know how to fix myself?

That was it!

I couldn't let him die now. That was certain, but with my experiment ruined, there was no point in letting the other two live. Filled with what most people would consider hope, I lifted the gun to the back of Dee Dee's head and pulled the trigger.

Boom.

Her head turned into a red cloud. Brains and blood sprayed over the walls and across the floor, raining down over Troy. He flinched at the noise. That was it. The woman landed on his shoulder before tumbling to the cold floor. Blood saturated his shirt.

Interesting.

I watched as Troy raised his hand and touched Dee Dee's limp form as if he didn't believe what had appeared next to him. Blood dribbled down his cheek and onto his neck. He reached up and touched his head. He touched his chest.

Then he turned toward me, his eyes wide. His skin flushed dark red, almost purple.

I expected him to remain silent. Again, my hypothesis was wrong.

He screamed. "Nooooo! Why? Kill *me*. Please. You shouldn't have killed Dee Dee. No, not her. Nooo."

Tears washed through the blood on his cheek as he pulled the woman into his arms. He tilted his head back and roared, gasping for breath between great desperate sobs.

I took a step back. I had never seen so much emotion.

At that moment, in a flash brighter than anything the end of my gun could have produced, understanding came.

I would never be fixed.

The thing that had brought Troy back to life, what made

him feel again and again with every part of his being, had been the loss of someone he loved.

I had never loved anyone, not even my own mother. Therefore, I would always feel nothing.

As that understanding sank in, something inside sparked to life. It started as a coldness, an emptiness, a sinking like a falling elevator. I thought it was disappointment, but it changed quickly. Almost as soon as I hit the bottom of the shaft, a fire exploded somewhere deep within my chest. It roared through my body, burning with lava-hot heat.

Rage.

I was angry with Benny, with Skid, with Roxie and Dee Dee, and especially Troy. All of them.

Nature had made me numb and would keep me numb. It wasn't fair.

If *I* could feel nothing but anger, *everyone* would feel my anger.

Kill them all.

Yes. I would start with the child. Let's see how much Troy could feel then.

With Troy still screaming on the floor, I stepped back toward Dee Dee's cage. The little boy was so obedient, still facing the wall. I leveled the gun and smiled at my star subject.

"Troy, are you still watching?"

35

S tella had one hand on the dashboard of the Explorer while the other held her phone to her ear. Her call was still waiting to connect. Sometimes, the world seemed to slow right down, and always when you needed it to move so much faster.

She scowled at Hagen. "Can't you hurry?"

Hagen pushed the gas, yanked the steering wheel, and raced past a pickup hogging the fast lane. The honking from the truck soon faded behind them. "If I had my Corvette…"

"We'd still be too late." She could feel it.

After just one ring, Slade's voice filled Stella's ear. From the background came a faint clatter of crockery and conversation.

"Stella, I was just about to call you. What have you got?"

"An address. They're at the old dog pound in Murfrees-boro, off Compton Road. Hagen and I are on our way."

Slade's voice turned muffled as he barked orders. "Forks down. Let's go." The sound of crockery grew louder. Slade must have been striding through the café, heading to the car. "We're close. Don't go in until we get there."

Stella glanced at Hagen. "Don't worry. The way Hagen is driving, you'll probably get there before we do."

Hagen lifted an eyebrow and stepped harder on the gas. The speedometer nudged past ninety. Stella swallowed. Perhaps she'd pushed him too hard. With her free hand, she held on to the "oh shit" handle over the passenger window.

"What were you going to call me about, Slade?"

"We've got another body. It was found near Roxie's trailer. No ID yet, but judging by the state of the corpse, we're assuming it's one of the kidnapper's helpers."

Stella lowered her head as her chest grew tight. She had promised Roxie that she would do her best to help Benny. "Right. Thanks for telling me. See you there." Stella dropped the phone in her lap and turned to Hagen. "How much longer?"

Hagen kept his eyes on the road. "Three minutes."

They drove on, Hagen zipping expertly between the passing and middle lanes of the highway. Stella rested her hand on her holster. Soon, she'd have to draw her weapon again, and this time, she wouldn't let someone take it from her. They'd have to shoot her first.

Hagen shot across two lanes and up the exit ramp. "There." He pointed to an opening on the right of the road. The tires squealed as he stamped on the brakes, forcing Stella toward the dashboard. Her seat belt slammed against her chest.

"Easy now. We don't want to spook him."

Hagen slowed and let the vehicle glide quietly into the parking lot. The one-story building looked abandoned. Wide cracks ran up the wall, and some of the bricks had chipped and crumbled, leaving gaps in the graffiti tags. Three sets of windows were secured with rusty steel bars, while a new steel door stood firmly closed. A black Lexus was parked closest to the door. Next to it was a brown pickup with a covered bed.

Hagen pulled up behind a different building. "Guess Benny's here."

Stella swallowed hard. "Let's hope so. If he isn't, then that's probably him out near Roxie's trailer."

As she opened the door, Slade's SUV slid into the parking lot behind them. Ander and Chloe leapt out before it finished moving, their hands already on their holsters.

Slade hopped out and put a restraining hand on Chloe's good shoulder. "You stay out here and watch the perimeter. Make sure no one gets out."

The agent looked like she might explode but nodded instead.

"Nice work, Stella." Ander peered into the pickup's cab.

Hagen pushed him away from the window. "What am I, chopped liver?"

"Yes, well done. Both of you." Slade nodded toward the entrance. "The chief's office says all the doors should be chained off. Let's hope this is the only one open. There's not enough of us to split up. Let's go."

Hagen was already on his way to the door. He pulled out his weapon and waited. Stella joined him. Ander and Slade took position on the opposite side of the door.

Stella gripped her Glock firmly, one hand supporting the other. Her heart thumped in her chest. She breathed slowly, calming herself. This moment, the moment before breaching the premises, was always the worst. After that, it was all movement.

Slade grasped the handle and eased it down. The door clicked open. Stella licked her lips and followed Hagen inside. He turned left while she went right.

The light from the doorway penetrated no more than a couple of yards inside the corridor. The air was sour with a stench as thick as an open sewer. Whatever had been going on in here, it had been a dirty business.

Hagen advanced, gun outstretched. Stella followed. Behind her, Ander's footsteps echoed softly off the walls.

"Shit." Hagen's whisper broke the silence. Still crouching, he scooted toward an open doorway.

Stella took two slow steps, then stopped. A body was facedown on the floor. The top of the head was missing, and a large puddle of blood stretched most of the way to the opposite wall. Was this Benny? Or was Benny lying near the trailer?

It didn't matter. Either way, she had promised Roxie that she would do her best to keep him safe. Now, he was dead, and her promise meant nothing.

Stella grasped her Glock tightly. Anger lit in her guts. Fear sent the flame a little higher.

Hagen slipped around the corpse and into the room. "Clear. But look at the floor."

A series of blood-stamped, crescent-shaped heel prints made a trail down the corridor.

Stella trod past the crimson stains until she reached a corner. The sound of sobbing drifted toward her. A woman. Somewhere down there, at least one hostage was still alive. Relief washed over her like cool water. They weren't too late.

Boom.

The gunshot was the loudest Stella had ever heard. The bang bounced off the walls of the corridor, the noise filling the air. The echo died away, but the screaming that replaced it was worse.

Stella sprinted around the corner, taking the point position from Hagen. Her ears still rang. She couldn't hear her footsteps anymore, couldn't hear her team. Only the muffled screams broke through her damaged eardrums. The vibrations from the gunshot were so strong and so thick she could have been running through syrup. Her legs couldn't move fast enough, no matter how much she willed them on.

She had to get there before the next shot. She had to.

At the end of the corridor, on the other side of an open door, a figure stood. He was tall and dressed in a long, white coat that was spotted with blood. Dr. S. His arms were outstretched, the gun in his hand pointing at someone she couldn't see.

Stella staggered to a halt, her legs apart. She aimed her weapon, knowing she wouldn't miss.

"FBI! Drop your weapon or I'll shoot!"

The man turned his head, but the gun didn't waver. Stella focused on his finger. It was outside the trigger guard. Her heart pounded, sounding like she had cotton in her ears. One move, one slide of that finger, and she would open fire.

A shout came from behind her. Hagen. "Drop it. Do it now!"

For a moment, the man stood there, his head facing one direction, his gun another. His finger moved, and Stella touched the Glock's trigger in response.

In the next heartbeat, Dr. S. opened his hand and released the gun. The weapon hit the floor, but she didn't hear it.

Only the wails coming from a man on the floor remained.

Stella's hands relaxed ever so slightly. She held her stance even as a bone-deep weariness rushed through her system, warring with adrenaline and leaving her feeling jittery but hollow.

It had taken too long to find the killer, and now more people were dead.

They'd won the final battle, but in the end, they'd lost the war.

36

S tella stood with Slade in the office of the old dog pound on the outskirts of Murfreesboro. A monitor rested on the table, its screen showing the carnage that had taken place over the previous few days.

A pool of blood covered the floor between the kennels. More blood sprayed the walls. The room looked more like a badly maintained slaughterhouse than a place to find a new pup.

In the middle of a crimson pool lay what was left of Dee Dee Bisgard. While the victims they'd found so far had been shot in the back, everyone they'd seen today had taken a bullet to the head.

Forensics swarmed the place, flashing bulbs and sketching the scene before digging into the small details.

The mess had to be the worst Stella had ever seen, and Dee Dee was only a small part of it. Behind Stella was the corpse they'd stumbled upon on the way. Most of the back of his head was missing too.

"Benny Ruggle." Slade stared at the young man's wallet. "Think he was out of his league here."

Stella wanted to smile but couldn't. Hagen owed her ten bucks.

"Like Roxie. I wonder what brought him back here. He should have been long gone once we nabbed her."

Slade put the wallet in an evidence bag and handed it off to forensics, signing a chain of evidence clipboard without really looking. "I don't think we'll ever know. The promise of free drugs, maybe. That was probably why our guy, one Dr. Horace Shannahan, chose them. Probably thought he could make a junkie kill his mother with the promise of a regular fix."

He pulled out his phone and read the preliminary report from Mac. "Horace Shannahan. Recently moved into town. Mother diagnosed with Alzheimer's. Psychiatrist, if you can believe that. Probably how he knew how to control these junkies."

"Yeah. Shannahan gave Benny something like a home and a purpose. At least for the weeks it took to plan and organize this thing."

"Maybe. Whatever the reason, Benny made a bad decision. The last in what I suspect was a long line of bad decisions."

Stella sighed. She turned around to look at the corpse. Benny wore the same black cargo pants and gray t-shirt she'd seen in the video at the diner. His mouth was partly open, revealing missing and blackened teeth. Not all the blood on his face had come from the big hole at the back of his head. Some were scabs, both fresh and old. He didn't look like a man you wanted to spend time with. For all Roxie's involvement in this horror show, Stella wasn't looking forward to breaking the news that her friend was dead.

Two of Shannahan's helpers were dead, and one was in custody. And Dee Dee Bisgard was dead too. This wasn't the FBI's best day.

Stella turned away from the body and rested both her hands on the back of the chair. "What about *our* bad decisions? We're supposed to find killers before they murder their victims. All we seem to have done on this case is get there late and find the mess."

Slade put his hand on her shoulder and looked her in the eye. "That's not true. We did the best we could. We got to Troy in time. We got to Ashton in time. We saved a child's life today."

Stella nodded. *Ashton. Did he even understand what he'd seen these last few days?* "Where is he now?"

"Chloe's riding with him in the ambulance to the hospital. Wayne and his grandparents will meet him there." Slade chewed his lip. "He's young. He'll be okay."

Stella jerked her head up. "Will he? We saved him, but who knows what kind of scars this place will leave? I can't even imagine what this will do to him."

Slade lowered his glasses and wiped a lens on the edge of his shirt. "He's very young, and the young are resilient. I think Troy, however, might be a different story."

Once he'd finally stopped screaming, Troy hadn't said a word. As soon as Ander dragged Horace Shannahan out of the room to drive him to the station, Troy had gone catatonic. A vacant expression had fallen over his eyes, heavy as a curtain. His mouth closed, and the muscles on his face relaxed until he did nothing but stare at some point by the door, which was directly in front of him.

"Troy will be okay, though, right?"

"It'll be a hard road for him. Turns out Horace Shannahan, our psycho psychiatrist, messed up brains instead of fixing them. I'm pretty sure that, once we swab Troy's fingers, we'll find that he shot all of them. The ones who got it in the back, anyway. That's a tough burden to carry."

"But he's clearly tough too." Stella desperately wanted the

young man to be okay. "He didn't have a choice. I've seen people do hard things and live full lives. Roxie said they were going to kill Ashton if someone didn't step up. He saved that little boy."

"I'm sure his psychiatrist will tell him that, but it's up to him to believe it. He's already on his way to the hospital with Hagen. I figured it was better if Ashton and the man who killed his father rode separately. Troy's state seemed more urgent."

"Right." Stella pushed a stray lock of hair behind her ear. "No news about Brenda?"

Slade pushed his glasses back onto his face. "No. The chief's got people out looking, but nothing yet."

Stella closed her eyes. Brenda Renelle wasn't in any of the cells, and they hadn't found her anywhere in the building. Did that mean Horace Shannahan or Skid or Benny had already dumped her somewhere? Or was there a chance that she had escaped or been released, still alive and waiting to be rescued?

Stella lowered her head.

Please let her be alive. Let Angela keep at least one of her parents.

The blood drying in the corridor gave the air a heavy, coppery smell. Slade patted her on the shoulder again. "Stella, let's get out of here. Forensics and the M.E. can take the files and deal with this mess. We've done our bit."

Stella nodded. Just the thought of fresh air lightened her mood. She stepped carefully past Benny's corpse, treading like a dancer between the dry patches on the floor the blood hadn't reached. The door at the end of the passage was open. The closer she got to the exit, the easier she moved.

From behind Stella came the sound of light jazz. Slade's phone. She stopped and turned just before the sunlight hit the corridor. Slade's voice was oddly firm and solid in a building where nothing felt solid.

"Uh, huh. Right. Okay, thanks for letting me know." As he tucked the phone back into his pocket, he added a final, quiet, "Damn."

Stella knew what Slade was about to say.

"That was the chief. A Tennessee highway patrolman just found Brenda's body in a field about a ten-minute drive from here. Cause of death appears to be the same as the previous victims. A shot to the back."

Slade's mouth continued to move. He said something about how long the body appeared to have been lying there based on a preliminary analysis, but Stella was no longer listening. She lowered her head into her hands and closed her eyes.

As much as Stella's heart broke for little Ashton, she held out hope that the child wouldn't be traumatized too badly. Like Slade had said, children were amazingly resilient, and if other family members wrapped him in their loving arms, maybe he'd be okay.

But Angela? That poor kid. Not only had she lost her father, but now, she had lost her mother as well. Both of them gone. And she was very much old enough to internalize the loss, guilt, grief.

Stella knew that all too well.

Horace Shannahan, orphan-maker. What a monster.

Stella lifted her head from her hands. "Does Angela know yet?"

"The chief's on his way to her grandparents' now. He wants to tell her himself."

"Rather him than me. I've got enough on my hands telling Roxie that we couldn't save her friend."

Not that the two were anything alike. Not even close.

She stepped out of the building and blinked from the

sunlight. The air was warm on her face, and, after the cloying stench inside the dog pound, it was fresh in her nostrils. Slade's Expedition was just outside the door, parked at a strange angle that only law enforcement officers used when they didn't have time to park at all.

Slade opened the door and fished a bag of salted peanuts out of the glove compartment. "I was an Eagle Scout. I'm always prepared." He tore the bag open and offered them to Stella. "Snack?"

Stella smiled and shook her head. If Slade was so prepared, why didn't he have a thermos of hot cocoa? She could definitely have gone for a cup of that now.

Slade picked a nut out of the bag and chewed it carefully. The sight made Stella smile. Hagen wouldn't have done that. He'd have flicked a peanut into the air, caught it in his mouth, and hoped that no one noticed his satisfied grin. Stella didn't envy him riding with Troy now.

Slade pulled out another nut. "I want to ask you something. How did you crack Roxie? I saw her when she came in. She was terrified. I thought she'd take the location of this place to the grave."

"She's got a sister. And she cared about Benny. I told her that I could protect them, but only if she helped us." Stella sighed. "I lied. I asked Chief Houston to make sure Roxie's sister was protected anyway. I couldn't protect Benny. It's all just wrong."

Stella dropped into a crouch, stretching her lower back.

Slade crouched next to her. His move relaxed her. Stella was used to seeing her boss standing tall at the head of a room, leading a briefing and barking out orders. Sitting shoulder to shoulder reminded her that he was another member of a team facing the same stresses, the same dangers, and the same disappointments.

He nudged her arm. "Keep that."

She didn't understand. "Keep what?"

"That empathy. Even for the nasties you bring in and toss into a cell. You care about them, too, and you should. This job has a habit of knocking that empathy out of us. It leaves us desiring nothing more than another collar, some revenge, a chance to get even that we can never find. Don't go that route, Stella. Keep your empathy."

She wasn't feeling particularly empathetic at the moment. Mostly, she had a hole in her gut carved out of disappointment and frustration. She nodded anyway. "I'll try."

"Remember, we saved two innocent people's lives on this case, three if you count Roxie. Five if you count Roxie's sister and her nephew. Roxie is looking at a long sentence, but I really wouldn't have rated her chances if you hadn't gotten her address or the location of this place. You did good."

Stella smiled. "Thanks."

"Now, have a nut. You've earned it." Slade offered the bag again.

Stella grinned and spilled a few in her hand. "Actually, sir. There is something else I'd like." She took a single nut and balanced it on the tip of her finger. "Any chance of a couple days off now that this case is solved? There's a trip I need to make."

"I think we can manage that."

She flicked the nut into the air and caught it in her mouth.

37

The medical team had told Hagen to speak to Troy, but not about the case. Just get him to say something, anything, or it could be years before the young man spoke again. Trauma was getting a strong foothold.

Hagen grimaced at the thought of Troy's specific trauma. Camera footage could never capture the true damage. Only four people could explain what went on in those cells. The madman leader, Roxie, a two-year-old, and Troy. The young man was the best chance for a firsthand account.

But Troy's mind had to first come out of the deep well it had fallen into. They sat alone in the emergency room as doctors ran tests and gave him intravenous fluids to revive his body, even if his mind tried to disappear.

He tapped Troy on the knee. "Hey, Troy. It's Agent Hagen Yates. Remember? We were in the ambulance together."

Nothing.

"Listen to me. You're going to be okay. You're safe now."

Troy didn't move. His gaze remained still, his eyes blank.

Hagen leaned forward in the uncomfortable plastic chair where the ER team had parked him. He kept his voice low and calm. "Can you hear me, Troy? It's all over. You're in a hospital. After you're all checked out, you're going to get to go home."

Troy blinked. Was that a sign he was getting through?

"That's right. We've got him. He can't hurt you. You're out. You made it out."

Troy blinked again. His forehead creased. He slid his eyes from the wall to Hagen's face. Hagen wanted to punch the air in triumph.

Troy opened his mouth. His voice was weak, his throat hoarse. "I killed him. He was like the only dad I ever knew, and I shot him. I shot them all."

The confession dragged like sandpaper on felt, rough and destructive. Its honesty tore through Hagen and left him cold.

"And Brenda. She was so scared. Darrel tried to calm her down, and I…and I…"

Hagen leaned forward and lowered his voice. "Listen to me. You did what you had to do. I know it, and you know it. You saved a little boy. Sometimes, doing what has to be done is the hardest thing in the world. It might mean doing something terrible, something that goes against everything you believe. But you do it anyway because you must."

Troy's eyes were growing blank again. His voice faded. "Terrible. Terrible. Terrible."

Shit. Hagen was losing him. "Terrible, yes. But also necessary, so it was brave and noble. Y'hear me?"

Troy blinked. "Brave. Noble."

"That's right." Hagen nodded. "Brave and noble. The *right* thing to do."

Frowning, Troy's eyes fixed on Hagen and stayed there.

A bolt of electricity seemed to pass through Hagen's spine as though, by staring at him, Troy had plugged him into a socket and held him there.

"It was brave and noble? To kill the only father I've known? To kill his friends? His family? To live? That doesn't sound right. I should have killed *him*." Troy's eyes were focused, his voice clear. Something like anger flickered in his eyes. "Maybe I still will. That sounds brave, noble."

Hagen leaned away from the young man. The fury he saw, dark and razor-sharp, in Troy's face was the same fury he felt in his chest when he thought of his father's killers.

Troy nodded as if he saw the invisible bond between them. An understanding. "What terrible thing have you done? What brave, noble thing are you going to do?"

Hagen swallowed. Troy's stare seemed to dig all the way through him, reach to his very marrow.

38

S tella opened her apartment window. Even from the second floor, the stink of exhaust fumes made her nose crinkle.

A cherry-red Corvette sat right outside her building, gray smoke pouring out of the back as the driver gunned the engine. From behind the wheel, Hagen peered up past the coffee shop on the ground floor to her studio, one bare elbow resting against the open window. He waved. Why honk when you've got a muscle car's engine to rev?

Stella made a cutting motion under her chin. The roar of the engine died away.

Jeez, Hagen, it's not even eight o'clock on a Sunday morning. People are trying to sleep, some of them my neighbors.

She held up a finger to indicate that she'd be down in a minute and pulled her head back into the apartment.

A road trip with Hagen. *Am I crazy?*

She wasn't entirely sure about the answer to that question, but once Slade had agreed to give her some time off, once she realized she was about to go to Atlanta to hunt down the man she'd once known as Uncle Joel, she knew there was only one person to accompany her.

Hagen was a field agent. He could think on his feet. He was focused, and he knew how to get information out of people.

They'd made a good team on their last investigation, and they'd make a good team now on her personal case. She wasn't sure about spending four hours in a car with him, but she was certain he was the right man for the job. He trusted her, and she trusted him.

And a good-looking man waiting for you in a sports car outside your apartment isn't a bad way to start a Sunday.

She closed the window, took her bag from the bed, and scattered some food into the fish tank.

"See ya, Scoot. Little Emily will be around to give you some supper. Be nice to her. I don't want you giving her a hard time."

The goldfish flicked its tail and gulped down a morsel of food, content with the twelve-year-old neighbor girl coming in for a visit.

"And close your mouth when you chew. I don't want her thinking I haven't raised you right."

Stella shut the door and bounced down the stairs, relieved to be away from the work stress for a couple of days. After she'd left the crime scene, she'd gone straight to the interview room at the Stonevale Police Station, where she told Roxie her sister was safe, but Benny was dead, murdered by their former boss.

Roxie dropped her head on her arms and wailed uncontrollably as though she and Benny had been lifelong friends rather than two junkies who'd known each other for a few months and shared a supplier.

Eventually, Roxie's tears turned to rage. She called Horace

Shannahan more names and threw more curses at him than Stella had heard anyone spill in two years in a police uniform. The range of her vocabulary, at least in one area, was impressive.

Stella believed her, but more important than Roxie's claims of remorse was her promise to do everything she could to make sure that sonofabitch spent the rest of his life in a tiny cell, ideally with nothing for company but a cold, metal bucket.

The thought of Shannahan in prison was enough to put a spring in Stella's step as she pushed open the door and slid into the passenger seat of the Corvette. "See you got your car back."

He pulled away from the curb as she pulled her seat belt on. "That's right. No more old man SUV for me. If we're going to Atlanta, we're going in style. I think we deserve a treat after a week like that."

"Yeah, it wasn't easy. I dunno. I keep trying to find the silver lining. We got Shannahan in the end, and like Slade said, we kept Ashton, Troy, and Roxie alive. I just wish we'd done more. If we'd arrived just a few minutes earlier, we could have saved Dee Dee and maybe Benny."

Hagen shook his head. "You can't think like that. We move as fast as we can and do the best we can. The important thing is we got him. That's all that matters. That's our job. Nothing else, and certainly not saving a murdering junkie like Benny."

Stella said nothing. She had wanted to save Benny, despite his involvement in the deaths of so many people. Even in prison, he could have lived a useful life and found a way to do some good. Only the dead couldn't be rehabilitated.

They pulled onto Highway 24, a route that took them

back past Murfreesboro. Stella mentally shuddered. It wasn't a place she particularly wanted to go back to. Apparently, that went for everyone in Tennessee. In front of them was a single white Honda Accord, and behind them was a black SUV. The traffic was almost nonexistent.

A thought struck her.

"Hey, you never got to see your sister last week, did you?"

Hagen shook his head. "Got kind of busy, what with chasing down a psychopath and all."

"We could stop on the way if you want. We've got time."

Hagen drummed his fingers on the wheel. "Maybe on the way back." He lifted a shoulder. "Or not. You really want my sister asking what we're doing in Atlanta together?"

Stella hadn't thought about that. "No. Definitely not. I mean, I just don't like talking about my father's death. Not usually. It hurts, right? You know what I mean."

Hagen grunted in reply. "You could talk to my sisters. If anyone can understand what it's like to lose a father, they can."

"Right." Stella sighed. She was thinking of Angela Renelle, another teenager who now had to cope with the loss of a father. A mother too. And little Ashton. "You know what hurts most about that case? Gerry Renelle's suicide. We accused him falsely, and he took his own life because of it. I know we weren't wrong in looking at him hard, but I just feel so responsible. If he'd just spoken to someone and gotten help, maybe he would have found a different way to cope. I keep thinking that maybe there was some sign we missed when we talked to him."

"Don't. I spoke to him, too, and I didn't see anything. We're investigators, not psychiatrists, and I doubt it would have mattered, anyway. If Brenda leaving him and Angela not wanting to see him hadn't pushed him over the edge, the reason Horace picked the Bisgards would have been enough to do the job."

"What do you mean?"

Hagen glanced at Stella. "I talked to Ander last night. Horace Shannahan was quite chatty in the car to the station. You know Shannahan is a psychiatrist, right?"

"Yeah, that's what I heard. Though, let's face it, he should really have been a patient."

"Agreed. But Shannahan worked in the same hospital as Gerry Renelle. They'd often take lunch around the same time, and Gerry, being Gerry, complained a lot."

"That tracks."

"Doesn't it? He'd bitch about his work and about Stonevale, and, in particular, about one family in town. The Bisgards owned the local grocery store and, apparently, the fact that they were loving and generous, always willing to lend a hand, annoyed Gerry. The do-gooders always 'inserted themselves,' whether it meant coaching Little League or giving a job to someone who really needed it. Gerry thought they were stuck-up. Then, when they planned to set up his ex-wife with an accountant…"

"Shannahan decided to strike." Stella would never understand how some people's minds worked. "When Shannahan decided to perform his weird experiment, he picked what he thought was the perfect family, so he could watch them tear themselves apart. Christ, what a freak."

"Right. He figured he'd get a more emotional response working on people bonded by love." Hagen glanced over at her. "Or by affection."

An uncomfortable silence filled the car.

Stella cleared her throat if only to make some sort of noise.

Affection? Hagen had emphasized the word as though he'd rolled the notion around in his head for some time, trying to decipher the exact meaning. Now, the word had fallen out and dropped in their laps, and neither of them knew where to put it.

He cared about her. That seemed to be clear. But was affection really strong enough to make him spend the next couple of days trawling through Atlanta looking for Uncle Joel? Surely, that required more than mere affection.

Stella peered out the window. Billboards advertised burger bars and log homes and sprays for unblocking sinuses. The traffic increased but flowed smoothly. The black SUV that Stella had seen in Nashville was now two cars behind them, seemingly ready to ride the highway as long as it went.

Two days in Atlanta. Maybe in those two days, Hagen would open up and tell her exactly why he had wanted to tag along. She was sure his motivation wasn't just affection, but she was also certain that Hagen was a good man. If he was looking for closure for his own father's death, maybe they could help each other.

She yawned, remembering to cover her mouth only when she was almost done. "Oops, sorry."

Hagen grinned. "Glad I'm such exciting company."

Stella's cheeks warmed. "Sorry, I'm just beat. The week catching up with me, I guess."

Hagen nodded. "Catch yourself some shut-eye. I'll wake you up when we reach Atlanta."

"Thanks."

Stella leaned her head against the window. In the mirror, the black SUV kept its distance, the glare on the windshield hiding the driver's face. A knot developed in her gut before she shook her head and closed her eyes.

Enough.

The tough week had made her too jumpy. Soon, they'd be in Atlanta, and she wouldn't be there alone.

Hagen changed the radio station, switching from country to light rock. Stella opened one eye.

The SUV was still there.

The End
To be continued...

Thank you for reading.
All of the *Stella Knox Series* books can be found on Amazon.

ACKNOWLEDGMENTS

How does one properly thank everyone involved in taking a dream and making it a reality? Here goes.

In addition to our families, whose unending support provided the foundation for us to find the time and energy to put these thoughts on paper, we want to thank the editors who polished our words and made them shine.

Many thanks to our publisher for risking taking on two newbies and giving us the confidence to become bona fide authors.

More than anyone, we want to thank you, our readers, for sharing your most important asset, your time, with this book. We hope with all our hearts we made it worthwhile.

Much love,

Mary & Stacy

ABOUT THE AUTHOR

Mary Stone

Mary Stone lives among the majestic Blue Ridge Mountains of East Tennessee with her two dogs, four cats, a couple of energetic boys, and a very patient husband.

As a young girl, she would go to bed every night, wondering what type of creature might be lurking underneath. It wasn't until she was older that she learned that the creatures she needed to most fear were human.

Today, she creates vivid stories with courageous, strong heroines and dastardly villains. She invites you to enter her world of serial killers, FBI agents but never damsels in distress. Her female characters can handle themselves, going toe-to-toe with any male character, protagonist or antagonist.

Discover more about Mary Stone on her website.
www.authormarystone.com

Stacy O'Hare

Growing up in West Virginia, most of the women in Stacy O'Hare's family worked in the medical field. Stacy was no exception and followed in their footsteps, becoming a nurse's aid. It wasn't until she had a comatose patient she became attached to and made up a whole life story about—with a past as an FBI agent included—that she discovered her love of stories. She started jotting them down, and typing them out, and expanding them when she got off shift. Somehow, they turned into a book. Then another. Now, she's over the moon to be releasing her first series.

Connect with Mary Online

facebook.com/authormarystone
goodreads.com/AuthorMaryStone
bookbub.com/profile/3378576590
pinterest.com/MaryStoneAuthor

Made in United States
Troutdale, OR
09/28/2024

23220375R00146